"I'll never forget that day, Natasha, if I live to be ninety."

Jared's grip inadvertently tightened around the leather steering wheel. He spoke the truth—he continued to be haunted by images of that terrible day, and he probably always would be—but he was keeping a secret close to his heart. He hadn't left New York because of emotional distress over what he'd witnessed on 9/11.

He'd left because in the weeks following the terrorist attacks he'd found himself feeling more and more attracted to Tim's widow, and the feelings of guilt and stress had eventually become unbearable, to the point where he couldn't bear to be around her....

BETTYE GRIFFIN

ONE ON One

ARABESQUE®

ISBN-13: 978-1-58314-682-8
ISBN-10:   1-58314-682-2

ONE ON ONE

In memory of all those who perished in the
terrorist attacks of 09/11/2001

ACKNOWLEDGMENTS

I would like to acknowledge the following people:
Bernard Underwood, Mrs. Eva Mae Griffin, Elaine English,
Kimberly Rowe-Van Allen.

The homegirls and guys from Yonkers, New York,
who have been so supportive: Kim White Bledsoe,
Jim Britt, Karen Jenkins Shinault, Jayna Greene Rivera,
Detra Oliver, Lenore Lipscomb-Wilson, Dorothy Hicks,
Rebecca West Ogiste.

The Jacksonville connection: Cynthia White, Felice Franklin,
Lez Cunningham, Karen Bell.

The Georgia connection: Toni and Gerald Robinson,
Cynthia Abraham.

The Family Griffin: Dorothy Clowers Lites,
Donna Griffin Williams, Lynda Griffin Harvey,
Joanne Griffin McClain, Leslie Griffin.

And anyone else I may have forgotten. Forgive me;
it's 2:00 A.M. as I write this, and I desperately need
some sleep.

Chapter 1

Late summer 2005

"Take care of my sons."

Natasha's eyes flew open, and she shivered in the dark August night. Her dream seemed so real. She'd heard Tim's voice just as plain as she had that awful day four years ago, when he called her after the explosion six floors below him in the North Tower of the World Trade Center.

She reached for the remote control, wanting to get some light into the room. My goodness, if this kept up she'd have to get a night-light, like Gary and Gordon used. But her sons were mere children, almost nine and seven years old; one would almost *expect* them to be afraid of the dark. She, on the other hand, was a grown woman.

An infomercial aired on the TV screen. Natasha turned to the bedside clock: 3:00 a.m. No wonder.

She turned to one of the cable-movie stations. She gasped in fear at the sight of Wesley Snipes portraying a half man, half vampire in one of his *Blade* movies and quickly changed the channel. She decided that *Nick at Nite* had to be a safe choice.

Her heartbeat slowed to normal at the reassuring, nonthreatening sound of canned laughter. She recognized the seventies sitcom being shown. *Just another night in paradise,* she thought bitterly. Sitting up at three in the morning, alone in her king-size bed, haunted by a recurring dream of her last chilling conversation with her late husband as he awaited his own death.

Natasha's dreams began immediately after the nightmare of losing Tim. She would never know the precise moment that it occurred, but she prayed death came before the collapse of the World Trade Center's North Tower at 10:30 a.m.

By then Barbara, her mother-in-law, had arrived from Newark, where she worked as an assistant district attorney. On the way she stopped at the day care and retrieved Gary and Gordon, whom the family called Gordy. Both children knew something was terribly wrong, but no other details were given. Barbara put them in the master bedroom with the TV set tuned to the Cartoon Network, a channel she knew would be safe from any frightening news video of burning towers.

For the boys' sake Natasha tried to stay calm, but when she saw the South Tower collapse in a tremendous gray cloud, she lost it. If the South Tower, which had been struck about fifteen minutes *after* the North Tower, could fall, what was to stop Tim's tower from falling as well?

Just minutes later, her worst fear came true. Natasha gasped at the sight, then began sobbing uncontrollably. Tim, plus God only knew how many other people, was dead.

Gary and Gordy came running at the sound of her anguished cries. Together, she and Barbara tried to explain to the youngsters that their daddy had gone to heaven, something that children two and four could hardly grasp. For months afterward they both asked when Tim would be coming home.

Now that they were older, they had a better understanding of what happened, but they still felt the loss.

She shivered again. This same dream, which she used to have maybe once or twice a week, now interrupted her slumber at least three times a week, sometimes four. And each time it happened, it took longer for her to get back to sleep.

Her alarm went off at six forty-five. Natasha shut off the buzzing noise with a heavy hand. She couldn't be sure exactly when she fell asleep, but the last time she looked at the digital clock it said 4:07. After the boys left for school she would go back to sleep for an hour or two. She didn't like the idea of sleeping in the daytime, but she wouldn't be able to function if she didn't get back at least part of the sleep she'd lost.

"Are you okay, Mommy?" Gary asked as she yawned loud and long while pouring milk over their cereal.

"Oh, yes, I'm fine. Just a little tired."

"You should go to bed earlier," Gordy suggested.

She laughed. "I'll try that." She put the milk away and poured orange juice, then set the glasses on the table and sat down with her sons, ready to share her idea with them. "Boys," she said, "what do you say we fly down to South Carolina this weekend and visit Grandma and Grandpa Ed?"

"Ooh, can we, Mommy?"

Natasha smiled. "I guess that means you'd like to go."

"Yeah!"

She called her mother-in-law after Gary and Gordy left for school.

"Natasha! I was just going to call you," Barbara exclaimed.

"How'd you like to have some company this weekend?"

"We'd love it, Natasha! You know that." Barbara called out to her husband. "Ed, Natasha and the boys are going to come down this weekend."

Natasha easily heard Ed Langston's booming response. "Just tell us when their plane lands, and we'll be there to meet them." Her eyes suddenly became damp. How blessed she was to have such caring in-laws. They were the only family she and the boys had. If it weren't for them… She sniffled, an action not lost on Barbara.

"Natasha, are you crying?" she asked, concern in her voice.

"I'm fine, Barbara."

"That's not what I asked you."

"I'm fine, Barbara," she repeated pointedly.

"Natasha, tell me what's wrong."

She took a deep breath. She should have known her mother-in-law wouldn't be put off. "I keep having that dream about Tim's last day, about what he said to me."

"Why didn't you tell me, dear? I assumed that stopped long ago."

"It's never gone away completely, but I'm having it more often lately, every other night or so."

"I know why. It's Kirk," Barbara said flatly.

"Oh, I don't think so," she said quickly. "It's probably because of the anniversary coming up."

"You might be right. Does that usually happen around September? I know I find myself thinking of Tim more this time of year."

The sad note in Barbara's voice made Natasha wish she could reach out and hug her. As difficult as it had been to lose her life partner, she couldn't imagine losing Gary or Gordy. She said a quick prayer that she never would know the pain of losing a child, even a child who'd grown into an adult.

"I do, too," she said. "But it never affected my dream. I don't know what to make of it happening so often now."

"Like I said, it's Kirk. All that stress has finally caught up with you. I know you've tried to keep a stiff upper lip about it all, but sometimes you just can't be stoic, Natasha. I'm so disappointed in my son I don't know what to do. And that Tara! I could just throttle her."

"Barbara, it's old news. We need to forget about it and move on."

"He's disgraced his brother's memory," Barbara said, her voice quivering.

"I don't see it that way," Natasha said gently. "After all, Tara is his wife. Honoring her wishes takes precedence over his spending time with Gary and Gordy."

"I can't dispute that spouses should come first for each other, but if Tara had any humanity whatsoever she wouldn't be so jealous. That's the whole root of the problem, you know. I always told Kirk she was too possessive. He can hardly call his soul his own."

Natasha tried again. She found it unbearably sad that Barbara had lost one son and harbored such disappointment in the other. "I'd prefer to not even talk about it, Barbara. The boys are fine, and I am, too."

But Barbara wouldn't be swayed. "I'm not having it, Natasha. My grandsons are growing up. They're without the male influence they need because Kirk virtually abandoned them, and even after four years you're still having nightmares, reliving the worst day of your life, of all our lives." She sighed audibly. "But I'm so glad you're coming down. I wish you'd consider moving here. There's really nothing to hold you in New Jersey."

Natasha hesitated a moment, not sure if she should really share her thoughts with her mother-in-law. She hadn't even spoken to the boys yet. "Barbara, I thought that while I'm there I'd look at some houses."

"Oh, Natasha! Really?"

"I think a change of scenery would do us all good."

"Ed and I tried to get you to come down when we did. You've always been so reluctant to even consider leaving Montclair. I'm pretty sure what changed your mind."

"Now, Barbara—"

"Yes, I know. You don't want to talk about it. Instead, I'll tell you my good news. It's the least I can do, after you've made Ed and I so happy." She paused for effect. "Jared is moving to Atlanta."

"He is?"

"Yes, his employer offered him a position as director of IT at their Atlanta office. Ed and I are thrilled about it. He's been so far away all this time, but Atlanta is only two hours from here, you know."

"Yes, I know."

"And if you and the boys come, we'll have three of you close by. Kirk will never leave New Jersey, of course, and maybe that's for the best."

"I'm just happy that you and Ed put me in the same category as Jared and Corey and Kirk." The long-divorced, fiercely independent Barbara Lawrence married Ed Langston when Tim and his younger brother, Kirk, were still in college. At that time, Ed's son Jared had recently graduated from college, and his daughter, Corey, was in high school. The Lawrence–Langston offspring, despite not having grown up together, had formed a close alliance, particularly the boys. Distance separated Corey from the rest, for she chose to remain in South Carolina with her mother after her parents' divorce.

"You're more than just a daughter-in-law to me, Natasha," Barbara said. "You and Corey are the daughters I always wanted but never had."

When Natasha lay down to get some sleep, she considered the possible connection between her dream occurring more frequently and the fact that she'd never felt so alone in her life. She always tried to play down Barbara's vehemence where Kirk and his wife, Tara, was concerned. But Kirk's behavior still hurt.

Natasha was certain that it would have broken Tim's heart to know what happened after his memorial service. At first Natasha had plenty of male companions for Gary and Gordy, who were just two and four years old at the time. Gary turned five just two weeks after the attack that destroyed the World Trade Center. Between Kirk, Jared and Ed, they didn't lack for role models.

Jared, who at the time of the attacks worked in lower Manhattan, just blocks away from the trade center, had never really recovered from the horrible scene he witnessed that day. Although he'd lived in a third-floor walk-up on West Fifty-fourth Street, after the attacks he spent a lot of time in New Jersey with the family as they grieved the loss of Tim together. Within six months, he accepted a position in Houston and left New York for good.

Two years later Ed and Barbara retired and moved to Ed's hometown of Spartanburg, South Carolina. That only left Kirk and his wife, Tara, in New Jersey.

At first Kirk spent a few hours every Saturday afternoon with the growing Gary and Gordy, playing catch or taking them bowling or out for ice cream. Often Natasha would go along when they went out. But when Tara called one day while they were on the way home and heard Natasha's voice in the background, she lit into Kirk with such vehemence that he had to hang up, unable to prevent Natasha and the boys from overhearing Tara's tirade as she ranted.

Sitting next to Kirk in the front seat, Natasha could actually hear Tara's stinging words: "I've heard all about these 9/11 widows, latching on to any man in their social circle, whether they're available or not. They sashay past, flashing their cleavage and all that money they got from those financial settlements, and the men follow behind them like puppies. No one is immune, not their dead husbands' best friends, and certainly not their brothers."

The next day Kirk called and sheepishly said he wouldn't be able to spend as much time with the boys anymore because Tara resented the time away from home on his day off. Natasha said she understood, but she didn't. In her opinion Tara's behavior was unreasonable and selfish. Sometimes Kirk only spent an hour and a half with Gary and Gordy, and the most he ever spent was three hours if they went to a movie and got something to eat afterward.

Natasha didn't know at the time that she would barely see Kirk after that. As the weeks passed with no word from him, she painfully realized the truth. Even after a year, it still hurt.

Learning that Jared would be moving close enough to spend some time in South Carolina was definitely an improvement.

Chapter 2

Three months later

Natasha quietly opened the door to the boys' bedroom. The glow of the Spider-Man night-light made it easy to spot the outlines of Gary and Gordy sleeping in their twin beds. Earlier in the day she'd directed the movers where to deposit their beds, dressers and desk. Ed would be here tomorrow to attach their headboards, so the only things she had to unpack other than their clothing was the lamp for their desk and their computer. She'd get started on that tomorrow. She wanted the new house to feel like home to them from the start.

Natasha took a moment to be grateful she'd remembered to pack the boys' night-light in her tote bag. They never liked sleeping in a completely dark room, and she certainly didn't want them to wake up and feel disoriented on their first night in their new home.

She shut the door with the softest of thumps and ran a hand

lightly along the royal-blue walls. She'd closed on the new house three weeks ago, which gave her time to have the walls painted the colors of her choosing, and also to have new carpet and flooring installed. She'd even hung curtains.

The seventies era three-bedroom ranch house in Greer, South Carolina, was very different from her seventy-year-old two-story brick home in Montclair, but it suited them well. The boys shared a bedroom, she had her own bedroom and private bath, and the third bedroom would serve as her office. One of the previous owners had the basement completely finished, and the section not used for laundry would make a nice play area for Gary and Gordy.

They'd arrived in town the day before and spent the previous night with Barbara and Ed at their home in nearby Spartanburg. The Langstons tried to get them to stay another night and to tackle the unpacking the next day, but Natasha wouldn't be put off. The sooner she had the house in order, the sooner it would feel like home to all of them.

Natasha craved normalcy. Born to very young parents unable to care for her, she grew up in a children's home in Newark, vowing that one day she would have a family of her own. She formed one with Tim, but it ended with the terrorist attack over four years ago. After so many months of not hearing from Kirk, who had become more of an outlaw than an in-law, she began to consider moving closer to the family members who'd always made her feel like one of them.

When she finally got up the courage to ask the boys if they'd like to live near Grandma and Grandpa Ed, their excitement and enthusiasm delighted her. She looked at numerous homes in the days they spent in the area around Labor Day, and from the first moment she saw it she knew it was perfect.

The house in Montclair sold easily…and handsomely. She and Tim held a special insurance policy that paid off the mortgage in full if either of them died, so all the proceeds went directly to her. Natasha had carefully invested both Tim's life in-

surance and what she received from the 9/11 fund to provide for
Gary's and Gordy's education, plus a monthly supplement to her
part-time income. She guarded her nest egg carefully; it represented part of what was left of Tim's life. She knew she was considered wealthy. But financial independence had come at a steep
price, one she would have gladly exchanged for Tim being alive
if she'd had any say in the matter.

Boxes rested against the walls in every room. She'd spent six
hours unpacking. She was determined to host Thanksgiving
dinner for the family next week, and she wanted the house in
order. She'd get it done. She still had plenty of time, and she
didn't resume work until the Monday after the holiday.

Her bed looked wonderfully refreshing to her after a long
day's work. She'd sleep good tonight. Her nerves had been
twisting ever since the day the moving van came and loaded all
their belongings. She packed a box with their essentials—Tyle-
nol, Band-Aids, the boys' night-light—and put it in the back of
her Explorer. They all stopped to take one last look at their home
when she backed out of the driveway for the last time. "Will we
ever come back here, Mommy?" Gary asked.

"Oh, I'm sure we will. And we'll definitely drive past the
house. But we won't be able to go in. Another family will be
living in it."

"A family with a daddy?" Gordy asked.

His question brought tears to Natasha's eyes. Gordy, who'd
been just shy of three years old at the time of Tim's death, had
virtually no memories of his father. Now seven and in second
grade, knowing that most of the children he knew had daddies
as well as mommies, he felt the loss more acutely. "Yes, I
suppose so," she said.

As she undressed and got into bed, Natasha thought of how
happy Gary and Gordy had been to see their stepgrandfather,
whom they called Grandpa Ed. The youthful-appearing sixty-
two-year-old Ed Langston, a retired college basketball coach,
represented a welcome source of male companionship. Natasha

knew Ed wouldn't let her down. He wouldn't abruptly pull back, like Kirk had, leaving her hurt and the boys confused.

She rolled over to the center of the bed, closed her eyes and slept straight through to the morning. She dreamed of good things, of how nice life would be once the boys made friends and became involved in organized activities.

She had no idea what life held for her, but if Gary and Gordy were happy, she would be, too.

"I'll bring the macaroni and cheese," Natasha said into the receiver. "Are you sure there isn't anything else I can do?"

"Absolutely not," Barbara replied firmly. "We're all set. Corey is making her famous apple cake, and I'm doing the rest."

"That's a lot of work, Barbara."

"It'll be a joy. My whole family will be here for Christmas!" She practically sang the words.

It delighted Natasha that Barbara made no reference to her annoyance at Kirk, instead only expressing joy at the prospect of seeing him. She shared her mother-in-law's happiness, for in the month she and the boys had been in their new home, not one time had she dreamed of that last conversation with Tim.

She kept waiting for it to happen, but it didn't. In four years she had never gone so long without that dream disturbing her slumber. That convinced her she'd made the right decision in choosing to leave Montclair.

"Jared is driving up Christmas Eve," Barbara continued. "And Kirk and Tara will be in on Christmas Day. They're going to hit the road before dawn."

"You and Ed are going to have a full house," Natasha remarked.

"No, just Kirk and Tara will be here with us. Jared plans to stay with Corey. They've always been very close, you know." Barbara sighed contentedly. "He'll have a nice long visit, too. Kirk and Tara only have a few days off, but Jared doesn't begin work until the first Monday in January. He promised to stay at least a week."

"Has he found a place to live in Atlanta already?"

"He's looking. His employer owns a condo there, and they're letting him stay there for the time being."

"That's nice of them. My, I'm looking forward to seeing him. It's been a long time."

"Here they come, Mom!"

Natasha put down the package she'd been wrapping, a softly muted knit sweater for Corey. She hastily got to her feet, a hand going up to smooth her braided bob. Gary had already opened the front door. "Hi, Grandma! Hi, Aunt Corey!" he and Gordy said in near unison, but Natasha could tell from how high their chins raised that their attention rested on someone tall, the step-uncle they barely remembered.

Natasha watched as her mother-in-law entered the house, followed by Corey. Then a rangy figure appeared, bent then scooped up both her sons in one motion. As the figure straightened, she recognized the face of Jared Langston under the goatee and the rim of the Atlanta Hawks baseball cap.

"Hey, how're my boys doing? You two probably don't even remember your old Uncle Jared."

"I remember you," Gary said. "But Gordy doesn't. He's too young."

"I am not," Gordy protested.

"Oh, I think your brother might be right, Gordy," Jared said. "But what's important is that you'll remember me from now on, because you'll be seeing me a lot more often." He tossed both boys up a few inches, then quickly caught them. "You fellas are really growing up, you know that? I'll bet y'all can give me some real competition in basketball."

"I'll bet we can beat you!" Gordy said with the confidence of a seven-year-old.

Jared chuckled. "Oh, I don't know about that, but we'll try it while I'm here, okay?"

"Okay!"

He lowered them swiftly to the floor. For a moment he merely smiled at Natasha, then held out his arms. "Natasha, my favorite sister-in-law."

"You'd better not let Tara hear you say that," she said with a grin as she hugged him warmly. Then she stepped back to look at him. "It's good to see you, Jared. It's been way too long between visits." He'd filled out a little, she noticed. Gone was the reed-thin man she remembered. In addition, his face bore a maturity that hadn't been there before the terrorist attacks, courtesy of the streaks of gray in his goatee and the vertical lines running between the outer corners of his eyes and the sides of his mouth that appeared when he smiled.

"I know. I'm sorry, Natasha. I didn't mean anything by staying away so long. I had a lot of things to work out." After Jared relocated he never returned, not even to visit. Barbara, Ed and Corey had all been to Houston to see him, but Natasha hadn't seen him since he left three years before.

"I think I understand. I hope you won't be a stranger any-more."

"No, I promise." He reached out to touch her braids, which were chin length at their longest at the sides of her face, tapering up to a shorter length that barely covered her nape. "I like your hair."

"Thanks."

"What do you think of your nephews, Jared?" Barbara asked proudly from the living-room sofa.

"I think they're great kids," he said as he lowered his tall frame into an easy chair. "I'm looking forward to spending time with them."

"Do you think you'll ever have kids of your own, Jared?" Corey asked.

"Come on, sis, you're putting me on the spot."

"Just following the natural course of conversation. You know how much Mom and Dad would love grandchildren."

"Corey, this may come as a surprise, but any children *you* have will be their grandchildren, too."

Natasha and Barbara both laughed. Corey looked embarrassed. "I'll have kids one day," she said. "But I'm only thirty-one. You're thirty-seven. By the time you have kids Gary and Gordy's age, you might be too old to play ball."

"Corey, you have to be optimistic," Barbara said. Natasha knew her mother-in-law hoped to diffuse a potentially dangerous situation.

"I'm sorry, Jared," Corey said contritely. "I didn't mean to imply that you're over the hill."

"Don't worry about it," Jared said easily. "Hey, Natasha, this looks like a pretty nice house. Why don't you show it to me?"

"Sure. Barbara, Corey, will you excuse us?"

The two women nodded consent.

Natasha showed Jared the kitchen, dining room and the boys' room, with him nodding approval and making positive comments until, as they entered her office, he suddenly said, "Are you really all right, Natasha?"

She faced him confidently. "I'm better now than I've been in the last four years. But I think I know what you're getting at. You're wondering how I feel about Kirk and Tara coming tomorrow."

"I think what Kirk did was rotten. And that wife of his is certifiable."

"Maybe she is, but there's no reason for our first Christmas as a family since Tim died to be ruined." They were all together the year Tim died, just three months after the attack, but she didn't count that. It just hadn't felt like Christmas. Tim had been gone only three months. The boys didn't yet understand the finality of death as they asked Santa Claus with heartbreaking childlike hope to bring their daddy back, while every day she braced for a call from the medical examiner's office stating that Tim's remains had been found...a call that never came. "Even your mother has softened toward them. And we all have to think of Gary and Gordy."

"What did you tell them when Kirk stopped coming around?"

"I told them that Aunt Tara wasn't well, and that Uncle Kirk had to spend most of his free time with her. It probably wasn't the best reason, but it was the only one I could think of."

He grunted. "She's not well, all right. Listen, Natasha. I never told you this, but Tim called me that last morning."

"He did?" she said, genuinely surprised. "When? After the plane—"

"Yes. He'd spoken with you, and with Barbara, and with Kirk, too. He said it had gotten hot as Hades in there and it was getting very difficult to breathe, but he wanted to tell me something, the same thing he told Kirk and Barbara. He asked me to look out for you and the boys because he knew he wouldn't be getting out of there. Then he said he wanted to call you one more time."

She practically collapsed against the wall, like a one-legged doll. Tim had asked Kirk to look after her? "He called," she whispered. "Just before the South Tower collapsed. I told him his mother had picked up the boys and they were home with me, but he said he thought it best if he didn't talk to them. He was afraid he'd only frighten them. He could barely get the words out. I could tell he was struggling to breathe. It had gotten much more quiet than it had been the first time he called. That's when it all came true for me, that people around him were unconscious and dying from the smoke, that he wasn't going to be rescued and come home to us. He actually said goodbye to me, and he told me to take care of his sons." Tears she could no longer hold back rolled down her cheeks at the memory. "But I never knew he called you and Kirk and Barbara to ask you to take care of us."

"I'm sorry, Natasha. It wouldn't be an issue if Kirk had done as Tim asked. But he reneged because his wife is too insecure to allow him to give a few hours' attention to his own nephews." He paused. "I'm not excusing myself, either. I was only around for a few months afterward, and I never went back. So Barbara is really the only one who honored Tim's request."

Natasha wiped her face with her palms. "I understand things

clearer now," she said. "Why Barbara is so disappointed in Kirk. Why you're so concerned about my seeing him and Tara tomorrow. But I want everything to go smoothly. I don't want my children to know the real reason their uncle stopped coming around to see them, and I don't want them to sense any tension in the air." She knew a thing or two about childhood disappointment herself. "We're still a family, Jared. We've lost Tim, but we're still a family."

"Okay, Natasha. I promise to be on my best behavior. It's the least I can do. And I'm sorry I upset you."

"I'm all right. I needed to know. I may look at things differently myself, now. But I still want us all to get along tomorrow. And, Jared…"

"Yes?"

She wrapped her hand around his forearm. "Don't feel guilty about leaving New York. I know how heartsick you were by what you witnessed that day."

Natasha felt confident that neither Barbara nor Corey noticed anything amiss in either the length of time she and Jared had been gone, or in the fact that she had shed tears during the episode.

Corey stood next to her while Jared and Barbara said goodbye to the boys. "He looks great, doesn't he?"

"Yes, he sure does," Natasha agreed wholeheartedly. "Some lucky girl in Atlanta is bound to snap him up."

Chapter 3

Holiday spirit surrounded the Langston home, evidenced by the Nativity scene in their yard to the 3–D lights of Santa and his reindeer on the roof. When they reached the front door, Natasha, carrying a large aluminum dish full of macaroni and cheese, bent and spoke in a low voice, "Remember, boys, you don't need to ask Aunt Tara how she's feeling. It would probably be better if you didn't. It's a rather sensitive situation. Okay?"

"Okay," they said simultaneously.

Natasha rang the bell, and within seconds Corey answered, a welcome sight. Now that Natasha lived in Greer she'd had a chance to really get to know Tim's stepsister, and they'd become good friends.

"Merry Christmas!" Corey exclaimed, bending to scoop up Gary and Gordy in a big bear hug. "And what do we have here?" She tapped the large shopping bag Gary clutched in his small hands.

"Oh, just some gifts for you guys that Santa left under our tree by mistake," Natasha said cheerfully.

"Oh, Mom, come on. Santa?" Gary spoke with all the wisdom of a nine-year-old.

She rolled her eyes.

"Well, come in," Corey said. "Everyone is here." As Natasha walked past her, she added quietly, "And I do mean *everyone.*"

Natasha tensed, despite the comforting scent of warm spices of cinnamon and apple from the pies Barbara had baked. This would be her first face-to-face meeting with Tara in over a year and a half.

No one in the family had ever warmed up to Tara, whose standoffish manner made approaching her difficult. Sometimes Natasha thought Tara made a special effort to stay outside of the family circle rather than inside, just so she would have plenty to complain to Kirk about. She knew people existed who didn't seem happy unless they had a beef with someone.

She held her breath, releasing it when Jared appeared. "Corey, was that Natasha?" Upon seeing them he broke into a wide grin. "Hey!"

"Uncle Jared!" the boys shouted, running toward him. The unencumbered Gordy got there first. He squealed with delight as the six-foot-four-inch Jared lifted him high above his head.

Gary watched from the carpeted floor. "Hey, my turn!"

Jared obliged, but was unable to lift the larger, heavier Gary quite as high. Fortunately, Gary didn't notice.

"Merry Christmas!" Jared said as he lowered Gary to the floor, throwing in a swift somersault before placing him on his feet.

Natasha held her breath nervously as she watched her son being flipped like pizza dough, but Jared's hands held him securely on each side of his waist.

"Merry Christmas, Natasha!" he said, bending to kiss her cheek.

"Merry Christmas."

He spoke in a whisper, "Kirk and Tara got in about an hour ago."

"I know. Corey told me."

"Here, let me take that." He reached for the dish she held inside the oblong paper bag, tucking it under his right arm, then with his free left hand guided her by the elbow into the family room at the rear of the house, the center of the family's holiday celebration.

While Natasha greeted Barbara and Ed, her peripheral vision took in Kirk hugging Gary and Gordy. He held up his hand palm down a few inches above Gary's head, probably demonstrating how tall Gary would be in the near future. Like Tim, Kirk stood over six feet, and the boys' old pediatrician in New Jersey had already informed Natasha to expect Gary and Gordy to be at least that tall as adults.

She approached Kirk first. "Hello, Kirk. Merry Christmas."

Kirk's sheepish expression suggested embarrassment. "Natasha, hello." He took both her hands in his. "You're looking well. Spartanburg must be agreeing with you."

"Actually, I live in Greer. It's about fifteen, twenty minutes from here." Not only did Kirk not have her new address, but when she moved he didn't even offer assistance.

"Uh, yes, that's right. Mom mentioned you were a town or two away." He glanced to his right. "Look, Tara, it's Natasha. Isn't it good to see her again?"

"Hello, Natasha," Tara said, not acknowledging Kirk's last remark.

Natasha recognized the significance of the omission. Forcing herself to sound cheerful, she said, "Merry Christmas, Tara. Tell me, how was the drive?"

"Not bad at all," Kirk said. "I think most people like to be at their destination by Christmas morning, so traffic was light."

"How do you like living here in the sticks?" Tara asked.

Natasha knew she didn't imagine Tara smiling more with this question than she had when saying hello. Tara always preferred to dwell on the unpleasant side of life, or at least someone else's life. "The sticks are usually the perfect environment to raise children in," she said brightly, "so for me it's perfect."

"Are you working?"

"Tara, don't you remember? I worked at home when I lived in Montclair. I didn't have to change jobs when I moved."

"Actually, I meant nursing."

"No, not yet. I'll get relicensed when the boys are older, maybe when Gordy is about twelve. In the meantime, I think it's best that I be at home for them. Gary's class took a school trip to see a production of *The Nutcracker,* and I went along as a chaperon. I couldn't do things like that if I was working outside the home."

"Well, it's nice that you can afford it," Tara said.

Instantly Natasha knew the source of Tara's unpleasant attitude. She resented the financial settlements Natasha had received as a result of Tim's death. A quarter million dollars in life insurance benefits, the mortgage on her home paid off free and clear and the huge settlement from the 9/11 fund that made her a millionaire. What Tara clearly chose to forget was the price tag for that financial solvency—Tim's life. "Yes, well, excuse me," she said as she turned to walk away, not caring if she sounded abrupt.

She found Barbara in the large, bright kitchen filling a punch bowl with eggnog. "Don't mind me. I just came in here to count to ten," she said with a grimace.

"Oh, dear. Is Tara acting up already?"

"I don't understand why she dislikes me so much."

Barbara sighed heavily. "I don't think Tara is a very happy person, that's all. She doesn't like to see things go well for other people."

"I'll say. She just made a sarcastic comment about how I can afford not to work outside the home. I guess I should have asked her, would she prefer to have a lot of money and her husband dead, or would she rather *not* have a lot of money and her husband beside her every day and night."

"I know, dear," Barbara said sympathetically. "We both know Tara is just plain jealous. Although I've heard there's a lot of resentment over those settlements. A lot of people thought it was a bad idea because those poor folks out in Oklahoma City didn't get anything for the loss of their loved ones. I understand a lot of them lost their homes because of financial difficulties."

"That's because the people behind that bombing were home-grown terrorists, or, as the press said, like 'choirboys.' Crime is always made out to be more heinous when the defendants are people of color or of a different religion. Remember how the coverage of the trial of the Oklahoma City bombers got pushed to the back burner by the O. J. Simpson trial?"

"I remember."

"Timothy McVeigh and company killed over a hundred and fifty people, but America was more fascinated with a man accused of killing two people. It isn't fair. And I do feel sorry for the people out there who lost family members or were maimed for life themselves. I know that nobody raised funds on their behalf and that all they got was a break from paying income taxes for a few years. But I didn't make that decision, Barbara."

"I'm not siding with Tara," Barbara said quickly. "I'm just making an observation. My advice to you would be to not let her get to you. And my advice to myself is to stop wasting time wishing Kirk had married someone else."

Natasha laughed. "Barbara, you always have a way of making me feel better."

"Good." Barbara sprinkled nutmeg over the creamy beverage. "Why don't you help me carry out the food. Now that you and the boys are here, I think everyone's ready for some lunch."

"Is this lunch or dinner, Grandma?" Gordy asked when they sat around the oblong table, which Barbara had decorated with tall candles and festive red and green place mats.

"It's lunch," Barbara replied, "but I'll tell you a secret."

"What's that?" he asked eagerly, forgetting that the entire family would hear the "secret."

"For dinner we're going to have more of the same food."

"Ooh, neat! Does that mean I can have another drumstick?"

"Gordy, how many drumsticks do you think a turkey has?" Natasha said, and they all laughed. "Besides, you're barely done with that one. I see a lot of meat left on it."

"I'm gonna finish it."

"You don't clean your bones like Daddy did," Gary said. "*I* cleaned my plate. Daddy used to say that you have to eat good if you want to grow up big and strong, like him."

Gordy stuck out his thin chest. "I'm gonna be real tall, like Uncle Jared."

Jared grinned easily. "You guys will both probably be over six feet. Your dad was, and so is Uncle Kirk."

"How tall are you?" Gary asked.

"I'm six-four. But you have to remember, you'll take after your dad and Uncle Kirk, not me."

"Why's that?"

A startled Natasha began to reply, but Jared waved her off. "Because Uncle Kirk is your blood relative, and I'm related to you by marriage."

"But you're our uncle," Gordy protested.

"Let me explain it to you boys," Ed said in his amiable paternal manner. "You see, Grandma and I were both married to other people before we met each other. Grandma had your daddy and Uncle Kirk with her first husband, your grandpa, and I had Uncle Jared and Aunt Corey with my ex-wife. When we married each other, we blended our two families. That's how it's been even before you two fellows were born."

Gary nodded. "Is that why Uncle Jared and Aunt Corey call Grandma 'Barbara'?"

"And why you guys are named Langston and Mommy and Gary and me are Lawrences?" Gordy asked.

"That's right, sport," Jared said. "Your grandma is my stepmom. I'm going to take you to meet my other mom while I'm here. I think you'll understand how our family works a lot better after that."

Natasha relaxed. Jared and his father did a fine job of explaining. The boys seemed to understand the somewhat tangled roots of their family tree.

Kirk cornered her later that afternoon, despite her best efforts to avoid him. "Natasha, I hear you and the boys are thriving down here. I'm glad."

"Thanks. We gave it a lot of thought before we decided to move. I made sure Gary and Gordy understood they would have to go to a new school and make new friends. They were so happy about being close to Grandma and Grandpa Ed again that they didn't mind."

"I know my dad wishes he could be around more."

She shrugged. "Freeport, Long Island, is a good ways from Montclair. It's even farther from here. But we'll be sure to visit him and his wife when we go to New York."

Kirk glanced at Tara, who had spotted them and come to stand at his side, no doubt so she could hear their conversation. She didn't let him out of her sight. Natasha considered how trying that must be for Kirk. She wondered if he could even take a shower without her checking on him.

"Are you planning a trip?" he asked.

"I'm thinking about bringing them to Ground Zero, maybe for the next anniversary. I hoped to get there before the move, but there was so much to do."

"A lot to do?" Tara spoke up. "Barbara said all you did was call the moving people, and they packed for you and everything."

"There's more to moving than just packing, Tara," Natasha said calmly. "Electricity and telephone service has to be turned off at the old house and on at the new, mail has to be forwarded, the old house has to be left clean for the new owners…"

"Hmph. I'm surprised you didn't just hire somebody to do that, too, since you can afford it."

Natasha had enough of Tara's verbal taunts. "Yes, Tara, I can afford it," she said coldly. "Maybe you'll get lucky and lose Kirk to a terrorist attack, and then you'll be able to afford it, too." She gasped, her hand flying to cover her mouth. "Kirk, I'm so sorry. I'm so sorry."

He held out a hand, palm out, and nodded, then reached for his wife's upper arm. "Would you excuse us, Natasha?"

Gladly. She watched as Kirk escorted Tara into the hall toward their bedroom, then turned and nearly collided with Jared, whose facial expression reminded her of a thundercloud.

"Is something wrong, Natasha?" he asked, a suspicious eye on the retreating forms of Kirk and Tara.

"Do you think it would upset anyone if I went out for a few minutes? I have to get out of here and clear my head."

He took her arm. "Come on. I'll go with you."

Chapter 4

Kirk faced Tara in the privacy of his mother's guest bedroom, where they slept. "Tara, just tell me why you said that to Natasha? Why?"

"Because it's true, Kirk. Natasha can afford to pay for any service she needs. I thought it was ridiculous for her to make it sound like she worked so hard when she didn't do jack."

"Tara, you shouldn't have said that. You shouldn't even have been listening in the first place. I was trying to apologize to Natasha."

Tara placed her hands on her hips. "So now you're telling me I had no business getting into yours and Natasha's conversation? Tell me, what were you saying that you didn't want me to hear?"

"Like I said, I was about to apologize to her. I'm sure you had no interest in doing that, so you didn't need to be standing there eavesdropping."

"Eavesdropping! You're so blind, Kirk. You still can't see how Natasha is scheming. First she tried using her sons as a ruse to spend time with you, and she's still trying. If I hadn't come over she probably would have put on a helpless act to get you to feel sorry for her."

Kirk breathed out patiently. "Tara, Natasha doesn't have a helpless bone in her body. She's done a great job of holding it together after she lost Tim. And she's not interested in me. She never was."

She smiled unpleasantly as she brushed aside the curtains that covered the front-facing window. "Maybe not anymore. It looks like she's got her claws into Jared now."

Kirk crossed the room to look out the window. Natasha and Jared slowly walked down the driveway toward the curb, where Jared had parked his butterscotch-colored Crossfire. Both had their hands in their pockets, and they stood at least a foot apart. "She doesn't have her claws in him, Tara. He probably senses she's upset. He's watching out for her." *The way I should have done,* he added silently.

Tara turned away. "Hmmph. He's probably feeling guilty for running off to Texas barely six months after Tim got killed."

The crisp December air filled Natasha's lungs. She noticed Jared had parked on the street in front of his father and step-mother's home rather than in the driveway, almost as if he was anticipating having to take it out. Had he parked in the driveway he would have been blocked in. "Oh, what Barbara and Ed must think of me," she lamented, her palms brushing her braids back and simultaneously soothing the sudden pounding in her temples.

"No one will be upset with you, Natasha. I pulled Dad aside and told him I was taking you out to get some air. I'm sure he's told Barbara by now, and I'm sure they figured out it's because of Kirk and Tara." He unlocked the passenger door and held it open while she climbed in.

Jared quickly walked around to the driver's side. He started the car and drove, not speaking until he reached the stop sign at the corner. "Now, I'd like to know what happened to upset you so much."

"I don't know if it's so much what Tara said to me as what I said to her. Jared, I was so determined not to let them get to me, not to say anything that would put a damper on the day. And now I've done just that. Barbara so looked forward to having the entire family together for the holiday, and I ruined it with my big mouth."

"Whoa. I don't believe for one minute that you said anything that Tara didn't have coming to her."

She recounted what Tara had said and her own response to it.

"Where did she come from, anyway?" Jared asked. "You said Kirk came up to you and asked if he could speak with you for a minute. Didn't he mean he wanted to speak to you alone?"

"She just wandered over and joined us. You know how she is, at least with me. If she spots him talking to me she's on him like…mustard on a hot dog."

"It's not just you, Natasha. I remember Barbara saying that when Kirk brought Tara to meet her for the first time, she never had a free moment with him the entire weekend. She said she couldn't even tell Kirk what she thought because Tara was always right there, stuck to him like Krazy Glue." Jared shook his head. "I don't know how Kirk can stand being smothered like that."

"It's like she doesn't trust him for some reason. Or she doesn't trust me. But I've never given her a reason to be wary of me, Jared. I was married to her husband's brother, for heaven's sake."

"That's just the way Tara is. I'm sure Kirk has been nothing but patient with her."

"I feel so badly about having put a pall over the holiday," she repeated.

"Natasha, no one will blame you for what happened."

"I should have had better control of my impulses." She noticed the passing countryside for the first time, homes built on sloping hills with spacious front lawns, children riding brand-new bicycles and rolling along on new skates. "I hope you're keeping track of where you're going. I know Wade Hampton Boulevard—that's what U.S. 29 is called in Greer—and that's about it."

"I know where we are. Natasha, what kind of life do you have down here?"

"Oh, I work while the kids are at school. We spend the afternoons together. Gary usually has homework. In the spring he wants to get into softball, and Gordy wants to join a soccer league, so I'll be shuttling them to practice after school and to their games on Saturday mornings. Fortunately, they'll be playing at the same field."

"What about socially?"

"Corey's been a big help with that. Sometimes we go out to dinner or to the community theater. I joined the book club she belongs to. We meet once a month and have a lot of fun. Barbara and Ed are always happy to sit with the boys for me. I've joined a church and sing in the choir, and because I'm available during business hours I can sing at funerals." She chuckled, realizing how awful that sounded. "Fortunately, there's been no need for that yet."

"Well, that's promising," he said with a smile.

"The church sponsored a bus trip to a big mall in Atlanta last month. Barbara and I went, and the boys stayed home with Ed. And Gary and Gordy had parts in their Christmas pageant. So I stay pretty busy."

"Do you like it here?"

"Yes, I really do. It's not all that different from ho—from New Jersey. The climate is milder, which is a plus. And the boys love it. They're so happy to be near their grandparents again." She smiled at the thought, and then she realized that Jared had gotten her mind off of Tara and Kirk, which had probably been the whole idea behind his rather abrupt change of topic. "So tell me all about Atlanta."

"I'm afraid I haven't been there long enough to be able to tell you much. But I think I'll like it. I'm glad to be geographically closer to the family. I've missed you all."

"We've missed you, too. But we all know how deeply affected you were by 9/11. After all, your office was so close, and you didn't live that far away. I'm sure you could see the cloud of smoke from your apartment."

"I'll never forget that day, Natasha, if I live to be ninety." Jared's grip inadvertently tightened around the leather steering wheel. He spoke the truth—he continued to be haunted by images of that terrible day, and he probably always would be—but he was keeping a secret close to his heart. He hadn't left New York because of emotional distress over what he witnessed on 9/11.

He left because in the weeks following the terrorist attacks he found himself feeling more and more attracted to Tim's widow, and the resulting feelings of guilt and stress eventually became unbearable, to the point where he couldn't bear to be around her.

And in the brief time they spent together this afternoon it had already become apparent that he still had the same problem.

Chapter 5

Natasha and Jared returned after being gone nearly an hour. Kirk appeared so quickly—the moment they stepped into the foyer—that she had to consider that he'd been looking out the window waiting for them to return. "I just wanted to say I'm sorry, Natasha," he said, taking her hand. "For everything. The way I behaved last year, and for the things my wife said a little while ago."

She took in a deep breath, aware of Jared's towering presence beside her, of the increased pressure he exerted on her upper arm. She felt equally cognizant of Tara standing down the hall glaring at her. "I accept your apology, Kirk," she said, "but as long as I live, I'll never understand why you treated Gary and Gordy the way you did."

Having had her say, she gently pulled her hand away and continued walking, eager to join the family members who loved her and her sons unconditionally.

* * *

Fortunately, Natasha did not see any more of Kirk and Tara during their visit. The day after Christmas she and Corey hit the post-holiday sales at the mall while Jared entertained Gary and Gordy. Corey and Jared had gone home and Natasha was cleaning up the remnants of the take-out pizza order they ate for dinner, when her telephone began to ring. She picked up the kitchen extension, breaking into a huge smile when she recognized her friend Terry's voice on the other end of the line.

She met Teresa Brown at a local support group for people who had lost loved ones in the terrorist attacks. Sadly, after the attacks, Natasha found that her existing friends' attitudes toward her changed. Her girlfriends seemed suddenly embarrassed to have husbands when hers was dead. Others displayed suspicious glances if Natasha exchanged more than two words with their husbands, as if she had suddenly become a predator, a predator who now had millions. Saddened by these new developments and feeling like a pariah, Natasha simply allowed the friendships to peter out. She and Terry might not have known each other very long, but Terry had a better understanding of how it felt that awful morning, the fear, and then the sickening certainty that their loved ones could not possibly survive the collapse of the buildings.

Terry hadn't been married, but she and Wendell Williams had dated for two years, and she felt confident a proposal would be forthcoming in the near future, perhaps over the holidays. But whatever plans Wendell may have had for the future died with him.

"Hi, Natasha!" Terry greeted. "How was Christmas?"

"Hey! It was…pretty nice."

"Uh-oh. You must have seen Kirk and his wife."

Natasha sighed. "It went a long way toward spoiling the day. Tara kept making nasty comments about my having money, and I finally lost my temper and told her off."

"I'm sure she had it coming."

"That's what Jared said."

"That's right, Jared is there. How is he?"

"He's great. As supportive as ever. It's hard to believe he and Tim were just stepbrothers, because Jared has been there for me more than Kirk has, at least in those early days after everything happened, before he moved away." She sighed. "But enough about me. How was your holiday?"

"It was nice. I ate too much, and now I've got a rock in my gut." Terry laughed. "I miss you something awful, Natasha, but I'm glad you and the boys are happy down there."

"Thanks, Terry. We miss you, too. You have to come down for a visit soon."

"I don't suppose you have any reason to come up here."

"Well, the boys' grandfather is in New York."

"But you never saw that much of him after the attacks."

"No. He took Tim's loss very hard. I got the impression he almost couldn't bear to look at Gary and Gordy because they remind him of Tim and Kirk when they were kids. But he called this morning and said he hopes we'll be able to get together next summer. I think the roughest time has passed, and he realizes that he needs to see his grandsons."

Jared called midmorning of the next day. "I just wanted to let you know that your two favorite people left a few hours ago."

She knew he meant Kirk and Tara. "Did you go over and say goodbye?"

"You're kidding, right? No, Corey talked to Barbara from work, and she just called me. Now I'm calling you."

"Our family communication works like a carrier pigeon," Natasha remarked.

"So what are you doing, working?"

"Yes. It's generally difficult to get anything done when the boys are out of school, but they're still sufficiently fascinated by the computer games they got for Christmas that they're not knocking on my office door every ten minutes. Although Gordy has been in twice to complain that Gary is hogging the computer."

"What are you doing for lunch?"

"The same as I do every day. I'll make myself a salad and the boys some sandwiches. Turkey, of course." Barbara insisted that both she and Corey take generous portions of food home with them. Natasha's refrigerator contained plastic containers of turkey, ham, sweet-potato casserole, green bean casserole and other dishes from their lavish holiday dinner. "You sound bored. Why don't you join us for lunch? The boys will welcome your company. I work for a few more hours after lunch, but I knock off by three."

"What is it you do again?"

"I edit medical transcripts. I fill in blanks, correct punctuation, things like that."

"Didn't you use to transcribe them?"

"That's how I started, but I'm better suited for editing." A registered nurse by profession, Natasha left her job after giving birth to Gary to care for him at home. At the time, she and Tim lived with Barbara and Ed while they saved to get a home of their own. Unhappy with day-care options but needing to go back to work because she and Tim had found a house in Montclair, Natasha found a stay-at-home position transcribing medical records for a local service. Shortly after Gordy was born, Tim received a promotion that allowed her to cut back to part-time. But Natasha wasn't a particularly fast typist, not a good thing in a field where production had a direct impact on the size of one's paycheck. She applied for a promotion to editor, filling in passages the transcription staff could not understand, correcting words, and generally cleaning up the formatting of reports. Natasha enjoyed editing much more than transcribing, and it paid better.

When Tim died she worked with a financial planner to invest her money and set up college and trust funds for Gary and Gordy, as well as health insurance benefits. Although she had become financially independent, Natasha continued to work part-time, mainly to maintain some sense of normalcy after losing Tim. Besides, working gave her a sense of accomplishment.

"Do you think you'll ever get back into nursing?"

"Probably, when the boys are older. Of course, I'll have to start from square one and get relicensed. I only worked for a few years, you know."

"That's right. You stopped when you had Gary."

"That's right. But when I do get back into nursing I doubt I'll do direct patient care. Utilization review is more my speed, especially since I've been reading patient transcripts all these years anyway. I figure it isn't too big a jump from checking word use and punctuation to reviewing the actual content and making recommendations.

"But enough about my career plans," she said. "Sorry for running off at the mouth like that. Sometimes I forget that I still have thirty years to contribute to the workplace. I feel like I've lived a lifetime already." She sighed heavily.

"Don't go getting morose on me."

"I'm not. So, will we see you this afternoon?"

"Sure."

"I'll let the boys know. They'll be tickled. You know, Jared, they kept telling me how much fun they had with you yesterday while Corey and I were out partaking in all those post-holiday markdowns. They're really getting used to seeing you every day."

"That won't be possible when I go back to Atlanta, but I can promise you I'll be up here at least one weekend a month to spend time with them."

Natasha realized too late that her words carried an implication she hadn't meant to make. "That's sweet of you, Jared, but I wasn't trying to paint you into a corner, even if it sounded like I was."

"I know you weren't. I enjoy being with Gary and Gordy. They're a lot of fun. I guess they bring out my inner kid."

Jared came over and spent the afternoon playing with the boys and giving them strategy tips for their computer games. After lunch he insisted on cleaning up the kitchen and that the boys help him. "I'm not one of those men who feels out of place in the kitchen, and I'd hate for Gary and Gordy to grow up feeling its unmanly to cook, or wash dirty dishes."

"I'm sure their future wives will thank you," Natasha said with a smile.

"I'm even making dinner for Corey tonight," he bragged, "since she had to go back to work today."

The next afternoon Jared showed up just as Natasha completed her work for the day and suggested they all go for a ride. They climbed into Natasha's Explorer because Jared's two-seater could not accommodate the four of them. "Wow, somebody short sat here," Jared teased as he adjusted the driver's seat for ample legroom.

"Jared, I'm five-nine. No one has ever called me short."

"Next to me you're short."

She playfully poked his arm. It did feel awfully good, having a man sitting in the driver's seat…almost like they were a nuclear family. Anyone who saw them would think just that, and a good-looking family at that. How nice it would be if it could be true and not just a mistaken observation….

Natasha stifled a whimper as she realized that she had become attracted to Jared, her brother-in-law. Well, technically her step-brother-in-law, but any way she looked at it, it wasn't appropriate. Just because Jared and Tim didn't share a bloodline didn't make Jared any less family.

She stared straight ahead, too upset to even speak. What in heaven's name was wrong with her, imagining Jared was her husband? In an instant she had become the vixen her old friends feared and Tara spoke of that day to Kirk.

She wished the ground would open up and swallow her, bucket seat and all.

Chapter 6

"Where are we going, Uncle Jared?" Gordy asked, leaning forward eagerly in the back seat.

"Remember the other day when I said I'd take you to meet my mom? Well, that's where we're going."

"To meet your mom?" Gary repeated.

"And my grandmother. I'll bet you didn't think I had a grandmother, did you?"

"Everybody has a grandmother," Gordy said, his high-pitched voice sounding quite serious. "Some people have two. Except Mommy. She doesn't have a grandma because she doesn't have parents."

Natasha suppressed a smile. She'd long since pushed aside the pain of growing up with an absent father and a mother who only occasionally visited. It hadn't been easy, but she made the best of it. She had Robin Harmon, who until this day remained her best friend. She and Robin used to pretend they were about to be adopted by a wealthy couple and that they would become sisters who had everything they could ever want. Talking about the lives they dreamed of helped ease the pain of being rejected.

In truth, neither girl was eligible to be adopted. Robin's mother had abused both alcohol and drugs and refused to give up her parental rights, even though she rarely visited, and even after Robin's father, to whom she had not been married, bled to death after being stabbed in a bar fight. As for Natasha's own parents, her father, Fred Pace, was never more than the name listed on her birth certificate. Natasha had known her mother, Debra Miller, who came to visit her maybe once a month, always painting a bright picture of what the future held.

Natasha's parents had both been only seventeen at the time of her birth. Debra managed to complete high school, then went on to college to study nursing. "My family wanted me to put you up for adoption," she told Natasha on one visit, "but I said no. It's always been my dream to bring you home with me and take care of you myself. That's what kept me going all through school, working part-time at night and studying whenever I had time. You'd like that, wouldn't you?"

"Oh, yes, Mommy! When can we go? Tomorrow? And will Robin be able to come visit us?"

Debra had laughed, a husky sound Natasha found fascinating. But then, everything about the pretty lady who was her mother fascinated her. At the time, she didn't realize how much she resembled her mother, and that one day she, too, would be pretty. "It's going to take a little more time, sweet pea," she'd said. "I haven't been working all that long. I'll have to get a good deal of money saved so I can get you all the things you'd like to have." She'd put her arms around Natasha. "Who knows? Maybe soon I'll meet a nice man who'll want to take care of both of us. I hate Newark. I'd like nothing better than to get out of here. But you and me, we come as a package. Where I go, you'll go."

From that moment on Natasha abandoned the idea of going to live in luxury with loving adoptive parents. She found it much more appealing to visualize living with her mother in a little apartment, just the two of them, with Robin coming over often to spend the night. No more than six or seven years old at the time, she could have no idea it would never come to pass. But she dreamed of it for years before giving up in defeat and bitterness.

She returned her attention to the conversation around her.

"It may be true that your mother doesn't have a mother of her own," Jared was saying to the boys, "but it's also unusual for people our age to still have a living grandparent."

"You mean, when Gordy and I get grown we might not have Grandma and Grandpa Ed?" Gary asked seriously.

"I hope you do, but you might not. You'll understand better when you're older."

"I know. They're going to go to heaven, where my daddy is," Gordy said knowingly.

"That's the final destination for most of us," Natasha said. "If you don't mind my asking, Jared, how old is your grandmother?"

"She's eighty-eight."

"Wow, that's really old," Gary said.

"Really old," Gordy agreed. "In two years she'll be ninety."

"She's lived a long time, but she's sharp as the proverbial tack," Jared said. "And she gets around pretty good, too. With that cane she uses, most people have to skip to keep up with her."

"I hope I'm active like that if I get to live that long," Natasha murmured. She and Tim used to talk about how they would sit around in matching rocking chairs on their front porch and watch the world go by. But of course that never came to pass. Tim died at the young and vigorous age of thirty-two. She was a year older than that now, and eventually their sons would be older than that as well, but as she aged, Tim would stay forever young in her memory.

Funny how you never knew what life held for you. One day over fifty years ago Jared's grandmother had been her age, and she probably never imagined she would live to be nearly ninety.

"You all right?"

Natasha blinked at the sound of Jared's low voice paired with his palm covering the back of her hand. "Yes, I'm fine. My mind was just wandering." The way his expression fleetingly changed and he gave a sad nod made her regret her choice of words. "I'm sorry, Jared. I don't mean to sound secretive. I was just thinking that some people live a long time and others die young. It's really a throw of the dice…or maybe it's decided the day we're born."

"I guess no one really knows for sure."

"Uncle Jared, where does your grandma live?" Gary asked from the back seat.

"She lives with my mom, and they live in Spartanburg, not far from your grandma and grandpa Ed. So it's not a long ride." He smiled across the console at Natasha. "There's no need for any are-we-there-yets."

She relaxed, confident that any hurt feelings she'd caused by sounding so vague had been smoothed over. She was still reeling from that embarrassing realization she'd had the other day, and because she still had to sort out her feelings for Jared, she didn't feel comfortable talking about Tim to him.

Traffic on U.S. 29 moved nicely at this time of day, with rush hour not yet started. Within fifteen minutes Jared pulled into the driveway of a redbrick ranch house with glossy black shutters. "We're he-ere!" Jared said in singsong fashion as he shifted into Park and removed the keys from the ignition.

Within seconds Gary and Gordy both had their seat belts unsnapped and climbed out to stand on the ground. Natasha suddenly felt nervous. She hoped Jared's mother and grandmother didn't think anything odd about his bringing them to their home. She quickly decided she was just being silly. Her guilt at suddenly seeing Jared not as a brother-in-law but as an attractive, desirable man was making her prone to ridiculous thoughts. No one would read anything into her accompanying Jared. After all, just because she had allowed herself to get carried away didn't mean *he* entertained such outrageous thoughts about *her*.

It would just be her secret crush, and in time she would get over it. Maybe seeing Jared in this new light and the cessation of her dream was nature's way of telling her it was time to start seeing men. And maybe she'd meet a man she really liked.

But even as she entertained that notion, she couldn't imagine becoming enamored with anyone other than Jared.

She hung back a little as he rang the bell and simultaneously opened the door with his key. Swinging the front door open, he called out, "Mom? Grandma? It's me, and I brought company."

Natasha followed Jared and the boys into a tastefully decorated foyer with console table, ornate oval mirror and a Queen Anne chair upholstered in green and maroon stripes in a trellis pattern. High U-shaped doorways on each side of the foyer revealed a living room and a dining room. Jared led them to the living room, and the first thing Natasha noticed was a large portrait of a beautiful young woman hanging over the fireplace. The woman had luminous dark eyes, and her hair was styled in an upsweep typical of those favored by women during the war years of the forties.

A tiny woman with a full head of gray hair sat resting in an armless chair in a corner. Jared bent his tall frame to kiss her cheek. "Hello, Grandma."

"Hello, dear. Who's this you've brought with you?" Her sharp dark eyes took in Natasha and the boys. "Don't tell me you've been keeping a family under wraps all these years I've been pleading with you to settle down."

They all laughed, and Natasha suddenly realized this was the same woman whose portrait hung above the fireplace. She essentially looked the same, only older, with short gray hair and fuller eyebrows. Even as she approached her ninetieth year, she retained her small frame, with her large expressive eyes dominating her face.

"Grandma, this is Tim's family, his wife, Natasha, and his two boys, Gary and Gordy. Guys, this is my grandmother, Olivia Hampton."

"Nice to meet you, Mrs. Hampton," Natasha greeted, the boys echoing her words.

"Call me Olivia. It seems like there are so few people left who call me by my first name these days," she lamented.

"We'll call you *Miss* Olivia," Natasha said quickly.

"That's fine." Olivia reached for Natasha's hand and held it in both of hers. "So your husband was Barbara's oldest boy." She made a clucking sound with her tongue. "Awful thing, what those people did with those airplanes. I never thought I'd live to see another day like the one when Pearl Harbor got bombed. Even that seemed different somehow, because in those days Hawaii wasn't a state. And it seemed so far away. But Washington, D.C., is only about five hours from here." Olivia's big brown eyes looked Natasha up and down. "How are you doing, child? I know it's been a few years since it happened, but some things stay with you always."

"Grandma," Jared protested.

"No, it's all right," Natasha said. "Miss Olivia, the boys and I are doing just fine. We're carrying on, the way Tim would have wanted." Again she felt a stab of guilt. True, Tim would want them to go on, but that didn't include having carnal thoughts about his stepbrother.

"I lost my husband twelve years ago," Olivia said. "Sometimes I forget he's gone, that's how close I hold him in my heart. Some mornings I wake up and say to myself, 'I'd better get Charles's breakfast.'" She sighed, a hand with arthritic fingers resting lightly on her chest. "I manage to get out of bed anyway. But when my Charles passed on I knew that part of my life was over. You, on the other hand, are still a young woman. You'll marry again, I'm sure."

Gordy, never shy, piped up. "My mommy doesn't want to get married again. She's got Gary and me to keep her company, and now that we live in South Carolina she has Grandma and Grandpa Ed and Aunt Corey."

"And Uncle Jared is going to come back and see us," Gary added.

"You're a strong family unit," Olivia said. "I hope you'll come back and see us. Think of us as an extension of that family."

"Thank you, Miss Olivia," Natasha replied warmly. "We will."

"I thought I heard someone," another female voice said. Natasha turned to see a middle-aged woman she instantly recognized as Jared and Corey's mother. Much of June Langston's features had passed to her two children, including her button nose and wide mouth. "Hello, boys!" she greeted with enthusiasm. "I'm June."

Gordy's forehead wrinkled. "Are you our other grandmother?"

"We don't have another grandmother, silly," Gary told him. "Mommy doesn't have a mommy, remember?"

Natasha had been honest with her sons about her childhood, telling them that she grew up without her parents because they were unable to take care of her. When they asked who had taken care of her, she told them her best friend, Robin, whom the boys knew as Aunt Robin.

June laughed. "No, but I'd love to be an unofficial grandmother. Tell you what. You can call me Grandma June if you'd like. Now that you're living nearby I hope to see a lot of you, Gordy, and you too, Gary."

"Hey, you know our names!" Gary exclaimed.

"That's because I've heard so much about you from my son and daughter." June held out her hand. "Hello, Natasha. It's good to meet you at last. I don't know why my daughter didn't bring you by sooner."

"Because your *son* is the one who thinks of everything," Jared said, sticking out his chest in mock pride.

"Hello, Mrs. Langston," Natasha said warmly. "It's good to meet you, too."

"Please, call me June."

"I would have known you anywhere, June. There's a strong resemblance between you and Corey and Jared."

"Ah, my son, my son," June said, hugging Jared, whose height nearly dwarfed her. "Did you know I named him after a character on a TV western with Barbara Stanwyck, *The Big Valley?*"

"No, he never mentioned it. Unfortunately, I'm not familiar with the show."

"You wouldn't be. It went off the air before you were born. Two of the three brothers on that show had names I liked, but Jared was my favorite. If Corey had been a boy, I would have named her Heath."

"I'm glad you didn't name her Heather," Jared grumbled.

June offered them Sprite, which they accepted. They made conversation for about twenty minutes, at which time Jared said, "Well, Mom, Grandma, I think we're going to have to hit the road. I don't want to get caught in rush-hour traffic, even if a lot of people are off this week."

"I wish you could stay longer, but I understand," June said.

"What will you do the rest of the day, Jared?" Olivia asked.

He stretched his long legs lazily. "I'm going back to Corey's and relax. I made dinner for her last night, so tonight she's cooking for me. Not just me, but Natasha, Gary and Gordy."

Natasha looked at him in drop-jaw amazement. "Jared! Corey never said anything about inviting the boys and me for dinner."

"That's because it was my idea."

"But, Jared, Corey worked all day. It's too much to ask her to go home and cook for five people."

"Relax, Natasha. She's just making spaghetti and salad. Besides, she told me to ask you guys to join us."

"But, still…"

"Now, Natasha, don't you fuss," Olivia said. "I know Jared and I know Corey. If they say it's all right, then it's all right. They consider you family, and family has to take care of each other."

Natasha tried to smile, but she feared it looked forced and unnatural. She *did* want Jared to take care of her.

Just not in a familial way.

"Your mother and grandmother are both sweet, Jared," Natasha said at the start of the drive back.

"They're the best."

"Miss Olivia is just beautiful. Has she always lived with your mother?"

"Just for the last five years or so. Grandma is very independent, so it took a lot of convincing on Mom's part. Now that Mom's retired—she taught school for nearly forty years—it works out even better."

"She never remarried?"

"No. She's dated over the years, and there always seems to be an admirer hanging around, but nothing permanent."

Natasha felt a little sad that the happiness Barbara and Ed had found in their second try at marriage eluded the appealing June Langston. She knew that life worked out better for some people than it did for others, and she wondered if she would be one of the lucky ones.

She certainly hoped so.

Chapter 7

At Corey's apartment, Natasha helped prepare dinner. She filled a Dutch oven with water and set it to boil while Corey changed into jeans.

"So Jared brought you and the boys to meet Mom and Grandma," Corey remarked as she measured dry pasta.

Natasha presumed that June called Corey at work after they left. "Yes, and they couldn't have been nicer. Treated us like we were part of the family. I'll definitely bring the boys back to visit with them again." June and Olivia accepted her and the boys as if they'd known them always. She'd been awfully lucky to become involved with such wonderful, giving people. Natasha wondered if this was God's way of compensating her for a childhood haunted by dreams that never came true. Tara represented the only liability. Without her there would have been no estrangement from Kirk, and her boys wouldn't have been hurt.

"Mom called me after you left. She said I should have brought you over last month, when you first got here, instead of waiting for Jared to take over."

Natasha's shoulders slumped. "I didn't mean to cause any trouble between you and your mother, Corey."

"You didn't. That's just how Mom is." Corey chuckled. "She said Gordy asked if she was their other grandmother."

"He's still a little confused about who's who in our family. But your mother invited them to call her Grandma June, which I think is sweet." Natasha paused. "Your grandmother mentioned Barbara by name. Are the three of them friends?"

"No, not really. They don't see each other often, other than maybe running into each other at the supermarket or the bank. But when my grandfather died, Pop and Barbara came down from Jersey and were a tremendous help with the arrangements. Grandma never forgot Barbara's kindness. After Pop and Barbara retired and moved here, Mom and Grandma had them over to dinner."

"That was nice of her."

Corey shrugged. "My parents resolved all their issues years ago, Natasha. I don't know if I can say they're exactly friends, but I like to think that when I get married they'll at least be able to sit in the same pew. With Barbara, of course, and whomever Mom is seeing at the time."

"Are you seeing anyone, Corey?"

"Oh, I met someone the other week who put a sparkle in my eye, but I don't think he really noticed me. Oh, that reminds me, Natasha. In honor of Jared's being here, I'm going to have a few friends over to celebrate New Year's."

Natasha stiffened. Jared, here for New Year's? She hadn't realized he would still be in Spartanburg by then. The idea didn't particularly thrill her. No doubt he would give her a kiss on the cheek at midnight, and she would have to fight to control herself, to keep from pressing her body against his and feeling his arms around her—what she so desperately wanted every time she saw him. The long-dormant sexual feelings in her had arisen, and since Jared was the object of her desires it had caused a lot of tossing and turning at night because of a little voice inside her that said it was wrong.

She quickly turned her back to Corey, using the pretext of rinsing the cans of spaghetti sauce and tomato paste under the faucet. "That sounds nice, Corey. I'll be glad to help you, that is, if Barbara and Ed are available to babysit." Even as she spoke the words she knew they weren't. Barbara had already told her that she and Ed were going out for New Year's. Gary and Gordy, bless them, would give her an out. Better to miss the whole thing than to suffer through the torture of not getting what she knew she could never have.

"Actually, they're going out, but now you have a second set of babysitters. Mom and Grandma."

Natasha turned to stare incredulously at her sister-in-law. "Corey, I couldn't possibly ask June and Miss Olivia to sit with Gary and Gordy. We just met them a few hours ago. Don't you think that's being a little presumptuous?"

"You don't have to. I mentioned my plans for a party to Mom, and also that you might have a babysitting problem, and she volunteered. She said the boys can spend the night."

"That's awfully nice of her. But I'll call and make sure she really wants to do it. I don't want her to feel pressured."

Jared approached the pass-through to the kitchen. "Hey, what's with all this chatter? Y'all are supposed to be working."

"We *are* working, warden," Corey said, cowering like a frightened convict. "I'm making the salad, and Natasha is heating up the sauce and the meatballs."

Jared's eyes went to the bag of frozen meatballs Natasha poured into the sauce. "What's this? *Frozen* meatballs?"

Corey waved the knife she held at him. "Now listen, you, I've got a very sharp knife in my hand, so no more criticism."

Jared, who had been leaning against the counter, hastily straightened up and held out his palms. "Yes, ma'am."

Gordy called to Jared. "Hey, Uncle Jared, you said you were gonna play with me some more."

Jared went back to the boys. Corey rinsed off a tomato and glanced out at them. "You know," she remarked to Natasha, "seeing how my brother gets along with kids so well, maybe he should date women with kids instead of avoiding them like he does. But he says women with baggage aren't for him." She chuckled, then turned back to the cutting board.

Natasha's heart sank. So Jared didn't date women with children. It shouldn't have stung, but it did, and terribly. She might have a crush on him, but she dreamed her feelings would one day be reciprocated. In light of what Corey just said and the other big problem that couldn't be ignored, her hopes seemed destined to remain just that.

After dinner Natasha and Corey relaxed in the living room while Jared, per the terms of his arrangement with his sister, cleaned the kitchen. "Natasha, why don't you call Mom now?" Corey suggested.

Natasha dialed the number Corey supplied. As Corey had said, June insisted she would welcome the opportunity to care for the boys. "Sometimes Mama and I both go to bed early on New Year's," she explained, "but the last couple of years we've been staying up in time to see the ball drop at midnight. I think Mama is excited just to be seeing another year. A friend of mine will be here, too, and I'm sure the boys will want to stay up to see the new year in. They strike me as night owls."

"They are. Gary used to sleep through it, but Gordy has always managed to be up hollering on New Year's Eve, even his very first year. He was born November twelfth, so by New Year's he was only about seven weeks old." She sighed. "He's always been a handful. Tim used to worry about what would happen when he became a teenager."

"I'm glad you brought Tim up, Natasha. I didn't tell you this before, but I really am terribly sorry about what happened, how you lost him."

It seemed odd to be accepting condolences more than four

years after the fact, but she knew June meant well, as had Olivia. "Thank you, June."

"Well, Mama and I would love to have the boys spend New Year's with us. You know—" June's voice dropped lower, as if she was about to share a confidence "—I always thought that by now I'd be a grandmother and Mama a great-grandmother. I've always envied Barbara for having grandchildren. Sometimes I wonder if I'll ever get to hold another baby."

"Well, Gary and Gordy aren't babies, but I'm sure they'll be thrilled to spend the night at Grandma June's."

"Natasha, I do hope I didn't confuse them by suggesting they call me that. They do realize I'm not really their grandmother, don't they?"

"Yes, just like they know that Grandpa Ed really isn't their grandfather. They do have a grandfather, but they haven't seen much of him the last couple of years."

"All right, then. We'll expect the boys New Year's Eve. You bring them over whatever time is convenient for you. See you then."

Natasha said goodbye and hung up. "It's all set," she said to Corey.

"See? I told you. My mother loves being around kids. She wants grandchildren."

Natasha chose not to share the thoughts June had expressed on that very topic. Instead, she glanced through the pass-through kitchen window and saw Jared busily wiping down the counter. "So Jared is staying for New Year's," she remarked casually.

"Yes. Everybody's so happy he's sticking around for a while. Dad, Mom, Grandma, Barbara. He's got a lot of lost time to make up for, and they've all missed him terribly."

Natasha's imagination immediately began to run rampant. Having Jared here for the holiday might not be so bad after all. And wouldn't it be wonderful if the real reason Jared remained in Spartanburg over New Year's was to be near her a little longer?

She knew that couldn't possibly be true, but nevertheless she enjoyed thinking it.

* * *

The night before New Year's they went to Barbara and Ed's for an informal family dinner, "the last one of the year," as Barbara put it. Ed, wearing a leather jacket and turtleneck sweater to guard against the December chill, grilled rib-eye steaks on the patio, while Barbara baked potatoes and cut up vegetables for a salad.

Sitting around the table, they all watched in amazement as Jared downed a second steak after cleaning his plate of salad, loaded baked potato and steak number one. "I've seen it before," Corey remarked, "but I can still hardly believe it."

"Most other kids say 'mama' and 'dada,' but Jared's first word was 'meat,'" Ed joked.

"I wasn't there to hear it, of course," Corey added, "but I'm told his second word was 'more.'"

Jared, his jaws steadily rocking in a chewing movement, shrugged. "Why is everybody looking like they've never seen anyone eat before?"

"After watching you, I feel like I really *haven't* seen anyone eat before," Natasha said with a laugh. "Do you often eat two steaks in one sitting, Jared?"

"Only when Dad makes them this good."

"Well, they were awfully good, Ed," Barbara said. Everyone echoed her sentiments, even Gary and Gordy, for whom Barbara had thoughtfully gotten steaks cut to a quarter inch, which she served on hoagie rolls.

"Steak was my daddy's favorite food," Gary announced.

Gordy nodded. "That's right."

After dinner, Corey insisted on helping Barbara with the cleanup. Natasha, too, offered assistance, but both women insisted that cleanup would be a snap between the two of them and urged her to relax with the boys.

Jared walked a few paces behind Natasha as she ambled to the living room, his eyes fastened to her swaying hips. Natasha sure could fill out a pair of jeans, he thought with admiration.

She appeared a little heavier than he remembered, but the hour-glass figure still existed, just more of it. Tim used to fondly say that his wife was built like the proverbial brick house. Seeing the two of them together had made Jared wish he would one day find someone who made him as happy as Natasha did Tim.

He'd waited a long time to get married—he could hardly believe he was only three short years away from turning forty—but he only wanted to marry one time, and he wanted to be certain that he made the best possible choice of a wife. He'd opt for the happily-ever-after over divorce any day.

He would never forget the constant arguments between his parents in the last months of their marriage. He and Corey were kids then, she about five and he six years older. They sought relief from all the tension at the home of their maternal grandparents, where all was peaceful. Charles and Olivia Hampton assured them that the trouble between their parents had nothing to do with them.

Still, Jared had been crushed when his parents sat he and Corey down and announced their plans to end their marriage. In spite of all the recent arguments, he remembered plenty of happy times together and spent endless hours lamenting about if only things could be like they used to. When he got married, he told himself, he and his wife would stay married the rest of their lives.

He'd liked Natasha Miller from the first time Tim introduced him to her. They seemed so happy together. It made him feel a little envious, not because he coveted Natasha but because of the bond she and Tim shared. He was two years older than Tim and had yet to meet his own Ms. Right. He had no way of knowing that Tim's days with Natasha would end in the smoke and heat of a terrorist-orchestrated plane crash…and that he would have to fight his attraction to his widow.

He sat on the arm of Natasha's chair and spoke to her in a low voice. Something Gordy said during dinner made him put a thought together, and Natasha could confirm it for him. "Gordy doesn't remember Tim at all, does he?"

"No, but he hates admitting it. That's why he agreed so readily with Gary about steak being Tim's favorite. He always will whenever Gary says anything about Tim." Her gaze focused on the floor. "It breaks my heart."

She caught her breath when he covered her upper arm and gave it a reassuring squeeze.

Just then Ed went by. He slapped Jared on the back. "We're all glad you're spending New Year's here in town, son."

"It's good to be here with everybody. Besides, better to ring in the new year with Corey and Natasha than in a strange city by myself. I haven't had a chance to meet any people yet."

"I presume you mean females," Ed prompted. "What's it been, a week since you've relocated? Shucks, even *you* can't operate that fast."

Natasha abruptly turned away, not wanting anyone to see her crestfallen expression. She knew she'd been foolish to even entertain the notion that she had anything to do with Jared's decision to remain in Spartanburg over the holiday. Once again she'd been painfully reminded that Jared would soon have a busy social life that didn't include women with children from previous relationships, like herself, or as Corey had so bluntly quoted him, "baggage." Even though she knew he didn't include Gary and Gordy in that unflattering category, it still hurt. But she had no one to blame for that but herself, because she'd allowed herself to entertain ludicrous thoughts and had been tossed back to reality with a thud.

Jared waved goodbye to Natasha and the boys as he backed the Crossfire out of his father's driveway. He waited for her to back out in front of him and then followed her until it came time for him to turn off for Corey's apartment, tooting his horn to alert her of his departure. Natasha honked back as she drove straight ahead.

"Well, that was a nice evening," Corey said with a satisfied sigh. "The last quiet evening of the year. Tomorrow night all hell will be breaking loose."

He chuckled. "You live in Spartanburg, South Carolina,

Corey. The way you talk you'd think you lived three blocks from Times Square."

"You really miss New York, don't you, Jared?"

"Not anymore," he said honestly. "But sometimes I wish I'd toughed it out longer." At least, he wondered if he should have shared his feelings for Natasha with her instead of simply leaving town. If he'd confessed his feelings to her before he moved, it surely would have come as a shock, but perhaps it wouldn't have appalled her. He considered that perhaps she wouldn't have reacted by slapping his face and telling him she never wanted to see him again, the way women did to men who got out of line in all those old movies his mother watched. Sure, it would have been awkward between them initially, but by now enough time might have elapsed for the impact to have softened and be replaced with a "Why not?" He could have been miles ahead of where he was now.

Which was nowhere.

Chapter 8

Natasha passed a tray holding filled champagne flutes and noisemakers to the guests. Corey's small apartment was comfortably filled with about fifteen revelers dressed in their finest, waiting for the old year to turn into the new. She was very much aware of the handsome figure Jared cut in his tuxedo with its white jacket. The last time she'd seen him dressed in a suit was when he escorted her to Tim's memorial service, a sad event held three weeks after the day the World Trade Center collapsed. She did not allow the just-turned-five Gary nor three-year-old Gordy to attend. Even after all the remains and debris of the trade center had been analyzed, a process that took several years, no traces of Tim's body were ever found.

"I think everybody has a glass," she said to Corey.

"Thanks for helping me, Natasha."

"No problem." She lowered her voice to a loud whisper, "Hey, is your friend here? The one you told me you met recently. The one you were, uh, semi-interested in?"

"Oh, him. No, he's not here. I don't really know him well enough to invite him over with my closest friends. Besides, I don't think he'd feel all that comfortable."

"Why not? It's a party, for heaven's sake."

"Uh…I don't really think he's the party type. I'm just guessing, of course, but he seems to be more of the quiet type who enjoys good conversation more than a lot of loud music. These are just my friends here tonight. No romantic interests."

"One minute!" someone yelled from the living room. Natasha and Corey both grabbed champagne glasses and noisemakers and joined the others in gathering around the large flat-screen television, where a big red apple slowly descended in Times Square.

Natasha easily spotted Jared, who stood out in his white jacket. He sat on an ottoman corresponding with a leather recliner. In the recliner sat Shontae Woods, one of Corey's close female friends who was also a member of the book club. Shontae reclined a few inches at a sexy angle, her legs crossed delicately at the ankles. Not only was she pretty, but petite, short enough to make Natasha feel like an Amazon in her three-inch heels. Fear stabbed at her heart. Did he find this woman pretty? Instantly she realized he *had* to think that. Shontae was a real stunner, with her light eyes and short sandy-brown hair that tonight she wore in thirties-style finger waves. Jared, of course, was a flesh-and-blood man. Would he leave here tonight with her phone number in his pocket, perhaps see her before he returned to Atlanta?

"Ten…nine…eight…" The guests chanted the closing seconds of the old year. Out of the corner of her eye Natasha saw Jared lean over and say something to Shontae. Even in the dark Natasha could see Shontae's disappointment and lingering glance when Jared got up and crossed to where she stood with Corey. Could he actually be coming to her…?

"…three…two…one…Happy New Year!"

Natasha held her breath, letting it out when Jared went to Corey, his arms outstretched. Of course. He and his sister had always been close, and like him, she had no date for the evening to share a first kiss with. "Happy New Year, sis," she heard him say.

Corey kissed his cheek. "And Happy New Year to you, brother of mine."

Natasha found herself hugging those who stood nearby, the festive occasion overriding the fact that she had never seen most of them before this evening. The other guests crowded in, separating her from Jared. Suddenly surrounded by strangers, she developed an overwhelming urge to speak to Gary and Gordy and let them know they were in her thoughts. June assured her that it would be fine for her to call at midnight, that she and her mother would definitely still be awake.

She worked her way out of the crowd, stopping to greet Shontae, who was clearly making her way to Jared.

Natasha entered Corey's bedroom, closing the door gently behind her, knowing Corey wouldn't mind her coming in to use the phone in the only quiet room of the apartment.

Coats covered Corey's full-size bed. Natasha pushed some of them aside so she could sit on the edge of the bed while she dialed.

Gary and Gordy had indeed made it to midnight, although they both sounded tired. They were thrilled to hear from her and proudly stated that they'd stayed up to see in the new year.

"I love you both so much," she told them. "Now, I want you to get a good night's sleep. You made it past midnight, so there's no need to stay up later. Miss Olivia and Grandma June are probably ready to go to bed, too."

She beamed when the boys told her they loved her, too. "Good night, my loves," she said, her voice ringing with affection. "I'll pick you up tomorrow after breakfast." Natasha knew it wouldn't be a late night; already she felt emotionally exhausted.

She hung up the phone with a little sigh, wishing she were with them. The sound of breathing behind her startled her, and she drew in her breath and whirled around.

"Natasha, it's me," Jared said quickly. "I didn't mean to sneak up on you. You were talking—well, you were talking to someone, and I didn't want to interrupt." He managed to sound natural, but inside he felt all stiff and uneasy. He'd heard her call the other party her "love," and he didn't like it at all. Who else would a woman speak to right after midnight on New Year's Day except the man in her life? She must have left someone special behind in New Jersey, someone none of them knew about. Why hadn't she told anyone?

"I was talking to the boys. Your mother told me it would be okay to call at midnight, that she and Miss Olivia would still be up. Gary and Gordy stayed up, too, but they sound tired, so I don't think they'll last much longer." She noticed a strange expression wash over his face, and then it was gone.

"When I went to wish Corey a happy new year you were right next to me. The next thing I knew I was surrounded. I looked for you to wish you happy new year and saw you rushing away. I wanted to make sure you were all right."

She suddenly felt embarrassed that he'd noticed her distress. She decided to make light of it. "Now, Jared, I could have simply been going to the restroom."

He grunted. "Nothing like waiting until the last minute. If somebody was in there you would have been up the creek."

"Yes, I suppose so," she agreed. "I just felt a very strong urge to speak with the kids all of a sudden."

"I know how important family is to you."

"The boys and I are so lucky to have Barbara and Ed and Corey and you in our lives."

He cleared a spot on the opposite edge of the bed, which was covered with coats. "Listen, Natasha, I don't want to get into anything I shouldn't, but I've always been curious about something. Did you ever see your parents while you were growing up?"

The mountain of coats between them made their sitting on a bed together seem less intimate. "I never saw my father," she admitted. "My mother says he came to see me once, but I was just a baby at the time. Apparently, after that, he went on and did his own thing. My parents were teenagers when I was born, you know."

"Yes, Tim mentioned that. Did you see your mother often?"

"Not a whole lot. She'd come maybe seven or eight times a year. Usually she'd have a little gift for me. She always used to say how she hoped that one day she could bring me to live with her." Her gaze moved downward, and she winced as she spoke. She tried not to think about those long-ago years, but when she did it still hurt. Oddly, she found that memory even more painful than losing Tim. "Eventually we lost touch."

"How did that happen?" he asked gently.

Natasha looked at him and shrugged. "She stopped coming around to see me when I was about eight. She'd married by then, and she was expecting a baby." It surprised her how clearly she recalled that last visit after twenty-five years. "She said her husband had a construction job in North Carolina, and they were moving there. She said she'd told him all about me and asked him if they could bring me with them. He said not now—something about all they had going on with the move and the new baby—but maybe later." Once again she lowered her eyes. "I felt so happy when she left, so certain she'd really come back for me and that we'd have a house with a yard to play in and I'd get to be a big sister. But…she never came back. I never saw her again."

"You haven't seen your mother since you were eight? Natasha, did you ever consider that maybe something happened to her?"

"Nothing happened. If she'd been in a car accident or something I would have known. I would have *felt* it." She pressed manicured fingertips against her chest.

"Do you think it was the new husband?"

"Absolutely. He just didn't want me around. After all, I wasn't *his* child. And she couldn't face me, so she went on and had a wonderful life while I spent every day hoping she would come for me." Her last words came out as a whimper, and she covered her face with her hands for just a moment, dropping her hands just as quickly and hugging herself instead.

Jared quickly rose and walked around to her side of the bed. He brushed the coats away and cleared a spot next to her, then sat and pulled her into his arms. What he wouldn't give to take her pain away. He knew Natasha grew up in a children's home, but he didn't realize her life had been filled with such pain. What an awful thing to do to a child.

"I'm all right," she said, her voice muffled against his shirt-front.

He rocked her gently. "Sure you are. Let's just sit here a few minutes." God, she smelled good. It was all he could do to keep from running his tongue over her smooth skin.

She raised her head and slid away from him. "No, really. I'm all right, Jared." She rubbed the lapel of his jacket. "I was afraid of that. Makeup."

Damn. Her sliding away from him meant he had to relinquish his hold on her. A moment of weakness for her had given him a brief period of bliss. "It'll come out," he muttered. "If you're sure you're all right, why don't we go back and join the party."

"Just for a little while. To tell you the truth, all the excitement has passed for me. I'd just as soon go home and go to sleep." She couldn't bear having to see him laughing and talking with Shontae. She knew she couldn't maintain a festive mood for very long. She felt heartsick at having to pull away from him. It felt heavenly to have him comfort her, but she had to break away. Having him hold her was too much to bear. It happened because she'd allowed her memories to overwhelm her and he wanted to calm her, not because he longed for her the way she did him.

If she was destined to want something she could never have, she'd rather not have the teaser.

To Natasha's surprise, at 1:00 a.m. when she quietly informed Jared and Corey of her plans to leave, Jared insisted on driving her. "But, Jared, it's only one o'clock," she protested. "The party will be going on for hours yet."

"I know, but there are plenty of nuts out on the road. All those people who get thrown out of parties because they're drunk and obnoxious have to go somewhere. I don't want you out there alone. I'll drive you. Corey and I will bring your car back to you later today."

Natasha recognized disappointment on Shontae's face when she saw Jared with his coat on. "You aren't leaving, are you?" she asked, her pretty face holding a hint of a pout.

"I'm going to drive Natasha home to Greer. I'll be back in about a half hour."

"I keep telling him it isn't necessary, but he won't listen," Natasha managed to say.

"Oh, that's all right. I understand." Shontae looked perfectly comfortable with the idea of Jared bringing his sister-in-law home.

And why shouldn't she be? Natasha thought miserably. *I'm no threat to her. I'm part of Jared's family. He could never be interested in me that way.*

"You're awfully quiet," he remarked on the way home. "I hope you're not sulking because I insisted on driving you."

"No, that's not it. I was just thinking how strange it seems for me to be going out for New Year's. It's the first time I've celebrated since Tim died."

"You shouldn't feel guilty for having a social life, Natasha, especially after four years. You're still a young woman."

She made a grunting sound.

"As time goes by you'll meet more people, start getting out more for occasions a little more exciting than church trips or women's book clubs. Or singing at funerals."

"You make my life sound so exciting," she said in a droll tone.

He glanced over at her. "I think you're just in a pensive mood, and nothing but time will change it."

"I think you might be right," she said with a sigh.

He pulled into the empty driveway of her home, lit by a dim porch bulb. A faint glow from behind the living-room drapes suggested more light.

They exited from the low-sitting sports car simultaneously. Jared rested his hand gently on her shoulder as they walked to the front door. "Do you think you should have picked up the boys? Or just stayed the night at Corey's? I'm not sure you should be alone right now."

"Jared, I'm hardly suicidal. You don't have to worry about me. I'm sure the boys are asleep by now, and your mom and grandmother probably are, too. I wouldn't want to wake everybody up at this hour. And there's too much going on at Corey's for me to get any rest there." She shrugged. "I'm probably overdue for a little case of the blues. I've been nothing but upbeat since I moved here. It'll pass, probably by tomorrow."

"Just don't let a temporary sadness cloud your outlook for the entire year."

"I won't." She unlocked the brass-framed glass storm door first, then the front door behind it. The sight of her familiar furnishings bathed in light comforted her immediately. "I feel better already," she said. "Maybe I just needed to come home."

She smiled at him for reassurance, and they fell into an impulsive embrace. "Happy New Year, Natasha," Jared said.

"Happy New Year, Jared. And thanks for being such a good and loyal friend to the boys and me."

Arms still around each other's shoulders, they pulled back so they could see the other's face. For a moment they merely smiled at each other. Then Jared leaned in and pecked her on the lips. Natasha didn't expect this, and she knew her surprise showed in her expression. It was merely a friendly gesture on his part, she told herself quickly, nothing more.

But just as her expression had changed to one of surprise in that swift moment, his changed as well, not to surprise but desire. She knew what would happen next in the seconds before he lowered his head once more and fastened his lips to hers, gently running his tongue over her lips, coaxing her to let him in.

With a breathless sigh Natasha did just that. Her arms tightened around his waist as she felt his grip on her shoulders intensify. Her hands roamed upward to grasp his broad back as her tongue joyfully mated with his, moaning somewhere deep in her throat. Oh, how she'd dreamed of this…

The fervor with which they kissed suddenly made it difficult to breathe, and they finally tore their mouths apart.

"Natash…I can't do this. We *won't* do this. Not after everything you and the boys have been through," he said in a choked whisper. "I forgot myself. Forgive me. Please forgive me."

Her happiness faded like a puddle in the sun. He regretted having kissed her. "There's nothing to forgive," she said softly, concealing her hurt.

He seemed unwilling to look her in the eye, instead focusing on something past her left shoulder. "I'd better get back to Corey's. We'll be over about nine to bring you your car." He turned away, speaking his last words to the air while walking toward his car. "Good night, Natasha."

Chapter 9

Jared slept badly. The feelings he'd tried so hard to fight, and that ultimately drove him out of town, had taken over full force. He'd finally kissed Natasha, pulled her into his arms and taken possession of her mouth as if he had every right to do so…except he didn't. She was Tim's widow, and that made her off-limits. When Tim asked him to look out for her, he hadn't meant for him to try and take his place.

But Natasha felt so good, so right, in his arms. For one crazy moment he'd allowed himself to believe she wanted the kiss as much as he had—but that was just his ego at work. Thank God Gary and Gordy weren't there to witness his amorous behavior. They probably would have jumped on him, especially that spirited little Gordy, for taking such brazen liberties with their mother.

At least he'd have another opportunity to apologize to her. Corey explained that she'd promised to help a friend prepare for guests she'd invited to watch the New Year's bowl games and asked if he'd mind if she skipped driving over to Greer to bring

Natasha her car. "I'm sure Natasha won't mind dropping you back here. She's got to pick up the boys at Mom's anyway. You might even want to go with her."

"No, I'm sure she won't." He sounded agreeable enough, but inside, his stomach churned. He had no intention of accompanying Natasha to his mother's house. He'd see his mother and grandmother later. It would be hard enough to be in the same vehicle with her for the return trip to Spartanburg. But he could hardly insist that Corey accompany him; she would want to know why. He'd planned on suggesting that Corey wait in the car, which would give him the opportunity to return Natasha's car keys and take a moment to apologize once more before leaving. Now he was faced with being alone with Natasha for the twenty-minute return drive to Spartanburg, which as a result would be much more awkward.

Tomorrow he would go back to Atlanta. It would be so easy to simply not see Natasha at all. Corey would go along if he suggested they drop off Natasha's car in the wee hours for her convenience, but that wouldn't be fair to Corey, who had been up until after 3:00 a.m. Besides, in his heart he knew that avoiding Natasha was the coward's way out. Besides, he *wanted* to see her. Jared still wrestled with the nagging feeling that he, in his own way, had dishonored Tim's memory by abandoning Natasha when he moved to Houston. He couldn't cope with his own growing feelings for her, but he was sure she'd be all right because his father and Kirk were nearby. Then his father retired and returned to his South Carolina hometown, and after that Kirk, the only remaining family member left in New Jersey, just dropped out of her life because he couldn't deal with his wife's insane jealousy. Natasha had needed him and he hadn't been there. No way would he do anything to hurt her ever again.

He lit a cigarette for the express purpose of having an excuse to hang back when he reached Natasha's door.

She looked around expectantly. "Corey didn't come?"

"She had just gotten up as I was leaving. She's helping her

friend Tameka get set up for the company she and her husband are having this afternoon for the football games. She wanted me to ask if you were sure you won't change your mind and come by."

"That's sweet of her, but I don't think so. After being away from the boys last night I'd really like to spend the day with them. Besides, I'm not that much into socializing. I did plenty of that last night."

"I understand. I'm sure Corey does, too. You don't mind dropping me back at her place, do you?"

She expected he would come along to his mother's and realized with a sinking heart that he didn't want to be alone with her any longer than necessary because of what occurred between them last night.

That was probably why he stood a few yards away from her front door. Natasha stood and watched Jared inhale, then exhale the smoke from his cigarette. She disliked smoking as a habit—she'd always tried to get Tim to stop—but Jared looked good enough to be in a magazine ad. She sensed his nervousness and felt equally ill at ease, but tried to hide it. "Are you about ready to take that ride?"

"Sure."

"I'll just grab my purse and house keys." A yawn inadvertently escaped from her lips as she climbed next to Jared in the passenger seat of her Explorer.

"Are you tired?" he asked.

"Just a little. I'm used to getting up early, but not staying up late." She paused. "Are you feeling better this morning?"

"No, I can't say I am. Natasha, about last night—"

"Jared, I'm going to interrupt you. What's happened has happened, we can't change it now. I don't think it's fair to either of us to beat each other up about something we can't do anything about."

"So you think we ought to just forget it."

Better that than have this tension between us. "Yes. Let's just forget it."

But as she said the words, she knew she'd never forget that kiss.

What she didn't know was that Jared, who concentrated so intently on the road ahead, had the exact same thought.

At his request she drove him back to Corey's first. "I'll be over to see Mom and Grandma later," he said. "I'm really tired. It was a late night last night. When the last guests left I helped Corey straighten up, since she can't bear to wake up to a big mess. I think I'll go back to bed for a couple of hours."

Natasha wanted to ask if he'd slept well last night. *She* certainly hadn't. She'd tossed and turned, trying in vain to rid herself of the memory of his lips and tongue mingling with hers, of his strong arms holding her close, and of what he'd said—not verbally, but with his body language.

Gary and Gordy were tired, too, going straight to their room when they got home. Natasha decided to take advantage of the quiet time to place a few Happy New Year calls.

Her closest friend Robin Harmon, who now lived in Raleigh, North Carolina, with her husband, Duane Davis, wasn't at home, but in New Jersey, Terry Brown answered the phone on the second ring with a happy-sounding "Happy New Year!"

"Ah, you stinker! I wanted to wish you happy new year first."

"Natasha, hi! How are you?"

"I'm good. But you sound fabulous, like you're just waking up from a really good night's sleep."

"Uh…I'm afraid I've been keeping a secret from you."

"Terry! You've met someone. Tell me all about him." Natasha felt certain the secret was a man. She felt genuine happiness for her friend, who had been cruelly robbed of her chance to be a wife to the man she loved, and mother of his children.

"You're right, Natasha. I am seeing someone. The reason I didn't tell you before was that we've been very closemouthed about the whole thing. We didn't know how people would react."

She began to feel alarmed. "React? Terry, you almost sound as if you're involved in something illicit. He isn't married, is he?"

"No. It's not illicit, Natasha. But some might consider it improper."

"Terry, you're making me nervous. Who is it you're seeing?"

"Larry Bishop."

For a moment Natasha was too stunned to speak. "Larry Bishop? Wendell's best friend?"

"It's the craziest thing, Natasha. In the months after the attacks we spent a lot of time together, having lunch or dinner, talking about Wendell, about what a good guy he was and how much we both missed him. I never told anybody this, but one night we kissed. We both felt terribly guilty and disloyal afterward, and we stopped getting together out of fear of our own emotions and where they might bring us. Then he started going out with some other woman, and I met Gregory."

"Yes, I remember him. Whatever happened to him, anyway?"

"Natasha, it doesn't matter. We went our separate ways when we realized we didn't really mesh, remember?" Terry paused. "You sound as if you want me to forget about Larry and look Gregory up. I take it that means you don't approve."

"It's not that. But I'm afraid for you, Terry. I lost a lot of what I believed were good friends because they became frightened that I would steal away their husbands once I became suddenly single and had money. A big part of Tara's problem is that she's heard stories about 9/11 widows coming between the friends of their dead husbands and their wives."

"I don't care about Tara and what she thinks. As far as I'm concerned she's a basket case. And your so-called friends obviously weren't true friends, or maybe they were just incredibly insecure, if they acted that way. Larry and I aren't cheating on anyone. We're both single adults," Terry said, a defensive edge to her tone.

"I know that, Terry. I don't mean to sound critical of you, really I don't. Even before this terrible thing happened to all of us, there have been situations where a man dies unexpectedly and his significant other hooks up with his best friend. It's just that with so many people being killed at one time and so many shattered relationships, it's become rampant, almost like the flu. I've heard that there's a lot of bad blood and shattered marriages within the fire and police departments."

"Natasha, you're not making sense. Larry and I aren't hurting anyone. He's not with the fire or the police department, nor is he leaving a spouse behind to be with me. And I'm not a 9/11 widow. Wendell and I weren't married, remember? I didn't receive any public sympathy, nor did I get a fat monetary settlement from the government."

Natasha stiffened. Never before had she heard Terry sound resentful of the money she'd received for Tim's death. If someone had told her Terry would ever say such a thing she'd argue against it. Hearing the implication now made her cringe.

She decided it was best to get off the topic of money. "Terry, are you sure it's really love and not just…are you sure you have more in common than just missing Wendell?"

"Of course I'm sure, Natasha. It's much more than that, and it's more than just sex. Larry and I are friends. We've been seeing each other for months, even before you moved. You just didn't know about it." She sighed. "Maybe telling you about this wasn't such a good idea after all. I'd better go. I'll talk to you later, Natasha." She hung up.

Natasha stared at the phone, aware of Terry's anger. Well, she'd reacted honestly. She couldn't help it if Terry didn't like what she said, or if she felt left out of all the public sympathy because she was a girlfriend and not a wife. The tragic events of 9/11 had destroyed families and friendships alike. Regardless of what Terry said about Tara being irrational, Natasha knew firsthand that Tara wasn't alone in her feelings that 9/11 widows weren't to be trusted.

She frowned. Wait a minute. Terry *wasn't* a 9/11 widow. As she said, she and Larry were both single adults. No one had been hurt by their friendship developing into something stronger. Surprised, yes, especially since it had been kept secret. Shocked, yes, because it was so unexpected. But not hurt.

She really had no call to react the way she did. With a sinking heart, she realized she'd tried to convince Terry to change her mind about Larry because of her own guilt over her feelings for Jared. How could she do such a thing? She'd put on a holier-than-thou act, suggesting Terry had been wrong to get involved with Larry, knowing all along that she practically lusted after Jared. But because she saw no happy ending for herself and Jared, she unconsciously didn't want to admit that Terry's affair with Larry *did* have a chance at success. No wonder Terry countered with that remark about the financial settlement she'd received. That shook her as much as her suggestion that Terry look up her old boyfriend must have shaken Terry. Her friend had scored a perfect *touché*.

She owed Terry an apology. She couldn't tell her why she reacted the way she did, it was simply too embarrassing to admit, to Terry or to anyone except maybe her best friend, Robin. But apologizing was definitely the right thing to do, and the sooner, the better.

But calling back right now might not be such a good idea. Better to give Terry a chance to cool off first, or else she risked making things even worse.

She'd better get a handle on her feelings about Jared before her entire life ended up in a shambles.

Chapter 10

The conversation floated around Natasha like champagne bubbles. The book club members, who went by the ungrammatical name We Be Readin', were discussing their selection of the month. The implausible yet believably structured storyline of divorced spouses who, through a twist of fate, find themselves living next door to each other with their second families touched many a raw nerve among the membership, who had either grown up with step or half siblings or were divorced themselves. But all Natasha could think about was Jared's impending arrival tomorrow, the first time she'd seen him since New Year's Day.

"Natasha, you've been awfully quiet," Corey pointed out. "What do you think?"

She shifted in her seat, embarrassed at having been found out. "Well, I didn't grow up as part of a family," she said, "but I belong to one now through my in-laws. I like the idea of everyone getting along, even though I know that isn't always the case. But isn't the idea of one big happy family appealing?"

She approached Corey after the meeting. "Barbara is keeping the boys overnight. Did you want to stop somewhere for a drink?"

"Can I get a rain check? I made plans to meet a friend."

"Oh, sure." Natasha hid her disappointment. Jared's upcoming visit tomorrow had her spirits soaring, and she hated the idea of merely going home to an empty house. Now she regretted letting the boys stay overnight at their grandparents'. It would be more fun to be with them and play a game than to sit in the house alone. The rest of the women in the book club seemed eager to get home after a long workweek, and she really didn't know them all that well anyway.

"Natasha, I hear Jared is coming up this weekend," Shontae remarked.

"Yes, he is."

"Please tell him I said hello."

"I sure will." She smiled at the smartly dressed Shontae. The youngest member of the book club—Natasha put her age in her late twenties—it was a cinch *she* had something to do tonight. What had Jared said the last time she saw him? One day she would have more exciting things going on in her life than book club meetings?

She didn't dare let on to anyone how exciting a prospect she found Jared's visit. They'd spoken on the telephone twice in the last three weeks, but only briefly. He spent more time on the line with Gary and Gordy than he did with her. She hoped the awkwardness of their last encounter would have diminished by now, as much for the boys' sake as for her own.

"Mommy, you look real nice," Gary said. Gordy echoed the sentiment.

"Well, thank you, boys," she said graciously. In spite of being flattered, she hoped no one else would notice that she had tried to look especially nice for Jared. She'd bought the royal-blue, seafoam-green and black-striped sweater set at Belk, and this was her first time wearing it. In a conversation she had with Jared Thursday night, they'd agreed that he would spend some time with his father and Barbara before coming to her house to spend the afternoon. "Mom and Grandma were hoping to see you," he said. "Mom invited us over for lunch. I figure we could take the boys out and do something fun afterward, before dinner at Dad's."

"Are you sure it's not too much trouble for her to fix lunch for all of us?"

"Are you kidding? She made baked ziti because she knows I'm coming and it's my favorite, and I know she's got a ton of it."

She laughed. "In that case, all right."

"Wow. You look nice, Natasha," Jared said when she opened the front door for him.

She felt heat pour into her cheeks. "Thanks."

"Uncle Jared!" Gary and Gordy raced from their room, each trying to be the first to reach him. Gary made it a few steps ahead of his younger brother.

"Hey, kids!" Jared wrapped an arm around each boy. "I want you to show me the progress you've made on that computer game you got for Christmas, and then we'll go over to my mom's house and get some of the best baked ziti you've ever had in your life."

"Natasha, you are positively glowing," Olivia said, her rich speaking voice expressing approval.

She laughed, making light of the comment and very much aware of Jared's presence in the room. "Thank you, Miss Olivia, but honestly, it's just my sweater. I think the colors agree with me. Actually," she added modestly, "royal blue flatters most people, regardless of their complexion."

"Oh, it's more than that," Olivia insisted. "I'm very happy for you, my dear. What happened to your husband was tragic, but it's time for you to be getting on with your life." She sat back expectantly. "Now, I want to hear all about him."

Her words mortified Natasha. She threw a desperate look at Jared in a silent plea for help, but he misunderstood her motives. "I know girl talk when I hear it. I think I'll go see how the boys are doing with Mom."

"My June raised that boy well," Olivia remarked as Jared's long legs carried him out of the room. "There's nothing worse than a person too dense to get the message that it's time to scram. All right, my dear. Don't leave anything out."

Natasha tried not to let the agitation she felt surface in her voice. "Miss Olivia, honestly, there isn't anyone. It's just the sweater. But I'm feeling pretty good these days. I confess, I had a little bit of the blues over the holidays but they're gone now and I feel very optimistic about the future."

"Jared, is that all you're going to eat?" June asked.

"I cleaned my plate, Mom," he said patiently. His mother's tendency to talk to him like he was a child could be annoying, although he knew she meant well.

"Yes, but usually you go back for seconds."

"I did," Gordy said.

"Me, too," Gary added.

"I guess that big breakfast I had this morning is still with me." Actually, once on the road Jared had stopped at a fast-food restaurant and eaten a single breakfast sandwich in four bites, but he could hardly tell his mother the truth, that it upset him to hear there might be a man in Natasha's life. His grandmother's hunches were rarely wrong.

He still remembered the sinking feeling in his heart when he'd heard her on the phone on New Year's, saying, "Goodbye, my love," instantly thinking she had a special friend back in New Jersey she hadn't told any of them about. He believed her when she told him she'd actually spoken to the boys at his mother's house. Natasha was no liar.

Even if she hadn't met anyone yet, eventually she would. Natasha was too vibrant a woman to spend the rest of her life alone after being widowed while still in her twenties. She'd find someone to take Tim's place in her heart.

He desperately wished it could be him.

"Barbara, I'm afraid none of us are very hungry," Natasha said apologetically after greeting her mother-in-law. "Jared brought us to Chuck E. Cheese this afternoon, and we couldn't resist getting pizza, even though we'd just eaten baked ziti at June's."

"It's my fault, Mom," Jared said. "I didn't eat much at lunch, and by mid afternoon I was starving. It was just a small pizza and I ate most of it, but I needed a little help."

"Don't worry about it," Barbara said amiably. "Just as long as you had a good time." She looked quizzically at Natasha. "You look lovely, dear. Is that a new sweater?"

"Uh, yes." *Not again,* she thought wearily.

Jared saw an opportunity to find out what Natasha had told his grandmother. Fortunately, Gary and Gordy were outside where his father had the sprinklers going, and thus safely out of earshot. "Grandma told Natasha she's glowing and asked her all about the new man she's seeing."

As he expected, his stepmother jumped on that like a cat pouncing on catnip. "New man? What new man, Natasha?"

"Barbara, take it easy," Natasha said calmly. "There is no new man. Like I told Miss Olivia, it's just the sweater. The colors are particularly flattering on me."

"Oh." Barbara glanced at her watch. "We can eat as soon as Corey gets here. And you know, Jared, we'll have to have June and Olivia over for dinner one weekend when you're here. And June's friend, too, of course."

"What friend?" Natasha asked. The boys had come in, and she playfully gripped Gary's shoulders.

"Calvin," Jared replied.

"Calvin is Grandma June's boyfriend," Gary said.

Natasha was incredulous at his statement. "Oh? How do you know that?"

"He was over the house on New Year's."

"He's real nice," Gordy contributed.

Natasha shot a surprised look at Jared. "I had no idea. The boys never mentioned him before." When June mentioned a friend of hers would be joining them to see in the new year it had never occurred to her that the friend was a male.

"He brought a bottle of champagne for Grandma June and Miss Olivia, and some ginger ale for us," Gary explained.

"Yoo-hoo!" Corey called out.

"Hey, Corey!" Natasha said as Corey entered the kitchen.

"Hi, everybody. It's getting cold outside. They're predicting a possible ice storm for later, you know."

"No, I didn't know," Natasha said. "How much later?" She thought of the steep hills en route to her home.

"Not until about midnight, they said. But it'll all melt in the morning. It's supposed to go up to the mid fifties."

"Don't worry, Natasha," Jared said, reading her mind. "I'll drive you and the boys home if it looks like the storm might be bad."

Corey announced she was leaving right after dinner.

"But, dear, it's so early," Barbara protested.

"Yeah, Corey, what's your hurry?" Ed asked.

"I've got a date."

"Isn't it awfully late for that?" Ed asked with a frown.

"Now, Dad, just a minute ago when Barbara said how early it was you nodded in agreement. Now all of a sudden it's so late."

"So, do we get to meet this friend of yours?"

"Dad, you have *two* grown children, remember? I don't ever remember you asking Jared to bring his dates home for you to meet."

"That's easily explained. There's so many," Ed stated matter-of-factly. "What's the point of meeting someone you won't ever see again anyway?"

Natasha shifted uneasily in her seat. She didn't like the turn this conversation had taken. What was wrong with her? After the unpleasant episode with Terry she realized more than ever the impracticality of a relationship between her and Jared, but still, she hated the idea of hearing about the many women he dated. Just like she wanted to look her best when he was around.

"Corey, you have to understand," Barbara said. "We don't mean to apply a double standard to you. But girl children are... well, different."

"I'm not a child, Barbara."

"When you become a mother you will *always* have children, whether they're grown or not. And sexist as it sounds, I do believe girls are different. I was divorced from Tim and Kirk's father when they were about the same age my two grandsons are now, and I handled most of the day-to-day responsibility of bringing them up. But while I did worry about some female trying to take advantage of my baby boys, I wasn't nearly as bad as I would have been if I'd had to worry about boys and my daughters. You and Natasha are our girls. We take an interest in anyone you might be involved with. It comes natural, so please don't hold it against us."

Natasha decided they all could use some comic relief. "I always dreamed of having a little girl to dress up in pretty clothes, but now that Barbara points out that they do grow up, suddenly I'm finding myself very glad that I had boys."

Laughter lightened the tension in the air. Corey hugged her father and Barbara to show she had no hard feelings, and left soon after without further objection from anyone.

After dinner, Natasha, Jared, Barbara, Ed and the boys played Uno. "It's nearly nine, Jared," Natasha said after checking her wristwatch. "I think we'd better get going. I'd like to beat that storm."

"I don't know," Ed said. "I walked Corey outside, and it felt like it's about to do something out there. There's nothing worse than an ice storm, especially in South Carolina. Folks down here aren't used to snow and ice. Of course, nobody stands much of a chance driving on icy roads, whether you're used to it or not."

"Of course, if you think the storm might come early, you and the boys can always stay here overnight, Natasha," Barbara suggested.

"Thanks, Barbara, but I'd really prefer to go home. I hate waking up without clean clothes or a toothbrush."

"I don't mind," Gary said quickly.

Natasha rubbed his head. "I know you don't. It's a girl thing."

"In that case, if it's still dry outside, Jared can drive your truck back here and bring it back to you tomorrow," Barbara said. "Or Ed and I can bring it back to you if he decides to leave early. But do let him drive you. I'd feel a lot better."

Natasha cast an uncertain glance at Jared. "Are you game?"

"Sure, let's go."

Precipitation began to fall as they neared Natasha's home. As it hit the windshield she could tell its composition was part ice. The Explorer slid a little as Jared maneuvered a turn off the main road. Frightened, Natasha reached out with both hands to clutch his upper arm as she drew in her breath.

"It's all right," he said quickly.

"Are we going to crash, Uncle Jared?" Gordy asked from the back seat, sounding equally anxious.

"No, Gordy. We'll be fine. You're almost home." Jared spoke reassuringly, but he gritted his teeth as he maneuvered the Explorer up the winding road. "No way I'll get back down this road until it thaws tomorrow," he remarked. "I guess I'll have to bunk on your sofa."

"Absolutely. I won't hear of you trying to drive back. Trying to get through these hills would be suicidal." She sounded calm, but could barely contain her excitement. Jared, sleeping in her basement...!

Chapter 11

"Boys, it's time to get ready for bed," Natasha said as she flipped on the living-room light.

"Aw, Mom. Can't we stay up with Uncle Jared and watch TV? It's Saturday."

"You can, but after you take your shower. But just for a little while. You know that if you stay up too late on the weekends you're still tired by school on Monday."

Gary and Gordy went off toward their bedroom. Natasha turned to Jared. "They might think they want to stay up till midnight, but they've had a busy day. I predict they won't last much beyond forty-five minutes."

"Let's put on the Weather Channel, see what they're predicting. It's too early for the local news."

"Okay." She picked up the remote control from its stand on one of the washed-oak end tables and flicked on the plasma TV above the fireplace mantel. A reporter pointed to a map as he gave details about the forecast in the Northwest. "It'll just take a few minutes for them to get to this part of the country," Jared remarked.

"Can I get you something while we wait?"

"No, not right now, thanks."

The meteorologist recited details of the forecast in the Southwest and Northeast before getting to the Southeast. They predicted dangerous ice storms overnight in the combined area of northwest South Carolina, southwest North Carolina and eastern Tennessee, but said it would all melt by the following afternoon, when the mercury was expected to rise to a balmy fifty-five degrees.

"That settles it," Natasha said definitively. "You're not going anywhere until tomorrow. I'll make up the couch in the basement for you. It's fully insulated down there, you know, so you'll be nice and warm."

The telephone rang before Jared could agree. "I'll bet that's Barbara," he said.

Natasha reached for the receiver. "Hello, Barbara," she said, her eyes twinkling as she shared an amused smile with Jared. "We had a feeling that was you. Yes, we're safe and sound, and no, Jared didn't try to drive back. He's right here. We just saw the forecast, and we both agreed he should bunk here for the night. Sure, just a minute." She held out the receiver.

He swiftly took it from her. "Hi, Barbara. You and Dad don't have to worry. I'm staying the night... Oh, I'm sure she's fine. I doubt they went out once they saw the freezing rain start. She's probably entertaining at home... Oh, she didn't answer? Then maybe she's at his place. All right. See you in the morning." He started to rise, but Natasha intercepted and took the phone from him, hanging it up. "I gather Barbara and Ed are worried about Corey."

"Yes. They couldn't get her either on her cell or at home. I didn't want to say it, but I'm sure she's home with her date and they just aren't answering the phone."

The implication embarrassed Natasha. What a wonderful night to be housebound with someone special, someone you could snuggle up to.

True to her prediction, Gary and Gordy became sluggish within a half hour after their shower. When Gordy dozed off and

Gary blinked furiously to keep his eyes open as they watched TV, Natasha said, "That's enough. I want both of you to get into bed. Come on. Tell Uncle Jared you'll see him in the morning." Gary obediently complied. Natasha stood up and took Gordy's hand. He rubbed his eyes and mumbled good-night to Jared as his mother led him toward the hall.

In the boys' room, Natasha helped them slip between the sheets. "Sweet dreams, Gary." She bent to kiss the warm cheek, then moved to the space between the two beds to do the same to Gordy, who appeared to already have returned to sleep. Natasha picked up their clothes, which they'd unceremoniously dropped on the floor, tossing the shirts into the hamper and placing the folded jeans over the back of the computer chair.

"Don't forget the night-light, Mom," Gary said sleepily.

"I've got it," she said softly. She switched the dim bulb into the on position. Red and blue hues from the Spider-Man figure clearly outlined everything in the room.

She quietly stepped out into the hall, closing the door gently behind her. As she turned to return to the living room the door to the basement opened, and Jared appeared.

"Boys in bed?" he said.

"Bed all made?" she asked at the same time. They laughed at their timing. "The answer to your question is yes," she said.

"And to yours, too." He smiled at her warmly. "Oh, Natasha. You're great, you know that?"

She beamed. It always made her feel good to be appreciated. This was almost straight out of her secret crush, the fantasy that would never come true. "I think you're pretty terrific, too."

He reached out to give her an impromptu hug, which she enjoyed thoroughly. Then, to her delight, she felt his arms tighten around her shoulders. "Natasha, Natasha," he whispered against her hair.

She had to ask. "Jared? Is something wrong?"

He pulled back, dropping his hands so that he held her wrists. "I'm not sure. But I've got to tell you something. Come on, let's sit down."

Natasha led the way to the living room, where they sat together on the sofa. Jared, on the end, stuck his long legs out in front of him and leaned forward, his elbows resting on his thighs, his head facing downward.

She began to feel alarmed. Was he ill? Almost as devastating, had he fallen in love with someone in the three weeks since they'd seen each other last?

"I thought I should tell you the reason why I left New York," he finally said.

"Wasn't it because of all the stress from the terrorist attacks?" She rarely referred to that day as 9/11. That sounded too clinical, too impersonal, and to her it was anything but. The events of that terrible day had changed the course of her entire life.

"That was part of it, yes, but not the whole thing."

She placed a soft hand on his shoulder and spoke gently. "Jared, whatever it is, surely it can't be that difficult to tell me."

At last he spoke. "You'll remember that after that day I spent a lot of time with the family, and I started to feel something I shouldn't have. I still do."

She struggled to grasp the meaning of his words, when he sat back and reached for her hand. "I began to have feelings for you that I thought were inappropriate, Natasha. Tim and I weren't blood relatives, but he was like a brother to me nonetheless. How could I possibly look upon his widow the way I looked at other women?"

Natasha could hardly speak. "You...you took that job in Texas because you were attracted to me?"

"I hope I haven't disgusted you."

"No, Jared. I'm just surprised, that's all. I had no idea." She hadn't, of course, but what should she say now? Should she confess that she, too, looked at him in a new light since his move to Atlanta? Besides, as much as she daydreamed about him reciprocating her feelings, the reality presented a whole new set of problems. It wasn't simply a man and woman deciding to become romantically involved. The feelings of a lot of other people had to be considered.

"It's been on my mind since I moved. I'm glad I finally told you. You see, Natasha, nothing's really changed. Being near you again has brought out that old struggle in me. Except now I think enough time has passed for things to be different, where I can tell you how I feel about you and maybe...maybe convince you to spend some time with me, not as a group with the boys, but one-on-one."

She didn't know what to say. Again she thought of the complications that Jared's attraction to her brought. How strange for him to use the term *one-on-one,* for that was the last expression he'd use to describe their situation, which involved more people than could fit comfortably together in a minivan.

"Natasha?" he pressed. "You're awfully quiet. Don't you have anything to say, whether good, bad or indifferent?"

She breathed out heavily. "Jared, I think I need time to think about this. Can we not talk about it anymore tonight?"

"Of course, if that's what you want." He reached for the remote control. "Let's see if anything's on TV."

They watched a movie on a cable network, a comedy that made them laugh. Natasha regarded the film as rather silly, but she couldn't deny its humor. It came as a lifesaver, for it meant she didn't have to think about Jared's confession, even if her laughter couldn't quite conceal the fact that he sat just inches away from her on the sofa. She could smell his woodsy cologne.

By the time the movie ended it was past midnight, and Natasha found herself yawning uncontrollably. She had put in a bag of microwave popcorn during the film and poured juice. Now she and Jared gathered up the drinking glasses, balled-up napkins and individual popcorn bowls and brought them into the kitchen. "I won't worry about washing these tonight," Natasha told him. "Putting everything in the sink is good enough for now."

"That's fine." He yawned. "Excuse me. I guess I'm kind of tired myself."

Natasha ran a damp cloth over the kitchen counter where she had placed the greasy bag of popcorn. She went to throw the bag in the trash can, then turned and promptly bumped into Jared, who was headed that way with some balled-up napkins. They laughed at their clumsiness, then in a swift change of mood he moved in and took her in his arms. "Don't be afraid, Natasha," he whispered just before his lips covered hers.

She gave in to the joy of being kissed and held by him, relaxing and exploring his back with eager hands, enjoying the feel of his tongue intertwined with hers, his strong body against hers.

"Mom?"

The sound of the sleepy voice made Natasha's shoulders jerk. She quickly broke away from Jared's embrace. "Gary? Is that you, honey?"

The pajama-clad Gary appeared in the doorway. He yawned and stretched. "I'm thirsty, Mom."

"I guess you should have had a glass of water before you went to bed," Natasha said, rubbing the back of his neck. "You woke up with a dry mouth." She exchanged a glance of relief with Jared as Gary took his favorite red plastic cup from the cupboard, filled it with ice and then water. He drank it, tossed the cup in the sink and mumbled "Good night" as he returned to his room.

"I'm going to turn in myself, Jared." My goodness, was that her voice sounding so high-pitched and unnatural, when just moments ago she'd kissed him so hungrily?

He nodded crisply, the strain showing in his dark eyes. "I understand."

Gary and Gordy stood in front of Natasha as they waved goodbye to Ed and Jared. By eleven in the morning the mercury had risen high enough to melt the thin layer of ice that covered the roadways, so Ed drove over to pick up Jared. Only she noticed Jared's eyes glued to her as he and his father drove off.

She knew she had to discuss the situation with someone she could trust. She decided to call Terry again.

She'd tried to reach Terry a week after their disastrous conversation New Year's Day, but was met with a phone that rang until it was answered by voice mail. Natasha left a message, but Terry hadn't called back.

She dialed the familiar number. "Hi!" she said brightly when Terry answered. "It's me, Natasha. Is it cold enough for you up there?"

"Well, this is a surprise. I didn't expect to hear from you anytime soon."

Natasha found Terry's blasé tone disheartening. She knew precisely what Terry was getting at. "Terry, I know you're annoyed at me for having doubts about you and Larry. I'm sorry if I hurt your feelings, but the news took me off guard. You have to admit how sensitive the situation is. Isn't that why you kept it secret?"

"I counted on your support, Natasha. You lost Tim that day. I was so sure you of all people would understand."

"In a crazy way, I do. And I do apologize for saying the things I did. There's…" She found she couldn't continue, couldn't bring herself to confide in her friend. "How is Larry, anyway?"

"Are you sure you really want to know?"

"No, I'm just asking to be polite. Of *course* I want to know, Terry."

"He's fine. He just left a little while ago."

Naturally lovers would spend the night together. Natasha felt a little twinge of envy. "Does anyone else know about you two yet?"

"Yes, we've gone public. All our family and friends were surprised, but no one suggested it might not be right. Only you."

She sighed. Instinct told her this not the time to bring up her own dilemma. "I don't know what else you want me to do. I've apologized already, and I meant it." She paused. "Maybe I should try this call another time."

"Maybe you should," Terry agreed defiantly.

"Goodbye, then." Natasha gently hung up the receiver. She couldn't talk to Corey or Barbara for obvious reasons. And her friend Robin had faced multiple stressors in her young marriage, including her husband's long-term unemployment and her late-term miscarriage. Fortunately, she and Duane had weathered it all and were about to celebrate their fifth anniversary with a large party, but Natasha didn't feel right burdening her with something that seemed so trivial in comparison.

She had never felt so alone in all her life.

Chapter 12

Natasha hurried across the large park. Gary and his team played softball in one corner, and diagonally across the way Gordy's soccer game was about to end. She estimated that she probably walked three miles every Saturday since their respective leagues began playing. Still, even with Barbara keeping watch over Gordy's game and Ed in the bleachers at Gary's game, she knew both boys wanted her to see them play as well. It wasn't easy, because the games started at the same time, nine-thirty.

She clapped her hands and shouted along with Barbara and the other parents as the children, wearing red sweaters for uniformity, kept the ball in continuous motion using knees, shoulders, feet and elbows.

"You must be Gordy's mother. I'm Gene Sanders, the soccer coach."

"Hello, Gene. Natasha Lawrence." She held out her hand. She recalled having seen him huddle with the team the prior week, but didn't get a chance to say hello.

"Gordy's quite a little powerhouse," he said as they shook. "I wish I could bottle his energy."

"It's only temporary," she said with a laugh. "He'll take an afternoon nap as soon as I get him home."

"He's got to recharge, I guess. How do you like it here in Greer? Gordy tells me you moved down from Jersey."

Even as she smiled she wondered what else Gordy told him. Something in his eyes hinted that he'd like nothing better than to sling her over his shoulder like a caveman and carry her off to his cave. "Oh, we like it fine. We have family here, and it's nice to be near them."

"I guess you'll be coming to all of Gordy's games?"

"I wouldn't miss it. His grandparents are here also. This is his grandmother." She placed a hand on Barbara's forearm. Barbara flashed a quick smile Gene's way and turned her attention back to the game. "But you'll have to excuse me. My other son is playing softball on the other side of the park. I like to keep up with both of them."

"Sure, I understand. I'll see you next week, Mrs. Lawrence."

She wondered if asking him to call her by her first name would give him the wrong idea. Ultimately, she decided that "Mrs. Lawrence" was simply too formal an address for someone who appeared to be around her own age. "Call me Natasha," she said.

Gene's face lit up as if someone had just plugged him in. "In that case, see you next week, Natasha."

She told an engrossed Barbara she was returning to the softball diamond, then set out back across the field to the diamond where Gary played, wanting to see his turn at bat. She got there just in time to see Gary make a hit on his second try. The ball flew toward the right, and Gary made it to first base before the ball bounced on the ground, was grabbed by the third baseman and tossed to the pitcher, who caught it.

Natasha squealed and jumped up and down, waving to him with both hands from the sidelines. He spotted her and waved back.

"Good job," one of the other mothers said. Speaking in a low voice, she confided, "My son struck out."

"Oh, I'm sorry. But that happens all the time in softball, so I hope he doesn't feel too badly." She paused to join the others in egging on the next player up at bat, clapping their hands and repeating, "Go, Jeff."

The game ended soon after, Gary's team the victors. Gary walked toward her, accompanied by a clean-shaven brown-skinned man in a baseball cap.

She held out her arms. "Good job, Gary!"

"Thanks, Mom!" He turned to the man beside him. "This is Keith. He's one of our coaches."

"Hello, Keith," Natasha said warmly. "I don't remember seeing you before. How many coaches does the team have?"

"There are three of us who volunteer. We take turns," Keith explained. He fondly patted the top of Gary's baseball cap. "You've got quite a slugger here."

"He's always loved baseball and softball."

"One day I'm gonna play in the majors," Gary announced.

"Well, that's going to be up to a number of factors, like if you can avoid breaking your arm over the next ten or twelve years, for one." Natasha glanced at the folding table that held gallon jugs of bottled water, paper cups and individual bags of potato chips. Ed stood there, munching on a bag of Lay's. "Gary, if you want some refreshments, get them now. We need to get back to Gordy."

"Okay. Be right back."

"Ah, so that's why you've been going back and forth," Keith remarked. "You have someone playing soccer."

"Yes, my other son. I like to see both of them play as much as possible."

"I find your intentions admirable, but it sounds stressful."

"It can be, yes. But I manage. My in-laws are here, too, so between us there's always a family member present to cheer them on." She noticed his face fall at her use of the term *in-laws*. A sixth sense told her that Gary either volunteered that his father was dead or Keith asked about him. He seemed interested in her, but hadn't demonstrated any obvious tactics to determine her availability, like straining to see her ring finger. That meant he already knew she was unmarried.

Natasha thought it amusing that both her sons' coaches made it a point to meet her. In any other circumstances she might be willing to choose one and get to know him, but she only had eyes for Jared.

She hadn't seen him in two weeks, not since Gary nearly caught them kissing in the kitchen. He'd found a town house in suburban Atlanta that he wanted, and was in the process of arranging a purchase.

It seemed a shame to waste the attentions of the two coaches. Natasha knew Corey was seeing the mystery man she hadn't invited to her New Year's party, but both her book club and her church included unattached women of the right age. Perhaps she could invite one of them to tag along to next week's game. She felt generous enough to even consider asking Shontae. Both Gene and Keith were reasonably good-looking, fit, and besides, what could be wrong with a man who volunteered his Saturday mornings to help children?

The following Saturday morning when Natasha and the boys arrived at the field, she was shocked to see Jared's tall form standing with Barbara and Ed. Even Corey, well known in the family for sleeping late Saturday mornings, had shown up.

Gary and Gordy both ran to their uncle, throwing their arms around his chest. Natasha stood back discreetly, suddenly shy. Seeing Jared unexpectedly brought back all the memories of their last encounter, when he'd kissed her and she'd kissed him back. She wasn't prepared to deal with that vivid private memory in front of the entire family.

"This is a surprise," she said after he finished squeezing the boys. She made no move to embrace him, not trusting herself to get too close. "A nice one. I didn't expect to see you until after you'd moved."

"I didn't think I'd get up here myself, but everything that can be done has been done, so I decided at the last minute to drive up. I got in late last night. That's why I didn't call. The boys told me about their leagues starting up when we talked on the phone, and I really wanted to see them play."

"We figured Jared and I would watch Gordy's game, and Barbara and Dad and you, Natasha, could watch Gary's," Corey suggested.

"Oh, I always go back and forth so I can see both of them."

"But you probably miss more than you see, walking across this huge field."

Barbara nodded. "I know how you feel, Natasha, but I really do think you're putting too much on yourself. You've got all of us to cheer the boys on."

"I don't know—"

"Natasha," Jared began, "you really should take it easy. There's no need for you to run yourself ragged when you've got family to help you."

His voice caressed her skin like a satin nightgown. She knew she would follow his advice even before Gordy spoke up.

"Yeah, Mom, it's okay if you're not at my game. Uncle Jared and Aunt Corey will be there."

"And next time they can watch me play," Gary added.

"All right, all right. I'll go along with the plan." She beamed at Jared. "Thank you."

The look in his eyes said it all.

Natasha held her breath as Gary stood poised over home plate, like she always did. Gary let the first ball pass. The second he hit high in the air, promptly dropping the bat and running. She followed the path of the ball as it sailed into the sky and then made its descent. Next to her in the stands, Barbara and Ed shouted in delight as catchers in the field failed to capture the ball before it bounced off the ground. Gary continued to run, stepping on second base and then third and then back home before the ball reached it.

As Natasha jumped up and down she spotted Jared's tall form with Gordy's small one, plus Corey, whose height was somewhere in the middle, on the other side of the field, cheering. How wonderful that the entire family had seen Gary's triumph.

Gary's home run put his team ahead and won the game. Natasha descended the bleachers, approaching her firstborn with outstretched arms. "I'm so proud of you!" she exclaimed, holding his face between her palms and kissing his cheek.

"Aw, Mom."

Natasha turned Gary over to the waiting arms of his grandmother, while Ed waited close behind.

"Did you see Gary's homer?" she asked Jared, Corey and Gordy, who by now had reached them.

"It was great!" Corey and Gordy exclaimed simultaneously.

"I tell you, that boy's gonna be the next Hank Aaron," Jared said.

"Gordy did pretty good, too," Corey added.

"Oh, yeah? Tell me, Gordy."

"I scored three goals, and my team won."

"Three goals! My goodness, both my sons are heroes." Natasha pulled her younger son into an embrace and planted a loud kiss on his cheek. "I'm so proud of both of you."

"Thanks, Mom. By the way, Keith said to tell you hi."

"Oh. That was nice of him."

"Ah, the coach. He seemed very interested to know why you weren't there, and who Corey and I were," Jared remarked. "If you ask me, I think he's a little sweet on you."

"Yes, Natasha, and he's real cute, too," Corey added.

"Maybe, but I'm not interested."

"Natasha, you always say that about everybody. Sometimes I think you're waiting for Will to divorce Jada or something equally unlikely." Corey sounded a tad exasperated.

She didn't have to look Jared's way to know his eyes were fixed on her. She could feel it, warm and powerful as the sun.

Eventually the entire family got a chance to congratulate Gary. Gene, the coach, circulated through the group to briefly speak with all the players and parents present, eventually making his way to where the Lawrence/Langston clan stood. He gave Gary a high five. "That was a heck of a hit, young man. Somebody should treat you to a nice lunch and let you order a banana split for dessert." His gaze caught Natasha's, and she braced for an invitation to be extended, an invitation she would have to politely decline.

"My uncle Jared is taking me and my brother someplace special this afternoon," Gary said. "But if I do it again next week, I know my mom will take me to lunch. Won't you, Mom?"

"Of course, sweetie." She beamed at him, delighted he had saved the day, even though she had no idea what he meant by Jared's taking him and Gordy somewhere special.

Gene glanced at the group. "I see you've got family here."

"Yes," she volunteered. "I hated to miss my other son's game—he did quite well today, too—but everyone insisted I watch one entire game. Next week I'll watch the soccer match and the boys' grandparents will be at the ball game."

Jared appeared at her side. "Do you have a minute?" he asked, nodding politely to Gene.

"Yes, sure. Excuse me, Gene."

"See you next week, Natasha."

Jared's hand rested comfortably on her shoulder as they joined the rest of the family a few feet away. "I was telling Gary while we walked over here… I'd like to take you and the boys out someplace special this afternoon, if that's okay with you."

"Ooh, someplace special!" Gordy exclaimed. "Can we, Mom?"

"Where is it, Uncle Jared?" Gary asked.

"I think that'll be fine," Natasha told Jared. "But I won't join you this time. I've got a ton of things to do."

Jared's surprise showed on his face. His eyes widened for a moment, then quickly lowered. "You know we'd love to have you along."

His comment was innocent enough, but delivered so convincingly she shivered in the bright sunlight. The way he made her react was why she knew it would be best not to go. If she'd had some warning he was coming it would be different, but she'd been all too aware of his presence all morning, anxiously waiting for him to appear at the baseball diamond if Gordy's soccer game ended before Gary's softball game.

"Yeah, Mom, come on," Gary said, tugging at the sleeve of her jacket.

"Not this time, boys. You go with Uncle Jared and have a good time. But I want you to eat first."

"That sounds like a good idea," Jared said.

Natasha looked at her in-laws, whom she had come to think of as her own family. "What's everybody got up for this afternoon?"

"I'm going to clean my apartment and do some cooking," Corey said. "I've got the book club meeting at my place tonight, remember?"

"Does your club meet Fridays or Saturdays?" Barbara asked.

"Usually on Saturdays. Sometimes we move it to Fridays if something's going on, like a concert or something, that some of our members are attending," Natasha explained.

"Oh, I see. Well, Ed and I are just going home and take it easy until we sit with the boys tonight."

They prepared to go their separate ways. Gary and Gordy simultaneously announced that they wanted to ride in Uncle Jared's Crossfire. Jared held up a hand. "I'll tell you what," he said. "Your mother can drive the Crossfire. You'll have to drive it this afternoon anyway, if you're not going to come with us, since the three of us can't fit," he said to Natasha. He smiled at Gary and Gordy. "You fellas can ride with me in the truck." Taking in their disappointed expressions, he said, "Hey, I thought you wanted to ride with me."

"In the Crossfire," Gary clarified. "But I can ride with Mom."

"No, *I* can ride with Mom," Gordy said, as Natasha knew he would.

"Mom will ride by herself," she said firmly. "You boys are too young to ride in the front seat anyway. You know that. That's why you always sit in the back of the Explorer."

"But, Mom," Gordy protested, "Uncle Jared's car doesn't have a back seat."

She playfully winked at her youngest son. "Exactly."

At home she fixed meat loaf sandwiches, spicing them up with crisp fried bacon and melted provolone and serving them on hoagie rolls. The boys ate quickly, anxious to take off with Jared, no doubt anticipating his surprise. They kissed her goodbye and climbed into the Explorer. All three of them waved as they pulled off.

She closed the door and went inside, trying not to feel hurt that none of them asked her one last time to join them.

Chapter 13

"Wait, wait, one at a time," Natasha said easily, trying not to look directly at Jared, who stood behind Gary and Gordy. The boys spoke simultaneously as they told her all about their afternoon with Uncle Jared, resulting in nothing she could understand.

They tried again, and although neither wanted to let the other tell her first, she gathered that Jared had taken them for a horseback-riding lesson.

"Jared, how thoughtful of you," she said. "I never would have thought of that in a million years. Did you go up north?"

"No, there are stables right over in Spartanburg. Their lesson lasted about an hour, and then we rode for another hour."

"You rode?" she asked incredulously. "As in *klippedy-klop*, galloping along at a nice clip? With no instructors around? Isn't that dangerous for novice riders?"

"We did a slow gallop at best. They were fine, Natasha."

She studied her sons carefully, looking for telltale signs of falls, like rips in their clothing or bruises and facial scratches, seeing none. She wished Jared had shared his plans with her. Gary and Gordy could have been hurt.

"Natasha," he said softly, "they're boys. Don't baby them."

"I'm not babying them," she said defensively. "But everyone knows horses can be dangerous."

"*I* rode a horse. The boys rode ponies," Jared corrected.

"Mom, our ponies were real small," Gary said.

Natasha smiled. She wished the boys hadn't sensed her distress, but Gary's attempt to calm her made it clear that at least he knew. She could speak to Jared about it privately, and she would. "I'm glad you guys had a good time. You've had a long day, with your ball games this morning and being on horseback all afternoon. I know you had a good lunch before you left, but by now you must be starved."

"Uncle Jared brought us to Applebee's," Gordy said.

Her brows shot up in surprise. "Oh, that was nice."

"The boys said you like the Santa Fe chicken salad, so we ordered one to go," Jared said, holding up a white paper bag imprinted with the Applebee's logo. "We're sorry you couldn't join us."

"Yeah, Mom, we had fun," Gary said.

"C'mon, Gary, let's play that NFL game on the computer," Gordy said. "On the last game I saved my team and almost made it to the Super Bowl."

The boys disappeared into their room down the hall. Natasha took the bag from Jared. "Thanks for thinking of me, Jared. Why don't you sit with me while I eat."

"I really meant it when I said I wished you had joined us," he said as he walked beside her to the dining room. "I didn't mean to take any liberties with choosing the boys' activities. I was sure you'd come along with us, and you would see for yourself that it wasn't dangerous."

The serious subject matter made her forget how close he stood to her. "Jared, maybe I do tend to be a little overprotective of the boys. But they're all I have. I can't put them in any situations that compromise their safety and well-being."

"I understand. But I hope you realize I love the boys, too, and I'd never put them in a dangerous situation. But I'll be sure to clear it with you before I take them up in a hot-air balloon."

Natasha looked up to smile at him, knowing he was joking, for neither Gary and Gordy would meet the height requirements to be allowed on a hot-air balloon. She placed the bag on the informal pine kitchen table, then stepped into the kitchen to pour a glass of fruit punch. "Can I get you something to drink?"

"Yes, but not punch. Do you have any beer?"

"Never touch the stuff. I do have liquor if you'd like a mixed drink. It's in the dining room." She led him to a cherry-wood buffet that matched the table and raised the top. A glass shelf slowly rose from inside, containing highball glasses, an empty ice bucket and several bottles of liquor and mixers, plus small cans of soda.

"Nice piece of furniture," he remarked. "I've seen bars like that in those old movies my grandmother watches."

"Actually, Tim and I found this dining-room set at an estate sale."

"Go ahead and eat," Jared said. "I'll be right with you."

He returned to the kitchen with a small amount of clear liquid in his glass, filled it with ice and then poured Coca-Cola. He pulled out a chair at her side at the square table, where she sat eating her salad. "Family is important to you, isn't it, Natasha?"

"It's everything to me," she said quietly. "When I was born my mother and father were both just seventeen. They were too young to be parents. I never even saw my father, although I'm told he came to see me once when I was a baby. I know his name—it's on my birth certificate—but he had no interest in being a father."

"What about your mother?"

"She visited every now and then, maybe five or six times a year. That isn't very often, of course. And I never met any of her relatives, my grandparents, aunts or uncles. I got the feeling I was an embarrassment to them. Still, my mother—Debra was her name— always told me she hoped to take me to live with her one day."

"But didn't you stay in the children's home until you were grown?" Jared knew some of Natasha's background from Tim. One couldn't help noticing the lack of guests on her side of the church when they married. He remembered Barbara instructing him and the other ushers to seat some of the guests on the left to minimize the disparity.

"Yes, until I graduated high school. My best friend, Robin, and I rented an efficiency apartment together while we went to college. It was too small for two people, but it was all we could afford."

"How did you afford college?"

"Fortunately, we had an excellent guidance counselor. We both had partial scholarships, and she set us up to get student loans for the balance. Plus, we both had jobs to pay for rent, food and carfare."

"So what happened to your mother?"

Natasha shrugged. "One day when I was about eight she came to visit. I'd never seen her look so happy. She had a glow about her." She tried to picture her mother as she had looked that day, but surprisingly the details of her face wouldn't come, only a gray suit trimmed in black braid and a black hat that hugged her head.

"She was full of news that day. She'd gotten married, and her new husband had gone to North Carolina to take a job in construction. She was going down to join him.

"I remember asking if I would see her again, because North Carolina seemed so far away. She said she was going to ask her husband if I could come and live with them. She said she was going to have a baby and that I could be such a big help to her, and that I'd have my own room and a big yard to play in." She sighed, aimlessly moving her food around her plate with her fork. "I never saw her again."

"Never saw her… Well, do you know if something bad happened to her? She might have had an accident or something on her trip down to join her husband."

Natasha's mouth set in an unyielding straight line. "It would make everything all nice and neat if she did have an accident, bumped her head and gotten amnesia that made her forget all about me, but that sounds like the plot of a bad movie. It's possible, but I doubt it, Jared. I think I'd feel something inside if she'd been killed in a car accident or something."

"But you don't know for sure. Did you ever contact her family?"

"No. They had no interest in me. They probably would have denied I was related to them. I'm pretty sure Debra reached North Carolina just fine." Her scorn showed in the acerbic way she uttered her mother's first name.

Jared's forehead wrinkled in thought. "So you think her husband just didn't want you around?"

"That's exactly what I think. He probably didn't want to be responsible for supporting me, since I wasn't his child. A lot of men feel that way." Natasha recalled Corey's comment to her last December about Jared. *He says women with baggage aren't for him.* She attacked her salad with gusto fueled by defiance.

"Well, I think that's a lousy way to be."

She looked at him, suddenly forgetting the years of anger and resentment toward her mother as the corners of her mouth turned up in amusement. "A lot of men feel that women with baggage aren't for them," she remarked innocently. She brought a forkful of lettuce and chicken to her mouth, noting that his expression didn't change. She made sure hers didn't, either. She chewed her salad, aware of the loud crunch the crisp lettuce, cucumber and other vegetables made.

"When you marry someone you marry their lifestyle, whatever that might entail," he remarked. "That's why it's never a good idea to marry someone with children if you don't get along. Sooner or later there'll be a showdown."

"So tell me, Jared, have you ever dated women with children?"

"Uh…not that I can recall."

"Surely you've encountered single mothers, in Houston as well as in Atlanta. Any particular reason you don't go out with them?" She gazed at him intently, almost enjoying his obvious discomfort.

He shrugged sheepishly. "I guess I'm the kind of guy who likes to keep life simple."

She chose that moment to bite into a piece of celery to disguise the anger that had suddenly returned, this time directed at him. "I'm sorry to be smacking, but this is really good," she said matter-of-factly.

"I'm glad you're enjoying it. So, did you get everything accomplished this afternoon that you hoped you would?" Jared felt relieved to be able to change the subject. He found all that talk about dating women with children disquieting. He didn't want to admit to Natasha that he generally made it a point to avoid dating mothers. He'd gotten involved with one woman whom he had no idea had two youngsters until he arrived at her home to pick her up. He soon learned she also had a jealous ex-husband. He broke it off and had evaded similar situations ever since, deciding it wasn't worth the hassle.

In asking Natasha how the afternoon had gone for her he carefully kept the doubt he felt out of his voice. It still smarted a bit that she'd declined to join them. He'd felt an invisible tension between them from the time he saw her, and suspected she still felt embarrassed about Gary's nearly catching them kissing. Holding her and kissing her had been wonderful, but in the end all he'd done was trade old stress for new.

"I had a very productive afternoon," Natasha said. "I took a Saturday class in Jazzercise, and when I got back I rearranged my closet and painted the boys' bathroom. And I confess, it was kind of nice to take a break away from parenting for a few hours. Remember, I have Gary and Gordy seven days a week."

"I can imagine that taking care of two active boys could wear on a person. But you wouldn't be avoiding me, would you?"

He noticed that she raised her chin slightly. "What reason would I have for ignoring you?"

"Because I kissed you the last two times we were together."

Natasha felt a sudden ache in her jaw. "We agreed not to talk about that."

"We agreed not to talk about the first time. But it happened again, remember? And I also confessed my deep dark secret about how my feelings for you changed after Tim died. We never really talked about that, either."

She glanced at the doorway, wanting to make sure their conversation wasn't being overheard. "Jared, I don't want the boys to hear this."

"We're alone, Natasha." He reached for her hand and massaged it between both of his, hearing her breathing quicken.

"Jared," she whispered, her voice holding a plea.

"We won't be able to put this off much longer, you know. Sooner or later you'll have to face what's happening between us." Drink in hand, he pushed his chair back and rose, leaving her to finish her dinner alone.

As she ate the remainder of her meal, she heard Jared's voice coming from the boys' bedroom. In spite of the seemingly never-ending stress and guilt she felt, she managed a smile. Her sons were crazy about their uncle. She could never risk that very special relationship.

Just another reason to keep Jared out of her heart.

She was washing out her utensils when Jared reappeared. "You know, you don't have to bring the boys over to Dad's. I'll be happy to sit with them while you go to your book club meeting."

"Well…that would be easier. Are you sure you don't mind?"

"Not at all. We'll have a great time together. Dad and Barbara get to see them all the time. They won't mind if I spend a little time myself."

"It pretty much amounts to the entire day. Jared, I can't tell you how much I appreciate your giving so much of yourself to Gary and Gordy. They really love you, you know."

"Natasha, you don't have to thank me. I enjoy being with them. They're great kids. And they seem really happy here."

"They are. Now I'm sorry I didn't relocate sooner."

"I've really gotten attached to them." Jared spoke the truth, but speaking about Gary and Gordy made him ashamed of his amorous behavior toward Natasha. His stepnephews had been through so much in their young lives, first losing their father so suddenly and then their uncle Kirk when he stopped coming around with an equal abruptness. He wanted to provide emotional stability for them, to let them know their Uncle Jared would always be a part of their lives. He felt fairly certain that even if Natasha began dating someone—a thought he found most unappealing—she would never banish him from their lives in favor of another man. She wanted them to have continuity even more than he did.

"Do you have a lights-out time for them on weekends?" he asked now.

"I don't like for them to stay up too late, but Gordy usually conks out first, and then Gary follows. They normally try to hang out late when you're here, but to tell you the truth, they've had such a long day, between their games this morning and horseback riding this afternoon, they'll likely fall asleep on their own. They'll probably stay up until I get in, which should be around ten." She smiled at him. "Are you going to send out the cavalry if I'm not in by then?"

"No, but I'll wait up. I'd like to talk."

Natasha kept hearing Jared's last words to her as she drove to Corey's apartment, as she greeted her fellow club members and throughout the discussion. The book selection, revolving around the personal and professional struggles of a young wife and mother after her husband's sudden death, was something she could relate to, and she'd enjoyed the book tremendously. Now that the group discussion was under way, she did participate, but her thoughts frequently wandered to a mix of anticipation and dread about what would transpire between her and Jared when she returned home.

Chapter 14

Natasha found Jared sitting alone in the living room when she let herself in a little before ten. "Hi."

"Hi. How was the meeting?"

"Fun. I brought you a plate. Corey had a nice spread." She glanced around. "Are the boys in bed already?"

"They told me to tell you good-night. Gordy was practically unconscious by nine o'clock, and Gary was struggling to hold up his head. I told them you wouldn't mind if they couldn't wait up for you." He reached out to accept the foil-covered heavy paper plate she held. "Thanks. Looks like a mountain of food."

"I piled on the baked ziti. I know it's your favorite."

"Thanks. I'll definitely eat it, even though—and don't tell her I said this—Corey's baked ziti isn't quite as good as Mom's."

"Are you kidding? Of course I won't tell her you said that. I'm not about to get in the middle." Natasha propped her purse in a chair and shrugged off her jacket, hanging it in the coat closet by the entry to the hall. She went down the hall and quietly opened the door to the boys' room. Gary and Gordy both lay fast asleep, their small chests rising and falling in rhythm. She closed the door equally silently.

"Boys all right?" he asked when she returned to the living room.

"Yep, they're sleeping like logs," she said cheerfully. She sat in one of the matching club chairs, curling her legs under her. "You mentioned when I left that you wanted to talk to me?"

"Yes. I wanted to know why you didn't come with us this afternoon."

"We already talked about that. I had things to do, and it felt good to get a break from Gary and Gordy. I love them with all my heart, but I'm human enough to want some time to myself once in a while."

"So you weren't avoiding me."

She inhaled deeply. "Let's just say that I was taken off guard when you showed up at the field this morning. I didn't know you were coming up this weekend. Maybe I would have gone along if I'd known ahead of time you would be there. I couldn't handle an impromptu outing. I have to be prepared."

"Because of what happened the last time I was here?"

"Jared…we should just forget about that kiss. And the one before it."

"I can't forget either one. Can *you?*"

Her lowered eyes gave her away before she even opened her mouth to reply. "No," she said softly. "But that doesn't make it right, does it? You and Tim were stepbrothers, Jared. That means you and I should be off-limits to each other."

"So you don't want to pursue what we both feel."

Her words came out choked. "No." She saw no point denying she felt anything; Jared knew from the way she'd responded to his kisses that she had.

He rose. "I'm thinking maybe I ought to be on my way. I can tell I've upset you. I didn't mean to.

"But, Natasha," he said as he stood directly in front of her chair, towering over her seated form, "one thing I've learned in life is that it's fruitless to ignore what's in your heart. I guess you haven't learned that yet."

He placed his long arms into the sleeves of his leather jacket. She got up as he turned to retrieve his plate from the coffee table. For a moment they simply stood facing each other. With his free hand Jared covered her forearm, gently fingering her warm skin with the pad of his thumb. "Barbara wants you and the boys to come over for breakfast tomorrow. And don't worry, Natasha. I won't press you anymore, I promise." Then he released her arm and disappeared into the night.

Natasha pushed aside the living-room drapes and watched him get into the Crossfire and back out of the driveway, considerately not putting on his headlights until the car faced the street. In another instant the car disappeared.

She knew she should be glad that Jared promised to not pursue her anymore, but instead she felt miserable. The sinking feeling in her heart made Natasha think of what Jared had said about the futility of ignoring what it told her.

Had Terry felt this same guilt when she found herself growing closer to Larry? Had she tried to fight what she felt out of loyalty to Wendell, only to give in to her heart later? And what would be the right thing for *her* to do?

The house, which just moments before had seemed so warm and alive, now felt cold and impersonal.

Natasha went to her room, moving with slow, lackadaisical steps. She read until her eyes felt heavy, but she lay awake in the dark for over an hour before she finally fell asleep.

As Jared had mentioned, Barbara called early Sunday morning with an invitation. "I know this is short notice, Natasha, but Ed and I are making breakfast for the family this morning. Can you and the boys make it over?"

She wasn't ready to see Jared, not after the determination with which he said he would never press her again, but she couldn't think of a believable reason to give for declining. "Sure we can. What time?"

Natasha felt relieved not to have to be alone with Jared, since the family gathered together in one room. She, as well as Corey, offered to assist Barbara in the kitchen, but Barbara refused, working alone until she called them all to the table.

"So, when do you move, Jared?" Barbara asked as they all sat around the table.

"Well, the unit is almost complete, and the builder promised a quick close. I'd estimate in about three weeks."

"I want to see your new house, Uncle Jared," Gary said.

"Well, it's not like your house or Grandma's house. It's a town house, with three levels, and it's attached to another house, at least on one side."

"Jared bought an end unit," Corey said.

"Three floors! That's really big," Gordy said. "Won't you feel lonely living all by yourself?"

"No, it's not that big," Jared answered. "You see, town houses tend to be narrow, so instead of being built out they're built up." He gestured width and height with his hands. "But you fellas will see it, all right. I'm looking forward to having you come and visit me."

"When?" Gordy asked.

"As soon as I'm in and unpacked I'm expecting everyone to come for a weekend. Of course, I can't accommodate all of you comfortably. I only have three bedrooms, and one of those is kind of small."

"The boys and I can get a hotel room," Natasha said quickly.

"No, Natasha, Ed and I will get a room," Barbara said. "I never pass up an opportunity to have someone clean up behind me."

"Of course, we don't all have to visit at the same time," Ed pointed out.

"Dad's right," Jared agreed. "I'd prefer for no one to have to rent a room."

"Is there a playground where you live?" Gordy asked.

"Yes, but it's pretty small. There's swings and a slide."

Gordy made a face. "Oh, like the park Mom used to bring us to when we were little. They don't have someplace with enough room where I can practice soccer?"

"Not on the grounds, but there's a school about a mile down the road. We can play soccer there, and softball, too," Jared said with a wink in Gary's direction.

Natasha offered to clean up the kitchen. "All this food you made, Barbara! Bacon, sausage, home fries, pancakes, scrambled eggs. You must have started cooking at dawn. Since you insisted that no one help you cook, at least let me clean up." She interrupted Barbara's attempt at protest. "I insist."

"I'll be in to help you out in a few minutes, Natasha," Corey said. "I'm so full, I've got to take a few minutes to digest."

Natasha suppressed a smile. She knew from past experience that Corey's digestive system kicked in just as she was completing the cleanup. It didn't really matter. They usually took turns, anyway.

She stood at the sink, holding each plate for a second or two under running water before placing it in the dishwasher, when she felt a sudden tap on her shoulder. Her body jerked at the unexpected contact, and at the same time she breathed in a familiar cologne.

"I didn't mean to startle you," Jared said softly. His palm moved over her shoulder, and he stood right behind her. If anyone were to enter the kitchen it would appear that they were embracing, she thought anxiously.

"I'm all right. At the last second I realized it was you." *But don't stand so close,* she wanted to add.

"So you'll bring the boys to Atlanta for a weekend?"

His words caressed her ears because he stood so close. "Of course. They're already looking forward to going. I have a trip to Raleigh coming up—"

"Oh?"

"Yes. I'll be attending my best friend's anniversary party there two weeks from now. Anyway, Gary and Gordy are feeling kind of left out because I'm going away without them, so I'd like to take them somewhere. But I think we should stay in a hotel."

"Aw, Mom, can't we stay at Uncle Jared's?"

Neither of them noticed Gordy come in carrying a tub of butter in one hand and a plastic syrup bottle in the other. Jared quickly stepped back, although his hand continued to rest on her shoulder. She could feel heat from his palm straight through her cotton man-tailored blouse.

Gary came in, carrying a glass pitcher containing a small amount of milk. "What's going on? Did Mom say we can't go to Uncle Jared's?"

"She says she wants us to stay in a hotel instead of at his house," Gordy answered.

"Oh, Mooooom."

Natasha turned her face toward Jared and gave him an exasperated glance.

"Don't worry, fellas," he said easily, removing his hand from its perch, leaving her skin momentarily tingly. "You'll come to Atlanta and stay at my house. Your mom is just being overly cautious. She's afraid you guys will disrupt my daily routine. I'll convince her otherwise."

"All right, Uncle Jared!" Gordy held up his small hand palm out, and Jared bent slightly to give Gordy a high five. He took the items Gordy carried and told him he would put them away. Gordy left, and Natasha loaded the dishwasher while Jared wiped down the counters. She couldn't help thinking that she and Jared worked well together. It hadn't been Tim's nature to help around the kitchen; he had been content to take out the trash and let her handle the cleanup...

"I guess you're about to head out," she remarked as they returned to join the family.

"Yes. I'll be home in time for lunch. I've got a lot to do, what with the move coming up."

"Will you be going to Houston to get your belongings?"

"No, I won't have to. The managers of the storage unit—a married couple—agreed to supervise the movers getting my furniture and boxes on the truck. I worked that out with them before I moved my things in. I probably won't be back in Spartanburg until after I move, so I hope you really meant it when you said you would bring the boys for a visit. I've gotten used to seeing them every couple of weeks."

"I really meant it." She smiled, but inside, her heart felt as if it had taken an arrow through it. "Bring *the boys* for a visit," he had said. Nothing about looking forward to seeing *her.*

She tried to tell herself she should feel relieved that he kept his word not to pressure her into giving in to her emotions, that he hadn't made her feel uncomfortable.

After all, wasn't that what she wanted?

Chapter 15

The episode with Jared bothered Natasha, to the point where hours later it was still all she could think about. When she could stand it no more she placed a call to Terry Brown. She missed her friend…and she needed her advice.

"Hi, Terry, it's me," she said brightly. Terry didn't even have to respond for Natasha to feel the chill. She continued, speaking quickly. "I know you're angry at me, but I really need to talk to you."

"Is something wrong?" Terry asked, concern in her voice. Being upset was one thing; turning your back on a friend in her time of need was something else entirely.

"No. Yes." Natasha's attempt at a chuckle sounded more like a short-of-breath. "I don't know," she admitted. "Terry, when you and Larry began to fall in love, how did you handle the guilt?"

"We couldn't. That's why we stopped seeing each other. But when we ran into each other again and I reminded myself that he was Wendell's best friend and tried to picture Wendell frowning at us, I realized I didn't have a clear picture of him in my mind anymore."

"You're not saying you can't remember what he looks like!"

"No, Natasha, only that I can't picture him as clearly as I used to. It's been almost four and a half years. His face is slowly fading from my memory. My therapist says that's normal. Think about it. Is it Tim's face you remember, or his voice?"

Natasha considered this for a moment. When she thought about Tim she thought about the things he said or things they did. "You're right. It's his voice I hear. I really don't picture him." But even as she said the words she tried to picture him, and while she could, his image was fuzzy, with slightly blurred features. She hadn't been able to clearly recall her mother's face, either. But that seemed so different. She hadn't seen her mother in two and a half decades, or nearly five times as long as the last time she saw Tim.

"Natasha, I'm not stupid. You're asking me this for a reason. I'm pretty sure I know what it is, and it would certainly explain a lot of things, but why don't you come out and say it?"

"All right." She took a deep breath. "Something is happening between Jared and me." She paused. "Well? Don't you have anything to say?"

"Not really. Things happen, Natasha. In the wake of 9/11, this type of situation has happened more often than you'd think. My situation is hardly unique, and neither is yours."

"But it's so much easier for you and Larry. Larry was a friend, but Jared is family."

"You're not blood relatives, and neither were he and Tim," Terry pointed out.

"Yes, but we nonetheless belong to the same family. What will Barbara and Ed think? And Corey? I've even met Jared and Corey's mother and grandmother. Terry, they're the only family I have in the world. I can't take the chance of them cutting me off. It would be just like the thing with my mother all over again." She felt herself tearing up and took a deep breath for its calming effect.

"I understand. At least I think I do."

"And what about Gary and Gordy? They've just grasped how our family works, with the second marriages of Barbara and Ed and their respective children. How can I confuse them by getting romantically involved with their uncle?"

"Larry and I kept our relationship a secret for months," Terry said. "It's true we had no family connections, but we were afraid people might criticize us and say we had been disloyal to Wendell."

"I'm not even sure that's the direction I want to move in," Natasha admitted. "I did find myself attracted to Jared during Christmas week. I even felt a little ill when his sister and father made remarks about his active love life. Fantasy is safe, Terry. Complications set in when it becomes real. I thought I was safe because it was nothing but a pleasant daydream. But Jared kissed me New Year's Day, and I haven't been right since."

"Might it just be that it was the kiss itself? That can matter sometimes when there's been no romance in a woman's life for a long time."

Terry's words stung a little, but Natasha knew she really couldn't blame her friend. Hadn't she initially thought the same thing about Terry and Larry, that it had all been about sex? "Yes, it's been a long time since I've been kissed, but there's more to it than just that. It hit me like a sock in the stomach that I'd begun to look at Jared in a different light. That happened before New Year's."

"Has Jared been back to South Carolina since New Year's?"

"Yes, several times. He was here this weekend."

"Did anything happen then, or was it just that one time?"

"No, it happened again," Natasha admitted.

"Would you like my advice?"

"Yes, Terry, I would."

"It's very simple. Follow your heart, Natasha. You deserve to be happy as much as anyone else."

A warm feeling of contentment washed over Corey as she and Bill walked hand in hand to his car on their way to dinner. Inadvertently she swung her hand, bringing his along for the ride.

"What's this?" he asked.

"I'm happy, Bill."

"If you're happy, I'm happy, too. But I believe in being cautious. We're just getting to know each other, Corey. There's a lot we have to learn, and a lot we might decide we don't like. And then there's the difference in lifestyle. So be happy, by all means. Just don't delude yourself into thinking you'll always feel this way."

"Oh, Bill, you're such a pessimist. We've been seeing each other almost two months, or since last year." She liked the latter expression, it made the duration of their relationship sound longer. "And I'm still mad at you for not coming to my New Year's party."

He dropped her hand to depress the remote that unlocked his Navigator. He opened the door and waited while she climbed in, then shut it and went around to the driver's side.

"Corey, we've been all through this," he said patiently. "If I'd come to your party I would have stuck out like someone in a red suit at a funeral."

She sighed heavily. "It doesn't matter, Bill. You and I are together. I want everybody to know it." Suddenly she felt anxious. "We *are* together, aren't we?"

He rested his right hand on her thigh. "Of course. But I don't see the point in letting everyone know about us so soon. You know that a lot of people are going to make us the butt of their jokes."

"I don't care," she said defiantly. "You make me happy, and I want everybody to know it. Including my family."

"Whoa, Corey. It's definitely too soon for that."

She stared at him, her forehead lined with confusion. "But you've invited me to the wedding. Your whole family will be there. Why is it okay for me to meet your family but not for you to meet mine?"

He gave her thigh a gentle squeeze before returning it to the steering wheel. "It's a delicate situation, Corey. My family will be surprised, but not necessarily shocked, to see me with you.

Your people, on the other hand, are sure to be shocked." He sighed. "To tell the truth, I'm a little apprehensive about bringing you to the wedding, but at least it's still a month away."

Corey relaxed. Knowing Bill had qualms about how people would view them made her feel better. Her old optimism returned. "I'll tell you what. It's only February. If we're still seeing each other at Easter in April, will you promise me now that you'll meet my family then?"

Bill smiled at her across the console. "All right, Corey. I promise."

"Hi, Corey!" Natasha said, pleased to hear her sister-in-law's voice.

"Hi. I was wondering if you might be able to come with me to the mall tomorrow afternoon after the boys' games. I need your help with something."

"Sure. What'd'ya need?"

"Advice. I'm going up to Atlanta next weekend."

Natasha's heart sank. "To see Jared?" Of course Corey would visit Jared. The two siblings had always been close. It was natural for Corey to want to help her brother shop for his new home, maybe give it a few feminine touches. His apartment in New York had contained practically no style. She just wished she could go along. Between his upcoming move and her plans to attend Robin's anniversary celebration in Raleigh, who knew when she would get to see him again.

"Actually, no. I'm not sure if I'll even get to see him. Bill is bringing me to a family wedding, and I need help choosing something appropriate. It'll be my first time meeting his family, and his ex will be there, too. I have to find the perfect dress, and you have such good taste."

Natasha knew Bill was the man Corey was seeing. She didn't know much about him other than that he worked as an administrative manager at Greenville Hospital. Corey didn't seem very forthcoming with information about him, and she didn't want to pry. "Well, sure. I'd love to help you pick out something. I might even get a new dress myself."

"That's right, you're going up to your friends' in…Charlotte, isn't it?"

"Raleigh."

"Oh. That's kind of far. You're not driving, are you?"

"No, I'm flying. I haven't had reason to get a new cocktail dress in so long, the more I think about the idea of getting something new the more I like it."

After their respective ball games, Gary and Gordy went home with their grandparents so Natasha could go shopping with Corey. Before Natasha could leave, Gordy's coach came up to her. "If you haven't made any plans, Natasha, I'd love to take you to lunch. And your boys, too, of course."

"That's sweet of you, Gene, but actually my sister-in-law and I made plans for the afternoon." She cocked her head in Corey's direction.

"All right, well, maybe another time."

She could think of no way to tell him it wouldn't ever happen. Hopeless as she knew it was, the only man who did anything for her was Jared.

She and Corey drove to Westgate Mall and went directly to the fine-dress department of Dillard's. Surrounded by racks of cocktail dresses, they began draping selections over their arms. Natasha had six dresses and Corey nine by the time they went to the fitting rooms, but they did not achieve satisfaction with any of them for assorted reasons.

"Oh, my goodness, this chiffon floral print makes me look like I'm wearing a nightgown!"

"This dress is shapeless. I might as well be built like a sack of potatoes."

"I can't get this zipper all the way up. And they didn't have it in the next size, damn it."

"This looked so nice on the mannequin, but it doesn't do a thing for me."

"I look downright dumpy in this."

"Whoa! This neckline shows *way* too much cleavage."

"It just hangs on me, like a pair of curtains."

"Now I know why I hate buying dresses," Natasha muttered as she pulled yet another discarded garment over her head.

"All I want is something elegant and sophisticated, but not old ladyish," Corey stated. "None of those shapeless tent dresses that cover every inch of skin and come with matching jackets, just to make sure nothing's exposed. Bill's mother will probably wear something like that. She's in her seventies. I see myself in something that shows I have a waistline without being overly sexy."

Natasha knew exactly what Corey meant. Something to show off her curves without demanding attention. At five-seven, Corey stood taller than the average woman, but not as tall as Natasha. She was smaller than Natasha, too, a perfect size twelve.

Their respective rejects eventually filled an entire rack. Natasha must have tried on twenty dresses when Corey happened upon a rack of velvet dresses in different colors and cuts that had been marked down. "Ooh, look at this one," she said, pulling a navy dress with sheer sleeves and a cut-out back off the rack.

"I like this one," Natasha said, choosing a simply cut maroon creation with a scoop neckline and full shirred skirt.

"Let's go try them on."

"Wait." Natasha began rummaging through the rack. "I want to get a size larger in case this one is too tight. Every dressmaker cuts their dresses differently these days, so there's no such thing as being a particular size anymore."

"That's not a bad idea. It would be awful if I needed a larger size and somebody else grabs it while I'm in the fitting room trying to squeeze my butt into this one." She found a larger size and went to try on the dresses.

Natasha held her breath as she reached for the side zipper.

Unzipped, the dress fit rather nicely, but this would be the real test. At least one of the dresses she'd tried on earlier had gotten stuck midway.

She much preferred side zippers to those in the back, although since Tim's death she'd mastered the awkward maneuver of zipping herself. Much to her pleasure, the zipper went all the way up without a hitch. The dress looked as if it had been made especially for her, hugging her bustline and draping nicely over her generous hips, falling to midcalf.

"Look, Corey," she said, stepping out into the hall.

"What do you think, Natasha?" Corey said at the same time as she, too, emerged. She caught her breath. "Natasha, it's perfect!"

She whirled around, enjoying the way the skirt of the dress swirled around her legs. "It is, isn't it?" she said, pleased. "Now, let me take get a look at you."

Corey obliged by turning around slowly. Her dress was shorter than Natasha's, the hemline ending just below the knee. The skirt was cut narrowly, with a three-inch slit in the back to allow for comfortable walking. The velvet bodice and skirt molded to her body without being too tight, and the sheer fabric covering her arms and upper chest and shoulders had an effect both sexy and modest.

"Corey," Natasha said, "I think we're going to be the belles of our respective balls."

"And the best part is that they're on sale."

"In that case, let's take some of this money we've saved and go get something to eat."

Chapter 16

Natasha realized after the fact that it had been a mistake to perform her exercise regimen so late. Now it was ten o'clock, and she didn't feel the least bit tired. She'd spent the morning at the hairdresser's getting her braids redone, and the afternoon packing for the weekend in Raleigh, her excitement growing all the while. This would be her first travel anywhere since that fateful weekend late last summer when she decided to take the boys to visit Barbara and Ed and to look at houses while in the Spartanburg area.

So much had changed since then, she mused. Back then she was haunted by that recurring dream of Tim's last moments on earth. She hadn't had the dream since she relocated, and now she believed she would never have it again.

No wonder the boys wanted to go to Raleigh with her. They hadn't been out of Greenville and Spartanburg Counties since their move. She should probably look into planning a trip for the summer, maybe a cruise with a lot of other kids on board, so they'd have something to look forward to.

Her own trip would be a quick one, over within forty-eight hours. The party would be held tomorrow evening. Natasha's plan was to drive to the airport to catch her flight immediately after the boys' games. Robin asked that she reserve Sunday afternoon to spend with her so they could catch up. Natasha would return home on Monday morning, her flight leaving in the mid-morning, after rush hour.

The packing process had put her behind schedule, and she didn't partake of her twenty-minute before-dinner exercise routine until nearly nine o'clock. Her restlessness resulted as a result of vigorous exercise combined with excitement about her trip.

She sat up in bed against plump pillows and channel surfed with her remote control. She stumbled onto a Bette Davis movie from the forties that was just beginning. Bette played an early twentieth-century novelist returning to her hometown for a visit with her best friend. Ten minutes into the film, Natasha found herself wondering how these two very different women had been able to sustain a friendship. Besides Bette's having taken the route of novelist and her friend the more traditional role of wife and mother, the latter's shrewish nature sharply contrasted with Bette's character's good nature. It came as no surprise when the friend's husband admitted to Bette that it was she he loved, not his wife. Still, Natasha sat enraptured in front of the TV, wondering how Bette, who obviously had feelings for her friend's husband as well, would handle a dilemma not too far removed from her own.

To her disappointment, after the husband divorced his wife and asked Bette to marry him, she turned him down, saying, "If you want to live decently, there are some things you just don't do." Natasha shifted her hips in discomfort as Bette Davis's character went on to explain that she would never be able to live with herself if she married her best friend's ex-husband, or the ex of any woman she considered to be a friend.

The heartbroken ex-husband eventually found another love. Bette's friend, with her as inspiration, also became a novelist, turning out popular romance novels that won her great financial success. The novels of Bette's character continued to be critically acclaimed but did not sell particularly well. Both women were unlucky in love, Bette having suffered the humiliation of losing her younger love interest to her friend's daughter, and her friend still in love with the husband who'd divorced her years before. The two middle-aged women toasted their lifelong friendship before the words *The End* appeared and the screen faded to black.

After Natasha turned off the set she kept hearing Bette Davis's voice saying, "If you want to live decently, there's some things you just don't do." She tried to tell herself that the situation depicted in the film had more to do with Terry and Larry than with her and Jared, since it involved the former love of a best friend. Of course, Wendell's death made it impossible for him to know what had transpired between his girlfriend and his best friend.

Still, Natasha couldn't help thinking of herself and Jared. She hadn't even spoken to him since his last visit two weeks ago. He'd called and spoken to the boys briefly, but apparently he felt it sufficient to ask them to convey his regards to her. She didn't really mind. She and Jared would have to limit their contact if they intended to stop the tension that flowed between them like electricity through power lines. If they continued to spend time together the inevitable would happen, which they had to prevent.

There's some things you just don't do.

Natasha rolled over to her stomach and formed a tent out of the covers, concealing most of her face while still getting a good supply of fresh air. Why had she watched that stupid movie in the first place? Now she'd never be able to get that line out of her head. It would come to her every time she thought about Jared....

Natasha settled in her seat. She'd paid an extra seventy-five dollars to upgrade to business class. This seat felt much more agreeable to her rather wide backside than those narrow little seats in economy class. She tried to concentrate on a novel she carried with her, but her thoughts kept going to Robin. She couldn't wait to see her friend again.

Natasha and Robin grew up together at the children's home in Newark. They'd been bosom buddies always, even sharing an efficiency apartment during their college years, trying to stretch the dollars from their part-time jobs.

Their lives ultimately went in different directions, but they never lost touch, although personal crises had prevented them from seeing each other in recent years. The first five years of Robin's marriage to Duane Davis had not been easy ones. Just months after their honeymoon Duane lost his job as a computer consultant, a casualty of the uncertain economy that followed the terrorist attacks of 9/11. Because Robin's work as a bank executive paid well, they managed financially, but Duane's pride took a blow as his wife went out every day to earn a living for them both. Adding to that, his period of unemployment dragged on for nearly two years. He took occasional temporary assignments out of town just to keep his skills sharp, and being apart for weeks at a time put another strain on their marriage.

During that time Robin became pregnant, but suffered a devastating second-trimester miscarriage at five months. Unfortunately, at the time of the loss Duane was doing some independent consulting in the Midwest. Not only did Robin hurt at the loss of her baby, but she resented Duane's not being there when she needed him so desperately. Duane, too, was heartbroken when their son died, and felt guilty for being so far away.

Eventually he secured a permanent position in Raleigh. Robin became pregnant again, this time taking an extended medical leave, and gave birth to a healthy baby girl.

At the airport Natasha rented a car and hit the highway. It felt undeniably good, for other than trips to Spartanburg while still living in Montclair, she had done essentially no traveling since Tim died. Maybe Raleigh wasn't the vacation capital of the world, but she felt comfortable going there alone. She wished she had more travel planned, but it was hard to travel without the boys. She'd passed on attending a literary event in Savannah that most of her fellow book club members were attending in the fall. The next time she took a getaway vacation Gary and Gordy would come with her, and it would be something *they* enjoyed.

Natasha looked around at the well-dressed attendees, a smile on her face. Robin and Duane held their party in the clubhouse of their community. To the delight of their guests, they renewed their vows. Natasha wiped away a tear as Robin and Duane once again promised to love, honor and cherish each other. How wonderful, after all they had been through, to be able to refresh and strengthen their commitment to one another. Everyone broke into wild applause when the newly remarried couple kissed. It was then, in the sea of happy faces, that Natasha noticed one that looked familiar.

She saw that same face every day in the mirror.

Chapter 17

She couldn't stop staring at the woman who resembled her so closely. The woman was slim in a way Natasha had never been and probably not as tall, but definitely stood taller than the average female. She'd heard it said that everyone had a double. She wondered if the resemblance she saw from a distance would hold up close.

She worked her way in the direction of where the woman stood. Maybe she should let the woman get a glimpse of her and see how she reacted.

"Lovely ceremony, wasn't it?" she remarked when she stood next to the woman.

"Yes, it was. I actually felt my eyes—" The woman broke off as Natasha's similar features registered. "Excuse me," she said. "I don't mean to stare, but you look a lot like me. I'm always seeing people who remind me of other people I know, but I've never seen anyone who looks as much like me as you do. It's almost…creepy."

"So I'm not imagining that we look alike."

"No, we really do."

The young woman's—Natasha put her in her mid-twenties— escort looked on curiously. The first thing Natasha noticed about him was that he appeared considerably older than she, she guessed in his late thirties. Perhaps he was an older brother.

"Cliff," the woman said, tugging on the sleeve of his jacket, "this lady and I were saying how much we look alike. Isn't it remarkable?"

"Yes, well, a lot of unrelated people have similar features."

That single sentence had Natasha thinking she didn't much care for this Cliff person. It was his tone, she realized. Not exactly rude, but dismissive, like she was a fly buzzing around annoying him.

"I guess I should introduce myself," she said. "I'm Natasha Lawrence. I grew up with Robin, and I'm here from Greer, South Carolina."

"My name is Genae Simms. I live here in Raleigh. And this is my fiancé, Cliff Allen. He works with Duane."

Cliff's curt nod did nothing to change Natasha's first opinion of him. She wondered why he seemed so eager to blow her off.

He placed his hand on Genae's upper arm. "We really should get settled at a table." He turned his gaze to Natasha. "It was nice to meet you, Natasha. Enjoy the party." He started to steer Genae away.

"Cliff, wait," she objected. "I'd like Natasha to come sit with us. We can trade backgrounds. Who knows, maybe we're related from way back when." Her wide grin suggested she didn't believe this for a minute.

"That's silly, Genae," Cliff said. "You have no family in South Carolina. Besides, I believe the seating has been prearranged."

Natasha stifled the urge to ask him what his problem was. "Actually, it's open seating," she said instead. "I think Robin and Duane wanted this to be pure celebration. They even asked for no gifts."

"Really? I wondered why I didn't see any packages. But I do

suppose five years is kind of soon to spring for another wedding gift," Genae said.

"Cliff, were you at their original ceremony?" Natasha asked. She felt she couldn't go wrong by trying to be friendly.

"No. I didn't know Duane then."

While not outright hostile, he sounded far from amiable.

She decided to forget about trying to make nice with him and concentrate on Genae. She fell into step next to the young woman as they approached a table, her sixth sense aware of the anger radiating from Cliff's pores like sweat during a workout as he walked on Genae's other side. "So you say you had no family in South Carolina, Genae?"

"No. My parents came down from New Jersey shortly before I was born. My mother's family is from Jersey, but my father came from Georgia."

Natasha gulped. Her saliva felt like lead going down her throat. She kept picturing her mother, her midsection swollen with a growing fetus, telling her that her new husband had gotten a job in North Carolina. And now here was Genae, saying that she'd been born shortly after her parents moved to that same state. She tried to remember if her mother had mentioned a specific city, but couldn't recall.

It occurred to her that there were other ways to find out if the baby Debra carried that last time they saw each other had grown up to be Genae Simms. They certainly looked enough alike to have a parent in common. Natasha didn't recall looking like her mother as a child. In fact, all she remembered about Debra was that she'd been pretty, but after twenty-five years she couldn't remember Debra's specific features. Unlike her distress at not being able to clearly picture Tim, this time Natasha felt no guilt. She supposed that if the mind had the ability to retain images that should fade, people would never be able to move on and leave the past behind. Surely fading memories were the mind's way of healing itself.

They paused in front of a round cloth-covered table. "Tell me, Natasha, where are *your* people from?" Genae asked.

"New Jersey."

"Really! This is so fascinating."

"Let me ask you something. Is your mother's name Debra?"

The startled look on Genae's face told Natasha the answer before she said a word.

"Yes, it is. But how did you…? Natasha, I thought seeing you was just a crazy coincidence, but…could it really be that you and I are actually related? Are we cousins or something?"

She sighed. "I was raised in a children's home in Newark. Robin Davis and I were roommates there. I was there because my parents weren't able to take care of me. They were teenagers when I was born. I never saw my father, but my mother visited every so often. The last time I was about eight. She had gotten married and was having another baby and moving to North Carolina. She said she hoped that one day soon I could come and live with them. But she never came back after that." She hadn't thought much about her mother's broken promise lately, but recounting it to Genae suddenly made her remember how much it had hurt.

"Oh, my God!" Genae said softly. "I was thinking we might be distant cousins or something, but you and I might actually be sisters!"

Cliff sat leaning forward, hanging on to every word they said. "Genae, you're getting way ahead of yourself," Cliff cautioned. "Just because your mothers have the same first name can easily be just a coincidence. Debra was a very popular name in your mother's generation."

"Just a coincidence? Cliff, did you hear what Natasha said? Her mother came to see her when she was pregnant, just before she came down here to live." Genae turned eagerly to Natasha. "If you don't mind my asking, how old are you?"

"Thirty-three."

"And I'm twenty-five. That means you were eight when I was born. It all fits. See, Cliff?"

He ignored her, addressing Natasha instead. "Tell me, what was your mother's *last* name?"

"Gee...I don't know."

He flashed an ugly little smile and turned to Genae. "See... what'd I tell you?"

"I do know her maiden name was Miller, but I don't know the name of the man she married."

Cliff shrugged. "Makes it kind of hard to prove anything, doesn't it?"

"No, Cliff, it doesn't," Genae said. "*My* mother's maiden name was Miller."

"Do you have any idea how many people are named Miller?" he said. "Debra Miller. There must have been literally hundreds of women with that name in New Jersey alone. Besides, has your mother ever said anything about having another child?"

"No, but I can understand why. She wouldn't exactly be proud of having a baby out of wedlock at seventeen."

"And she probably wouldn't want to be reminded of it now. Honestly, Genae, I think it would be a mistake to go to your mother about this. It'll bring out a lot of painful memories. She's never mentioned having had any children other than you," Cliff repeated, "nor did she make any other children part of her life. I feel you should let sleeping dogs lie."

Cliff's comparison of her to a sleeping dog was too much for Natasha to bear. She abruptly pushed her hips back, the legs of her chair scraping the parquet floor. "I think it would be best if I found another place to sit. Genae, I'll talk to you before I leave to exchange phone numbers." She picked up her clutch from the table and walked away, fuming.

Natasha soon found the friends of Robin's whom she'd met when they were in the wedding party five years ago, she as matron of honor and they as bridesmaids. They welcomed her warmly and invited her to sit with them and their spouses and dates. After the negative reaction from Cliff, she found their friendliness refreshing. Although thoughts of Genae and their possible relationship and what it could mean raced through her head, she still managed to enjoy the party.

Natasha rose early the next morning, excitement in her heart. Her sleep had been peppered with lovely dreams of an emotional reunion with her mother, of laughing and joking as she proudly posed for a photograph with Genae and Debra, then another with Debra, Gary and Gordy. Her dreams consisted mostly of a series of vague, disconnected images, with one spurt of dialogue just before she woke up.

Her mother was about to explain why she never came back to see her.

The common link between her and Genae still had to be confirmed, but in her heart Natasha felt certain she had found her mother. She couldn't wait to see her today. It might mean spending less time with Robin this afternoon, but Natasha knew her friend would understand and be happy for her.

She moved to the matching ottoman of the stuffed chair in the corner and began her daily routine of stretches, breathing deeply as she held each stretch for a slow count of ten. A ringing cell phone interrupted her midway through her regimen. She immediately jumped up and reached for the phone, always conscious that her sons might need her. "Hello."

"Good morning," a familiar male voice greeted.

"Jared! What a nice surprise!"

"Just wanted to make sure you were safe up there in the big city."

She chuckled. "You thought I might have checked in to a roadside motel where the door opens directly outside? Not me, Jack. Not without—" She broke off, realizing she'd been about to say, "Not without a man."

"Glad you're all right." He hesitated a moment. "It's good to hear your voice, Natasha."

She didn't know what to say to that. How could she? He hadn't asked to speak to her when he'd called the boys the last few weeks. She changed the subject. "When do you move?"

"I did an inspection on Thursday, but I told them there're some things they need to fix. Little things, like kitchen cabinets and the medicine chest opening from the wrong side, dual light switches where the second one controls the light instead of the switch closest to the door, things like that. I'm going back Monday, and the closing is scheduled for Wednesday. The truck should be here Friday. I figure I'll be ready for visitors by next weekend."

"The boys have been asking me every week when we're going to drive down and see you."

"I think Dad and Barbara are planning to come in the next week or two."

"What about Corey?"

"Corey's in love. I don't think I'll be seeing her anytime soon, unless she and her boyfriend break up. So how's everything going? Did you enjoy the party?"

"Yes, I did. And Jared, you'll never guess what happened. There was this girl at the party with her fiancé. She and I look a lot alike, and we got to talking about our backgrounds. Jared, I actually believe she's my sister."

"Your sister? You never told me you had a sister."

"I didn't know, myself. Remember, my mother was expecting a baby the last time I saw her. Genae—that's her name—told me she was born a few months after her parents settled in Raleigh from New Jersey. And her mother's name is Debra...her maiden name is Miller, which is the same as *my* mother. Of course, it could be just a series of coincidences, but my gut tells me it's not."

"Is your mother still alive?"

"According to Genae, she's alive, well, and living in Raleigh. She'd only be fifty or fifty-one, you know. Genae is going to speak with her this morning. She's the only one who can confirm I'm her daughter."

He was silent for a moment before asking, "What time is your flight back?"

"It's not until tomorrow morning. I just got here yesterday afternoon. Besides, Robin wants me to spend some time with her while I'm in town. It's been a long time since we've seen each other, and the circumstances weren't happy ones. She and her husband came to Tim's memorial service, and I spent some time with her when she lost her first baby. And of course Tim and I were at her wedding. Actually, we were *in* the wedding. I was her matron of honor and Tim was one of Duane's groomsmen. And hopefully I can see Genae and…Debra this morning." She couldn't bring herself to say, "My mother."

"Sounds like you've got a full day."

"Yes, I do. I'm waiting to hear from Genae after she talks to Debra. What about you? What are your plans for the day?"

"I'm going to pay a visit to a church a coworker invited me to. I'll probably attend services at different churches until I decide which one I like best. Then another coworker invited me over for a barbecue, so after I change clothes I'll probably stop by for a bit."

"You've got a busy day yourself." Natasha wondered if either of the coworkers Jared spoke about were women. People were certainly bending over backward to invite him places, but for an eligible, handsome man such as Jared that should be expected. She bit her lip. She had to prepare herself for the day when he would meet a special woman and bring her home to meet the family. It would have to be enough that he was a wonderful friend to her and the boys and always would be.

"Yes, but I want you to take down my cell number."

"Why?"

"So you can call me if you need to talk to me for anything."

"Jared, I'll be fine."

"I'll have to turn off the ringer when I'm in church, but I'll leave it on vibrate. If I see your number come up I'll go outside and call you right back."

He sounded so serious, and she didn't understand why. "Jared, I don't get it. Why would you think I'll need to talk?"

"I'm not saying you will. I'm just saying that if you do, don't hesitate to dial my number. And, Natasha…good luck with your mother. You know I wish you only the best."

She nodded knowingly. Jared wanted to hear all about her reunion with her mother. "Thanks."

After Natasha finished talking with Jared she found the waiting to hear from Genae almost unbearable. She went to the lobby for breakfast carrying just two items, her plastic room key and her cell phone. To her amusement, the phone rang just seconds after she returned to her room, as if the caller somehow knew she had finished eating. She hit the talk button and spoke eagerly, knowing it was too early for Gary and Gordy to be calling.

"Hi, Natasha, it's Genae. I talked to Mom, and she confirmed that she had a daughter named Natasha when she was seventeen. We're really sisters!"

"I knew it," Natasha said with excitement and relief. "I just held out a little bit, in case anything went wrong."

"I'm so excited. I said to Cliff last night, imagine going to a wedding—" she laughed "—I mean an anniversary party, and finding a sister I didn't know existed."

Natasha made a face. She could imagine Cliff's reaction. He probably cursed his decision for attending the party at all. Again, she wondered why.

"It was kind of lonely being an only child. I always wanted a big sister," Genae said shyly.

"And I always wanted to *be* a big sister." Natasha's entire body tingled with happiness. Those long-ago broken dreams she'd had of helping her mother care for the new baby didn't hurt as much now. The important thing was that they had found each other again. They could put the past behind them. "Would the three of us be able to get together for brunch or even an early lunch? My friends are expecting me at three. But if that's not convenient for anyone I'm sure they'll understand how important it is for me to see my family." The last two words almost stuck on her tongue.

She could hardly believe it. The word *family* previously only applied to Tim, Gary, Gordy and the blended Lawrence and Langston clan. After twenty-five years she would see her mother again, and she would get to know her little sister.

"Wait just a sec. Natasha, I'm afraid there's a problem."

"A problem?" Her brow wrinkled. Surely if either her mother or sister had previous plans they could break them. What could be more important than the three of them spending time together?

"Well, it's just that, um…"

A knot began to form in the pit of Natasha's stomach. Her idea of a happy reunion with the mother she hadn't seen in two and a half decades and the sister whose existence had only been a vague idea didn't include halting hesitations. Something was definitely wrong. Instinct told her it had something to do with Genae's fiancé, Cliff. What could she have done to make him dislike her so?

"Just tell me, Genae," she said evenly.

Genae sighed softly, hesitating once more before speaking. "Mom doesn't want to see you."

"Doesn't want to see me?" Natasha repeated, dumbfounded.

"She had a hard time telling me about you. How she got pregnant when she was sixteen, how her parents said she brought shame on them, and how her baby's father showed no interest in her afterward. She said finding out that I'd run into you was just too big a shock, and that she's not ready to see you just yet."

The distress Natasha felt transformed into anger. "Of course, that's it. She feels guilty for leaving me in that children's home after she'd raised my hopes that she would come for me and bring me to live with her in North Carolina."

"She didn't speak on it much, but I do think that's got something to do with it, yes," Genae admitted.

"I don't know why I didn't think of it sooner. If her husband didn't want me around all she had to do was tell me. She still could have kept in touch with me. Instead, she abandoned me.

And I'm sure it's not like she never returned to Jersey to see her family, but she never once came to see me, never tried to find out what happened to me once I became an adult. I was her big secret, her shame." Natasha didn't add that her mother's refusal to see her now made her feel as if she'd been abandoned a second time, but that was precisely how she felt.

No wonder Jared insisted she call if she needed him. He'd seen this coming. She'd been blinded by Pollyannaish thoughts of sugar and sunshine.

"Listen, Natasha. I'm not sure what's going on with Mom, but I'd love to get to know you, so if you're open to having brunch with me, I'm all for it. Then we can come back here and talk some more until it's time for you to go to your friends' house."

Natasha smiled through slightly blurred vision. Even if Debra didn't want to see her, she still had a little sister who wanted to get to know her. "Yes, Genae. I'd like that. Where should we meet?"

Chapter 18

Natasha frowned on hearing Genae's end of the cell-phone conversation. She and Cliff were obviously discussing the newly confirmed developments in her family, and a deaf man could tell Cliff didn't like it.

"She'll be fine, Cliff," Genae was saying. "She had a hard time telling me about Natasha, that's all. Learning that she and I met came as a shock. She has to cope with her actions of the past." Her eyes narrowed. "No, I will not come home. Who knows when I'll get another chance to spend time with Natasha. She lives in South Carolina, remember?" She exhaled loudly. "Listen, Cliff, if you're so worried that Mom shouldn't be alone, why don't *you* stay with her. I'll be home later. Goodbye." She clicked the off button of her cell phone. "Sorry about that, Natasha. For some reason Cliff is being difficult."

Natasha took another sip of her mimosa. "So," she said, an impish glint in her eye, "tell me what the deal is with him, anyway? You said he's your fiancé, but he acts more he's your father."

"His mother and my mother work together. They thought it would be a good idea if we met."

"I'm surprised they thought that, since he seems a little old for you."

"Mom liked the idea of me settling with a slightly older fellow, someone who could take care of me."

Natasha didn't know what to say to that. It struck her as outdated thinking for mothers to try to steer their daughters toward men who could take care of them rather than urge them to get the education necessary to be able to take care of themselves.

After about fifteen minutes of friendly banter in the Davises' living room, Duane Davis discreetly excused himself and left the room, giving Natasha and Robin the opportunity to speak privately. Natasha held the Davises' nine-month-old daughter, Cherisse, on her lap. "Oh, it's nice to hold a little girl," she remarked.

"Do you think that if…if it hadn't been for 9/11, that you and Tim might have had another child?" That question would have sounded insensitive coming from anyone else, but Robin spoke with the gentleness of a lifelong friend.

"Nah. After Gordy was born we agreed to shut down production. We even thought about Tim getting a vasectomy, but we held off, in case we ever changed our minds. It seemed too permanent."

"Duane and I would love to have another baby. The doctor said I probably could. We'd both like to have another boy." The baby they lost had been a boy. "I'm just so afraid something might go wrong again. I'm not sure I could handle it if it did."

"I know, Robin. You had a horrible time, and of course I'm speaking as a woman who sailed through both my pregnancies. I can't imagine how it feels to miscarry at five months any more than a person who grew up in a loving family can understand how you and I grew up. But I do know that you can't let fear run your life, or else you'll be afraid to try anything." Even as

Natasha spoke she heard a little voice inside her saying, "Hypocrite!" But surely she had the right to be afraid. Her situation, after all, involved other people.

"Yes, I guess you have a point. But what about you? You haven't so much as been out on a date since Tim died, unless you've been holding out on me. Are you afraid to fall in love again because of fear that you might lose another husband?"

"No," she answered honestly. "I know that bad things happen in life. There are some unfortunate women and men, too, who've been widowed twice, or even three times. I can't say I'm afraid of it happening to me a second time. I really would like to meet someone nice and have a relationship. But the one man I'm interested in isn't the right man for me."

"Why do you say that?"

"Because it's Jared."

Robin's eyes widened, like she was about to take a glaucoma test. "Jared? Really?" At Natasha's nod, she asked, "Is it mutual?"

"Yes. Actually, it was an issue for him long before it was for me. He said he took that job in Houston because of guilt over being attracted to me."

"Way back then? Wow, Natasha. If he hasn't moved on after more than four years, then this is no infatuation. It's the real thing. So what happens now?"

"Nothing, I'm afraid. There are too many other people to consider. The family is bound to be upset."

"It's awfully noble of you to be so concerned about everyone else's feelings, but nobility can't keep you warm at night."

"Robin!"

"I mean it. I don't see a big deal here. You and Jared aren't breaking any laws. Nor are there any morality issues. Nothing happened between you while Tim was alive. And we all know Jared had nothing to do with Tim's death."

Natasha, sipping a Sprite, choked at her friend's words. "I think you've been watching too many police-detective shows. What an awful thing to say."

"Okay, so I'm a big fan of *CSI,* but you'd be surprised how often men, and women, too, are charged with arranging to have spouses bumped off to clear the path for them to move on."

"I suppose, but it's not an issue with me. Jared is no stalker. And I'd rather not talk about him right now anyway. There's something else I need to tell you, something very important." Natasha recounted how she'd spotted a look-alike at last night's party and since had it confirmed that they had the same mother, a mother who didn't want to see her.

"I know who you're talking about," Robin said, leaning forward eagerly. "Duane's friend Cliff introduced her to us. I remember thinking how much she looked like you. But I never made the connection between her living in Raleigh and your mother moving here years ago. Did you know she moved to Raleigh?"

"No, all I remember her saying is North Carolina. I feel like a chump for thinking she would be glad to see me after all this time, to see how my life turned out. She has grandchildren she doesn't even know about, Robin. Doesn't she understand that I'm not mad at her for disappearing from my life, that I'd like nothing better than to see her again?"

"Natasha, for all she knows you've had a crummy life, while she came down here and lived the good life with her husband and baby. She feels both guilt and shame. Hell, she might not have even thought about you all these years, and she probably never told anyone, either. Did Genae know you were out there someplace?"

"No, she had no idea I existed."

"So it's true-confession time. That couldn't be easy, telling your daughter you had a baby at seventeen." Robin shuddered. "I'd hate to have to give Cherisse the details of *my* life when she's older. And your mother's husband must have had a fit, since he probably didn't want you living with them in the first place. Although I've always felt he did you a favor. If he didn't want you around, your life probably would have been a living hell."

"They're divorced now. Genae said it came when she was in

middle school. He doesn't even live in North Carolina anymore. He moved to Georgia."

"Hmmph. I guess your mother got tired of living under his thumb." Robin did a quick stretch and yawn. "I'm sorry, Natasha. I know this is difficult for you. I don't know which is worse, losing your mother to the streets, like I did, or having her choose a life that doesn't include you." Both of Robin's parents met premature deaths through street life. Her mother's drug addiction eventually killed her, and her father was knifed to death in a fight.

Natasha stared sightlessly at the wall. "Right now I'd rather trade with you. Better for people to be separated by death than because one of them just doesn't want to be bothered."

With a heavy heart, Natasha placed a call to the boys when she returned to her hotel room. Talking with Robin had been therapeutic, as always, but disappointment and bitterness still reigned over her emotions. This morning she imagined being able to tell them they would be meeting their grandmother soon. Now she thought it best not to say anything. She and Genae had had a wonderful talk at brunch and afterward, and Genae planned to come to Greer and meet her nephews, but they might have to put that off as well. How could she explain her mother's absence to Gary and Gordy? She wouldn't lie to them and say their grandmother was dead, and she couldn't say she didn't want to meet them. They would be hurt by that and wonder if it was somehow their fault. They'd already gotten the brush-off from their uncle Kirk. She couldn't let them be hurt again.

She forced herself to sound cheerful when she told the boys how she'd spent the afternoon with the woman they knew as Aunt Robin. "She sends her love, and so do I. I'll see you guys tomorrow, okay? I'll be there to pick you up from school."

"Grandma is going to drive us to school," Gary said. "We can't take the bus because it doesn't come to Spartanburg."

"No, Spartanburg has its own school buses. We'll do something special after school tomorrow, since we haven't been together the last few days, okay?"

"Like Chuck E. Cheese?" Gordy asked hopefully.

"Sure, why not."

"Yay!"

"I love you guys. I'll see you tomorrow, okay?"

"Bye, Mommy."

Natasha hung up with a relieved sigh. None of the torment raging inside her had been audible in her voice. The boys would never sense anything was wrong.

She readied her belongings for quick packing in the morning, showered and climbed into bed, moving to its center, as she'd done since Tim died. She opened the book club's selection for the month and read for a few minutes, when she was interrupted by the ringing phone. She reached for it quickly.

"Hi, it's me." Jared needed no further introduction.

"Jared! Hi! I didn't expect to hear from you."

"I've been thinking about you all day. Did you get to see your mother today?"

She didn't answer right away, and he prompted, "Natasha? Are you there?"

"Yes. Sorry. Genae had it confirmed that we have the same mother, and she and I spent a few hours together, but Debra—" after this latest slap in the face she didn't think she could refer to her mother as anything else "—didn't come. She…she didn't want to see me."

"Oh. Are you okay?"

"No, Jared, I'm not," she said flatly.

"No, I guess you wouldn't be. That was a rather silly thing for me to ask."

"It's all right. But if you don't mind, I'd really rather not talk about it."

"It might be therapeutic for you to talk it out."

"Jared, you're my friend, not my counselor. I don't want to be analyzed."

He began to feel annoyed, keeping his voice even only with effort. "I didn't say anything about wanting to analyze you. I just thought you could use a sympathetic ear."

"I had one. I talked to Robin about it. Believe me, she knows more about how it feels to be abandoned than you could ever know."

"Well, I'm glad you talked to *somebody*. And I hope you were more agreeable to her than you were to me. Good night, Natasha." He hit the end button on his cell phone, glaring at it as if everything was its fault.

He'd worried about Natasha all day. She'd sounded so happy this morning to have possibly found a blood relative who could connect her to her long-lost mother, but he'd feared Natasha's mother might not be pleased with her sudden reappearance years after making a new life for herself and leaving Natasha behind. He'd even worried that she might deny any connection to Natasha to save her own face, especially if her husband insisted she not own up to having given birth to Natasha. Still, she obviously felt hurt at her mother's refusal to see her. It wasn't fair for her to take it out on him, but regardless, he hated the idea of her being alone in a hotel room in a strange city as she struggled to cope with her pain. If he was there with her he would take her in his arms, stroke her hair and assure her he would be there for her always, no matter what happened. But Atlanta was a long way from Raleigh. He couldn't be with her, so all he could do was let her suffer alone and wait for her to reach out to him.

Natasha slept badly. Her hotel room was comfortable, but it felt strange simply because it wasn't home. She could deal with her mother's refusal to see her so much better if she were at home with Gary and Gordy, if she could hug them and tuck them into bed, and then retreat to the peaceful sanctity of her own bedroom.

Adding to her stress was the not-very-nice way she'd spoken to Jared, who'd called her out of concern. Obviously that was why he'd stressed for her to call if she wanted to talk, not because

148   *One on One*

he'd wanted to hear about her reunion with her mother, but because he feared it might not take place. Robin, too, hadn't been surprised. Only *she* had been caught off guard. If only she'd been astute enough to see it coming…she had let her emotions take over instead of using her head.

One thing for sure. She owed Jared an apology. She'd see that he got it tomorrow.

Chapter 19

Natasha picked up her car at the Greenville/Spartanburg Airport and drove home, arriving at 1:00 p.m. She unpacked her bags and went over the two days' worth of mail that sat in her mailbox. At two-thirty she left for the boys' school, stopping at the dry cleaner's along the way to drop off her party dress.

She moved mechanically and without enthusiasm, like a toy soldier marching. Nothing she did had much meaning to her until she saw Gary and Gordy emerge from the school building, and then suddenly she felt whole again. She broke into a happy grin and held out her arms. Happy tears formed in her eyes as she embraced them both. These two youngsters were her reason for getting up in the morning, for planning for the future, for doing virtually everything. It gave her pride and satisfaction to know she was a much better mother to her sons than her own mother had been to her.

After a fun afternoon spent playing games and eating pizza at Chuck E. Cheese's, they returned home. The boys did their homework, then showered and got into bed. When Natasha looked in on them and found them fast asleep, she went to the phone to call Jared.

"Hi, Jared, it's Natasha."

He sounded glad to hear from her, and she plowed on. "I owe you an apology for the way I acted last night on the phone. I didn't sound at all gracious, and I know you were trying to help. I'm sorry."

"I think I understand. To a degree you were right. My childhood was completely different from yours. I don't know how you must feel under the circumstances, and your friend Robin has a much better idea. On the other hand, I don't think I deserved to be spoken to like you caught me reading your mail or something. I'm glad you realize I only wanted to help."

"Yes, I do realize."

"How are you coping?"

She sighed. "Better, I think. Sometimes you just have to accept things as they are."

Jared didn't buy it. Her voice had a definite hopeful tinge to it, as if she held out hope that her mother might one day change her mind about seeing her. He recognized the feeling—for a long time after his parents' divorce he kept hoping they would reconcile and they could be a whole family again, but it never happened. He had no way of knowing if Debra, as Natasha referred to her mother, would change her mind, but he hated the idea of Natasha opening her eyes each morning and wondering if this would be the day her dream would come true, only to face more disappointment by nightfall.

"At least you've connected with your sister," he said.

"Yes. You know, years ago I used to wonder if my mother's new baby was a boy or girl, and now I know. I hope Genae will always be a part of my life."

"I'm sure she will." He silently cursed Natasha's mother for continuing to hurt her. A wound like that would never really heal, but Debra's refusal to see Natasha was like cutting into a faded scar. Natasha would probably devote much of her time to thinking about her mother, wondering, wishing. Jared suspected that human nature dictated that people think of their loved ones less frequently as time passed without any encounters. In time, Natasha would once again stop thinking about Debra.

At least he hoped she would, for he also believed that in certain cases time did little to heal the pain of missing someone you loved. With the stab of guilt that had become as familiar as his morning coffee, he wondered how often she thought of Tim.

Natasha spoke to Genae regularly in the following weeks, every few days. Each time, she was disappointed to learn that their mother still wasn't ready to meet her. "I guess I have to consider that she'll never be ready," she said sadly.

"I'm working on her, Natasha. I told her it's put you in an awkward position because I want to meet my nephews and they're going to want to know the whole story. I told her you didn't want to lie to them and say their grandmother was dead."

Natasha gripped the receiver tightly. "What did she say?"

"She said she understands, but she needs more time."

"Well, that's kind of encouraging. At least she didn't say to go ahead and tell them that."

"I'm so sorry. I don't understand her."

"I think she's trying to gather her courage. After all this time it's pretty obvious she never expected me to reenter her life. Tell me, Genae, how was your home life growing up?"

"It was pretty nice. Mom worked part-time as a nurse, and Pop was a construction foreman. Since I was their only child we lived rather comfortably. I can't say I wanted for anything."

"I probably shouldn't ask you this, but can you tell me why your parents got divorced?"

Genae's sigh filled the airwaves. "Pop has always been kind of domineering. The trouble started when I was ten and Mom wanted to start work full-time. She said they had to start thinking about my college education, that I probably wouldn't qualify for financial aid because our family was so small and our income high."

"He was against it?"

"He hated the idea. He wasn't a tyrant or anything like that, but the general rule was that what Pop said, went. Mom always did as he wanted. She never defied him. Except this time."

"She started working full time?"

"Yes. He left a few months later. You know, now that I think about it, she said something I didn't understand then, but now it makes sense."

"What was that, Genae?"

"Let's see…I can't remember her exact words, but during one of their arguments she said something like, 'Because of you I had to give up my other one. You're not going to interfere with this one, too, even if it's yours.'"

Natasha took a deep breath, her back ramrod straight. "Do you remember how he responded?"

"He told me to go to my room and close the door. I didn't get to hear what he said to her. Even though it was loud. I turned up my CD player to try to drown it out. It upset me to hear my parents argue."

"Thank you, Genae, for sharing that with me. I'm sorry if it brought up bad memories, but I really needed to know."

"It's all right. So, are you all set to go to Atlanta?"

"Yes. We're leaving Friday at 6:00 p.m. I figure by then we won't run into any rush-hour traffic, and it'll be nice to already be there when we wake up Saturday. The boys are so excited they don't even mind missing their games on Saturday."

"I went to Atlanta once. Nice city. Does your brother-in-law live within the city limits or in the suburbs?"

"He lives in a suburb, Duluth."

"Well, you guys be safe and have fun."

"Thanks, Genae." Although Natasha spoke to her half sister three or four times a week, they still had a lot to learn about each other. She hadn't confided about the tension between her and

Jared. Surely a day would come when she would want to share that part of her life.

When it stopped being so painful.

Natasha watched in amusement as Jared gathered Gary under one arm and Gordy under the other and lifted them like sacks of potatoes, their arms and legs dangling. "I've missed you rascals."

"We missed you too, Uncle Jared."

He smiled her way. "How was the drive?"

"Not bad. Not much to look at, though, since it was already getting dark when we left."

"I was a little worried about you driving in the dark."

"Oh, I think I've got a couple of good years left," she said with a smile.

Gordy piped up. "Hey, Uncle Jared, put us down. I'm gettin' dizzy."

Jared bounced the boys a few inches, catching them with strong arms, then simultaneously flipped them onto their feet.

"Your house is nice, Uncle Jared," Gary said.

"Come on, I'll show it to you." He gestured toward the overnight bag hanging from Natasha's shoulder, into which she'd stuffed a clean pair of jeans, two blouses, socks, underwear and toiletries. "Here, Natasha, let me take that."

She shrugged off the bag and handed it to him, careful not to let their fingers touch. She couldn't help noticing how he had greeted her verbally while he held the boys. Had relations between them deteriorated to the point where they could have no physical contact whatsoever? Jared's promise not to press her made her feel as if she was a typhoid carrier or something.

The entry of the trilevel town house was halfway between the first and second floors. The half flight of stairs going down led to an open room that Jared explained would be the den. For now the room held sparse furnishings; an oversize chair, a pecan-wood end table and a brass reading lamp. A laundry room and a full bath were behind the two doors against the long wall.

The second floor contained the living room, kitchen and dining room, and the third floor a master bedroom and two smaller bedrooms. The end unit contained plenty of windows, and Natasha imagined that the open layout provided for plenty of light during daylight hours.

"Uncle Jared, you don't have enough furniture," Gordy said. "Where are we going to sleep?"

Two of the bedrooms contained no furniture at all. The only bed in the house appeared to be the king-size one in Jared's bedroom.

"That big chair in the den downstairs opens to a bed. It's just a twin, but you fellas are still small enough to share it. You can sleep with your heads in opposite directions."

"What about Mom?"

"She'll stay in my room."

"Where will you sleep, Jared?" Natasha asked.

"In the recliner in the living room. It's very comfortable. I often nod off when I'm sitting there."

"Isn't it a little short for you?"

"Not if I position the ottoman to hold my feet."

They had a busy day on Saturday, going to the King Center, the Children's Museum and the Underground, where Natasha treated everyone to lunch at Johnny Rockets. After relaxing for a while at Jared's, they went to the local movie theater and saw a family comedy. Everyone was hungry when the movie ended, and Jared suggested they go to a Japanese restaurant. Gary and Gordy were originally skeptical, wanting to go to Fuddruckers. Natasha convinced them to try something different, and they enjoyed watching the white-jacketed chef in his tall hat prepare their meal before their eyes, especially when the flame rose up high each time the chef lit it. "I like this place, Mom. Is there something like this in Greer?" Gary asked as he bit into stir-fried shrimp.

"I'm sure there is. See what you might have missed out on?" Natasha smiled at Jared over their heads.

* * *

The boys, worn out from the days' activities, got ready for bed as soon as they returned to Jared's. They watched a little television, then went downstairs to bed. Natasha went with them to get them settled, then told Jared she was going to turn in herself. She told the truth when she said she was rather tired, but she also wanted to avoid being alone with him. This new distance he'd insisted on putting between them made her feel awkward and stiff. She was here because Gary and Gordy wanted to come visit Uncle Jared, and it made them happy to be here. She could put her own feelings aside for a day and a half if it benefited her sons.

She showered in the connecting bath, put on her pajamas and climbed into bed. Unlike the high footboard in her bed at home, Jared's bed had a low-riding pecan-wood footboard. She suspected that even at six foot four Jared's feet might come close to hanging over the edge, which would make a high footboard unpractical. She sat reading in the center of the large bed, both bedside lights turned on. When a knock sounded at her door she quickly pulled the covers up to her chest, although the long-sleeved red-and-black mandarin pajama top she wore wasn't a bit revealing. "Come in."

Jared opened the door. She couldn't read the look on his face at the sight of her sitting in his bed, but she suspected he liked what he saw.

"You look comfortable," he said approvingly.

She twisted her lower lip and shrugged in embarrassment. "For a long time after Tim…after he died I slept on my side of the bed, like he was still there. It made me miserable. Then one night I rolled over to the middle, and I've been doing it ever since. It feels much less lonely this way."

She was too lovely to be sleeping alone, he thought. She looked luscious.

"I just wanted to make sure you were comfortable," he said.

"Oh, yes. Just relaxing a bit before lights-out. I often read at night. Belonging to a book club means I've always got something to read."

He moved a few feet closer until he stood at the foot of the bed, looming over her.

Natasha laughed nervously. "For heaven's sake, Jared, if you want to talk, sit down. You look like a giant standing there like that."

He sat on the armless chair on the other side of the bedside table, leaning toward her and holding her gaze intently. "I've been feeling very confused lately, which isn't like me."

"Does it have anything to do with me?" she asked.

Something in her tone told him she felt fairly certain what his answer would be. "It's got everything to do with you, Natasha."

"Tell me," she said gently.

"I guess I'm about to break a promise I made to you a few weeks ago."

"I think if you have something on your chest you should get it off," she said softly. "I promise I won't be angry."

"All right." He was silent for a moment as he tried to gather his thoughts, figure out where to begin. "It's important that you understand that I never looked at you as anything other than Tim's wife in all the years you were married to him. But he's gone, and I can't help but see you in a different light. You're on my mind constantly, whether I'm there in South Carolina or here at home."

Her breath caught in her throat in a gasp loud enough for him to hear, but she didn't say a word. He reached out for her hand. For what he was about to say he had to have contact with her, feel her soft skin against his. "Natasha, I can tell from the way you react, those little nervous mannerisms you have, that you feel the same way. I really do want you to find another love, strong and lasting, like you had with Tim. You deserve it. The trouble is, as much as I want you, I can't offer you that.

"I just wanted to let you know that I'm here for you if you need me, or if you want me. No strings. No commitments." He rubbed the back of her hand against his cheek before releasing it as he rose. Then he quietly left the room, closing the door behind him.

Chapter 20

She stared at the door he had just walked through, not knowing what to make of his proposition. It was…well, practically insulting. Hadn't he just offered her the equivalent of a back-alley affair?

Her anger soon fizzled. Jared wouldn't do that. He only wanted to protect her from getting hurt. He knew that her main priority was the happiness and well-being of Gary and Gordy, who would undoubtedly be confused and hurt if they knew of an affair between her and the uncle they loved so much. Jared also knew that her body had gone untouched for more than four years. And finally, he knew that if anything were to happen between them it would have to be here at his home, for she could never invite him into the bed she'd once shared with Tim.

She turned out the light and tried to sleep, not succeeding. She ran her palm over the crisp sheets, a geometric design of black, tan and white that complemented the black-lacquer furniture. Few places could feel as lonely to a solitary person than a king-size bed, even when lying in the center. Life wasn't fair. She lost the love of her life, and her children lost their father, to the murderous schemes of fanatics who had nothing better to do than cause death and destruction. When she believed she could finally be happy with another man, she was bound by the parameters of polite society. She wanted those around her to be happy and despised the idea of scandalizing them, but what about herself? Maybe Robin had been right. Nobility would make for many lonely nights.

Jared definitely had been right. A person couldn't ignore what they felt in their heart. She tried to tell herself to forget all hopes of getting involved with him, tried to applaud his promise not to press her about it…but in spite of her best efforts she still wanted him.

She tossed and turned. Finally she could bear her restlessness and the cold, lonely feeling she'd had as long as she could remember no more. She pulled the covers of the bed back and tossed her legs over the side. Now she wished she'd brought something sexier than pajamas with a mandarin collar. But when she packed she chose them specifically because they *weren't* sexy, just attractive-looking red satin with black piping, more like loungewear than sleepwear. She didn't even have to pack a bathrobe; the fabric was not sheer, and the long sleeves of the high-necked tunic top with bottoms that came to her ankles covered virtually every inch of her except the base of her throat.

Natasha padded barefoot down the carpeted stairs. She paused at the second-floor landing, but Jared made no sound or movement. She continued downstairs to the den where the boys slept.

Gary and Gordy lay asleep in bed, their heads in opposite directions, Gordy's feet just inches from Gary's face. She had brought their familiar night-light from home, and she could see the peaceful expressions on their faces.

She stood there silently in the semidarkness for several minutes, just gazing at them. In only a few short years they would go from children to adolescents, and one day they would be fine young men. That day would doubtless come quicker than she realized, and she would have the rest of her life ahead of her. Damn it, she did have a right to be happy, even if only for a few hours.

She turned and quietly ascended the stairs to the second floor. A T-shirt-clad Jared lay back in the leather recliner, his feet propped up on the matching ottoman, a quilt thrown over his lower body. Although the television was turned to a war movie, his eyes were closed. No wonder he hadn't noticed her on the stairs; he had dozed off.

For a moment Natasha considered turning around and returning to the bedroom, but she quickly decided against it. She simply couldn't spend another night alone. Even if all she got was one night, that would have to sustain her.

"Jared," she said softly.

His eyes opened immediately. "Am I dreaming?" he whispered.

"No." She held out her hand. "No strings, Jared."

He sat up, the chair back returning to an upright position. The quilt fell to the floor, exposing gray sweatpants. Seconds later they stood facing each other, her hands in his. "I want you, Natasha," he said softly, his eyes fastened to hers. "I've wanted you for a long time."

She moved closer and placed her arms around his waist. He buried his face in the crevice where her neck met her shoulder, his large hands pressing against her back. For a few moments they simply stood still, getting acclimated to this new intimacy. Then Jared's hands slipped beneath her pajama top and made contact with the bare skin of her back. Natasha gasped aloud, unable to contain her excitement as her skin tingled from his touch. She glanced up at him. His eyes were closed and his lips parted, soft moaning noises escaping as his large hands moved to her front, where they covered her breasts and gently squeezed. He abruptly opened his eyes, removed his hands and began fumbling with the buttons of her pajama top.

She threw her head back when he bent and took one of her breasts into his mouth. "Jared," she said between breaths, "we shouldn't be standing out in the open like this. What if the boys get up?" That seemed unlikely, judging from the way Gary and Gordy slept just minutes earlier, but she could never predict when one of them might wake up with a dry throat.

In a swift movement, Jared wrapped one hand around her back and the other one over her hips and lifted her in the air. She looped her arm around his neck and rested her head against his chest.

He climbed the steps rather slowly, and Natasha guiltily wished she were more svelte. It couldn't be easy for him to carry a woman her size. If he didn't go to the gym regularly and bench-press he probably couldn't do it. Still, Jared seemed to be breathing normally as he gently deposited her on the bed.

"I'm going to take a shower," he said.

"Make it quick."

He chuckled deep in his throat, then kissed her hard. "Got that right. I'm not about to give you a chance to change your mind."

He disappeared into the adjoining bath. Natasha used his absence to remove her pajamas and climb back between the sheets.

True to his word, Jared emerged within five minutes, a towel around his waist. He stood so tall and graceful.

In one motion he yanked away the towel and tossed it on the floor, then sat on the edge of the bed. "Are you cold?" he asked, taking in the quilt that covered her from the neck down.

"No. Shy."

"This is no time for shyness, Natasha." He reached for the quilt and pulled it away, his eyes lingering on her breasts, rounded hips and the dark triangle where her thighs met. The enraptured look on his face made Natasha feel more beautiful than she had ever felt in her life.

She caught her breath in her throat when he raised a palm and gently traced her body, beginning at her collarbone and ending at her thigh. His palm barely touched her skin, but she found the action incredibly erotic. Her nipples expanded, her stomach went taut. "Jared, I have to tell you something," she whispered.

"I'm listening."

"Your grandmother thinks I had a boyfriend, but there's been no one. No one since…" She couldn't bring herself to utter Tim's name. Instead, she said, "That's the truth."

"Grandma's hunches are often right, but I knew you were telling the truth. I don't mind telling you, though, that when I thought there might have been another man in your life I wanted to knock him out." He shifted position, lying down on his belly and throwing one leg over hers, his upper body atop hers. Holding himself up on his elbows, he cupped her lovely face. "It's been longer than you think for me, too. I can't tell you how beautiful you look lying in my bed. And you probably wouldn't believe how many times I've wished you were here." He gently massaged her cheekbones with long tapered fingers. He could tell she felt nervous. "Relax, Natasha. I promise you we won't go any further unless you're completely at ease, even if we have to lie here all night."

She shook her head, her hands gripping his upper arms. She felt his sex pulsating against the soft flesh of her inner thigh. "I'm all right, Jared."

He lowered his head, speaking with his lips mere inches from hers and moving closer. "You sure?" he murmured just before kissing her.

Natasha soon became so lost in the pleasure of his kiss that her remaining apprehension dissolved like yeast in warm water. Her arms looped around his neck, and she traced the outline of his mouth with her tongue, as she had longed to do for months.

They kissed so long, Jared playfully drawing portions of her lips into his mouth and sucking them, so that her lips began to feel swollen. She knew he deliberately took his time to put her completely at ease. Her toes bent backward in wild anticipation at the mere thought of what would happen when he acquainted himself this thoroughly with the rest of her.

Jared began exploring her breasts while still kissing her, gently squeezing the full flesh and flicking her nipples until they stood tall and erect.

"Jared," she managed to say between gasps.

"It's all right, Natasha. Just let me make love to you." He kissed her lips yet again, then lowered his head to nuzzle her throat. A strong hand grasped her thigh, then moved upward to squeeze her buttock. She instinctively raised her leg, bending it at the knee, allowing him better access. When Jared's hand crossed to her front to gently tug at the curly black hair and tease the little nub that represented all things female, she thought she would weep with joy.

She cried out so loudly as Jared continued fondling her femininity that she took a moment to be grateful the boys slept two floors below.

He slipped a finger between her soft folds and found her moist with anticipation. He fought the urge to relieve the pounding ache in his groin, the wild desire to have her this moment. He swore that he'd go slowly with her, reacquaint her with the joy of all things carnal, and he intended to keep his promise.

He licked the sides of her breasts, moving toward her pebbly nipples and tracing the pattern of the dark circles of the surrounding areola. He never could have imagined how lovely her breasts were. One hand remained lower, his long middle finger happily buried inside her eager flesh. Their gasps and moans filled the room.

Natasha startled him by suddenly propping herself up on her elbows, her right hand reaching out until it touched his thighs. He quickly realized what she sought and lay down on his side facing her, his erect organ jutting out proudly. She panted as her hand closed around the male muscle, her eyes closing, moving the skin of his shaft up and down as she gently squeezed.

A breathless Jared felt himself surge against her hand. "I've... got to...get a condom," he said between gasps.

"I think it's time," she whispered.

Disappointment filled him when she released him, but of course he couldn't sheath himself if her hand remained attached to him.

He turned away from her to open the drawer of his nightstand, where he'd placed the supply of condoms he purchased last night.

He savagely tore open the package with his teeth. To his surprise, Natasha appeared on his left, lying on her stomach, propped up on her elbows, her face just inches from his groin. Once more she reached out for him, this time to point him closer to her mouth. She flicked her tongue over the tip of his sex for a few delicious seconds, then fastened her lips around it and eased her mouth downward. The condom slipped out of his hand as he braced himself with his palms to keep from falling. He whispered her name and words of encouragement as he watched her mouth slide halfway down his shaft and then back up again, moving in what appeared in his rapturous gaze to be slow motion.

She allowed him to slip out of her mouth with one final flick of her tongue. "I don't know what came over me. I saw you, and I just had to taste you." She flashed an impish smile. "I guess I shouldn't have skipped dessert."

"Not only am I glad, but I'll never offer you chocolate cake again." He bent to retrieve the condom packet from the floor and quickly applied it. When he turned to her, he found her lying in the center of the big bed, again propped up on her elbows. His gaze wandered over her form, the lovely breasts with their dark nipples, the rounded belly, the ample hips and thighs, the shapely legs and arched feet. He felt those legs part for him as he moved over her. "I've wanted you for a long time, Natasha," he said softly, his face close to hers.

Her arms went around his neck as her knees bent. She pulled him closer. Within moments she felt the sensation she'd dreamed of for months...his sex entering her body. Happy tears filled her eyes. She'd almost forgotten it was possible to feel this good. She wanted to tell him she loved him, that she was all his, but his no-strings edict stopped her like a glaring red light.

Instead, she gave in to the immense pleasure he gave her with his body. He moved with almost maddening slowness, pouring vitality into what had previously been an empty crevice. She wanted to meet him halfway, but found she could not move.

Jared gritted his teeth as he sank deeper and deeper inside her. It was a tight fit, but her moans told him it pleasured her. Holding back from the frantic pace with which he wanted to bury himself in her tortured him, but her fulfillment came first. Sweat rolled off his chest as he accelerated his movements, building to a crescendo that made them both cry out.

And then all was still.

They settled into a joint embrace as they lay facing each other.

"You know I can't stay with you all night," he said.

"I know," she said regretfully. It wouldn't do for the boys, who usually arose early, to wander in and find them in bed together. "But we have a little time, don't we?"

"I'll set the alarm for six."

"That's fine. The boys won't be up before then." She tightened her grip on his shoulders. She wanted to tell him all the things in her heart, that she was glad he had been the one to reintroduce her to the joy of sex, that she appreciated the wonderful patience he'd demonstrated with her.

But she couldn't say any of that, because falling in love with him went against his edict of "no strings."

"Bye, Uncle Jared!" Gary and Gordy waved frantically as Natasha backed the Explorer out of the guest parking area.

Her head at an angle where Gary and Gordy could not see, Natasha kissed the back of her fingers and then turned her hand so that the area she kissed faced Jared. She puckered her lips and blew out air. His smoldering gaze told her he recognized the private signal.

Natasha straightened the steering wheel and prepared to drive off. The boys called out to Jared once more, and she gave a jaunty wave. He made a handsome sight standing there in a pair of crisp jeans and a long-sleeved polo shirt.

"I had fun this weekend, Mommy," Gordy announced.

"Me, too," Gary said. "Can we do it again soon?"

"I'm sure we'll go back before too long," she said confidently, bolstered by the memory of being in Jared's arms, of his back muscles rippling beneath her hands. "When it gets warmer I'll take you to Six Flags. I think the one in Atlanta is even bigger than the one in Jersey."

"Yay, Six Flags!"

As she drove north on I–85, Natasha entertained herself with wonderful thoughts. She and Jared could spend another blissful night together the next time she and the boys visited. Eventually he'd come to feel the same way about her as she did about him. They'd tell the boys first and the rest of the family second. Everyone would be happy for them. There'd be no objections, no accusations. She'd learn all her fears had been for nothing.

The warm, fuzzy feeling that engulfed her began to fade around the time she crossed the Georgia border into South Carolina. She'd slept with Jared. She had actually embarked on a secret love affair with the stepbrother of her late husband.

No, she reminded herself. It couldn't even be referred to as a love affair. Unrequited love didn't count, and he didn't love her. "No strings," he had said. That was code for, "Don't fence me in." He found her attractive and desirable, and he knew there had been no man in her life since Tim died. Making love to a woman who had such a long hiatus was the closest he would come to deflowering a virgin. That notion was supposed to make men crazy with lust. Sexual cravings aside, Jared probably just felt sorry for her.

She cursed herself for giving in to her weakness, for allowing loneliness to overpower her to the point where she'd gotten out of bed, where she was safe, and gone downstairs to virtually ask him to make love to her. So now he felt satisfied…and she felt like a fool.

What in heaven's name was wrong with her, entertaining romantic notions that their family would accept their affair without objection, leaving her and Jared to ride off into the sunset with Gary and Gordy in tow. Hadn't Corey said that Jared didn't like women with "baggage"? And still she'd gone willingly into his arms, accepting his "no strings attached" terms.

She wished she could go back in time to last night. She would have kept her behind right in that bed and gone to sleep instead of making a fool of herself.

Chapter 21

Natasha's thoughts became more lucid by the time she approached Greenville. Jared wasn't out to take advantage of her. He just knew how delicate their situation was, and he didn't want her to get hurt. He wanted to protect her, not take advantage of her vulnerability. Shame on her for thinking anything else. Guilt could be a terrible thing, make a person believe awful things.

She forced herself to face another truth, too. Her being in love with Jared when he didn't love her would cause her nothing but unhappiness. But how could she not love him? He was kind, considerate, honest and she couldn't forget sexy. If not for their connection, she would shout it from the rooftops.

But they *were* connected, and therein lay the problem. It wasn't so much the feeling of disloyalty to Tim, which had gradually lessened. What worried her was how the others in the family would react. What would Kirk say? And Corey? Would Barbara and Ed be upset at her moving from her son to his? And now she had the feelings of June and Miss Olivia to consider. Would they find the idea distasteful? And, most of all, what about Gary and Gordy? How could she even begin to explain to them how the relationship between her and Jared had changed? The more she thought about the situation, the more futile it seemed.

At last she turned into her driveway, emotionally exhausted. "Don't forget to call Uncle Jared and let him know we got home safely, Mom," Gary reminded her.

Her shoulders tensed. She simply couldn't handle talking to Jared right now, not with all her conflicted feelings. "I'm really beat, fellas," she said. "I'm going to lie down. But why don't you call. The number's in my cell phone. After you talk to Uncle Jared you can call Grandma, to let her and Grandpa Ed know we made it back okay."

"I'll call Grandma," Gordy said quickly.

Gary took the phone Natasha handed him. "Okay, but *I'm* gonna call Uncle Jared."

"I'm going to bed," Natasha said cheerfully. She noted that in their anxiousness to call Jared the boys seemed to have forgotten all about the hamburgers she'd bought for them at the Sonic drive-in. Any other time they would eat first and then get on the phone, but where Jared was concerned food came second. "I'm going to put the same rule into effect that I do when I'm working."

Gordy recited the rule he and Gary had grown up with. "Don't bother you unless the house is on fire or somebody's bleeding."

Natasha slept soundly for three hours. Part of her fatigue came from the late night she'd had with Jared, part from being tired after a two-hour drive, and part from emotional turmoil. The sun was setting when she opened her eyes. For a few minutes she allowed herself the luxury of staring at the sunset, remembering how many a night she had awakened in fright, hearing Tim's voice, imagining how terrifying it must have been for him as the heat and smoke intensified. How odd that the dream stopped when she relocated to Greer. It was almost as if fate had known she was about to fall in love again and wanted to tell her somehow that it was all right to move on with her life.

She abruptly got up and went to check on the boys. The kitchen table was littered with hamburger wrappers, cardboard French-fry holders and empty packets of ketchup and mustard. She found Gary and Gordy in the basement, watching *The Parent Trap* on TV. "You boys left a mess on the table. Be sure to clean it up."

"I put your food in the fridge, Mom," Gordy said in that angelic way of his.

"Because I told you to," Gary pointed out.

Natasha knew they both wanted to get into her good graces. "I do wish you boys would be better at picking up after your-selves, but I'm not going to make a big deal out of it, okay? Just be sure to clean up that mess as soon as your movie is over. By then it'll be time for you to get ready for bed." She paused. "Did you talk to Uncle Jared and to your grandmother?"

Both boys nodded. "Grandma said for you to get a good rest," Gordy said.

"And Uncle Jared said he'd call later," Gary added.

Natasha kept her expression impassive. "All right."

She tried to concentrate on a new magazine that had come in the mail, but she kept thinking about Jared and what had happened between them. Her breath caught in her throat when the phone rang. "Hello."

"Hi, Natasha, it's Terry."

She immediately picked up on the happy note in her friend's voice. "You're calling with good news," she guessed.

"Yes. Larry and I got engaged last night."

Happiness filled Natasha's heart. "Oh, Terry, that's wonder-ful news. I am so very happy for you." Terry had been as devas-tated at losing Wendell as she had at the loss of Tim, but at last she would get to have the family she'd always dreamed of.

"You really are, aren't you?"

"Absolutely. Have you set a date yet?"

"No, but I already know I don't want to wait too long. I'm thirty-four years old. We've already decided to wait at least two years before we have our first child."

"Was that really a mutual decision, or is it just what *he* wants?"

"No, it's mutual. Our courtship has had its share of stress, Natasha. We want to make sure we have a solid base before starting a family."

"I'm sure it'll be fine. You be sure to keep me posted when you set that date."

After Natasha hung up she sighed deeply. She truly felt happy for Terry, but her friend's good news only drove home the hopelessness of her own situation.

Gary and Gordy had gone to bed when Jared called back at nine-thirty. "Hi, are you okay? Gary said you were knocked out when he called."

"Oh, yes, good as new. I just needed to recharge after the drive home."

"Natasha...I have to know. Do you regret what happened last night?"

"No, Jared," she said honestly. "Not at all."

She spoke the truth, for it wasn't the past that haunted her...it was fear of the future.

Kirk embraced his wife. He closed his eyes and said a silent prayer. A few hours ago she called his office and gave him the best news a wife could give her husband. They'd waited a long time for this. The first time ended tragically for them, and he'd begun to fear it might not ever happen. He knew Tara felt lacking somehow because of her difficulty getting pregnant and the ease with which she miscarried. Maybe now she wouldn't be so jealous of every woman who crossed his path.

"Have you told your parents yet?" he asked her.

"Yes, right after I called you."

"I guess we need to call Mom and Ed."

"No!"

His body suddenly went stiff. "What do you mean, 'no'? You just said you told *your* parents. Isn't my side of the family entitled to know about the baby as well?"

"No, Kirk, not yet. I don't want anyone to know outside of immediate family."

"Tara, you're not being fair. Why is your family more immediate than mine?"

"Because they'll hope everything goes all right for us. Your mother and stepfather will, too, but Natasha and Corey don't like me. I'm afraid they'll wish bad luck on me."

"Tara, that's not true. I've known my stepsister and my sister-in-law for a long time. They don't dislike you. They just treat you with the same standoffishness you treat them. I know you don't mean to come off that way," he added tactfully, "but you've never really felt comfortable around them. They did try to welcome you to the family, but when you didn't respond they gave up." He didn't want to point out that his mother didn't much care for Tara, either. Better to let Tara point to Corey and Natasha as the bad guys.

"Corey wishes she had a husband so she could have some kids, and Natasha wishes she had a husband to be father to Gary and Gordy. I know they'll be annoyed that I have both, and they'll hope something bad will happen. I mean it, Kirk. I don't want them to know anything until I'm in my fourth month."

He sighed. The notion of his stepsister and his sister-in-law creating voodoo dolls in Tara's likeness to induce a miscarriage couldn't be more ludicrous. More likely, they felt sorry for Tara because of her difficulty achieving and maintaining a pregnancy. He suspected Tara knew as much but preferred to think that they hated her, simply because it wasn't as painful.

His life was becoming more complicated by the day.

Chapter 22

"Honestly, Natasha," Barbara lamented, "I don't know what's come over my family these days. I hardly ever see Corey anymore. And Jared just called and said he won't be up this weekend."

Natasha's spine went rigid. "He won't?"

"No. Ed and I are so disappointed…we were expecting him. I guess we've gotten spoiled. Since he relocated he's never gone more than three weeks without driving up. We haven't seen him in over a month, since we visited him a few weeks after you and boys went down." She sighed. "But I suppose it's only natural. He's feeling at home in the city now, and he's probably met a young lady. It's about time."

Natasha swallowed a lump that suddenly appeared in her throat. "Did he mention if that's the case?"

"No, but you know Jared. He's always been closemouthed when it comes to his personal business. We probably won't know anything until one day out of the blue he'll announce he's getting married." Barbara's cheerful tone demonstrated how appealing she found that idea.

Natasha felt grateful they spoke on the telephone and not in person, so she didn't have to hide her anguish at the very thought of Jared with another woman just weeks after their intimacy. What had kept him away for so long? Did he fear that she wouldn't be able to live up to her end of their no-strings bargain? Did he view her as a lonely widow he took pity on?

She felt as if she couldn't stand it another minute. "Barbara, a UPS truck just pulled up in front of my house," she lied. "I'll have to sign for this delivery. Can we talk later?"

"Sure, dear. You go ahead."

Natasha hated to lie, but she felt there was no recourse. If Barbara said just one more thing about Jared's love life she surely would have begun to feel ill. At least now that she was alone she could control her tear ducts, but she *couldn't* control the sadness that threatened to engulf her like a blanket suddenly thrown over her head. Sleeping with Jared had been the equivalent of getting on a merry-go-round. Her emotions vacillated between bright happiness and deep despair.

And there was nothing merry about it.

Jared's call that night after the boys were asleep caught her by surprise. "Hello there."

"Hi." Despite her best efforts, her voice sounded flat and cool, almost accusatory.

"Something wrong? You sound funny."

"No, I'm fine." That sounded better. "What's up?"

"How do you know I'm not just calling to hear your voice? We've spoken every day, haven't we?"

He spoke the truth. They did speak daily, sometimes innocently when he called the boys, but mostly late at night, just the two of them. But Natasha's conversation with Barbara weighed on her mind. "Yes, we have. But when do I get to see you?" She waited expectantly, eager to hear why he wasn't coming to South

Carolina this weekend. She didn't even care that she sounded possessive.

"Hopefully this weekend."

His reply took her off guard. "Huh? Barbara just told me you wouldn't be up."

"That's because I'm keeping it a secret. I've got to be in Charlotte Monday morning on business. The job will get me an airline ticket, but if I get to see you it'll be worth driving. It's only about four hours from here. I can drive to Greer Saturday. Dad and Barbara will keep the kids for you. We can have dinner and go back to my hotel. No one even has to know I was there."

Natasha bit her lower lip. She wanted to scream at him that she wasn't going to be his South Carolina squeeze, that he couldn't just pass through her life like a ship gliding past an island on its way to its final destination. But hadn't she agreed to his edict of no strings? Hadn't she deliberately held back calling him every night because she didn't want to appear clingy or demanding? Besides, his plan wouldn't work anyway.

"I'm afraid that wouldn't work. It's my turn to host the book club Saturday night. Our discussions usually run kind of late."

He listened to her explanation, knowing that what she didn't say was as important as what she *did* say. She seemed to be keeping him at arm's length. Maybe she experienced guilt pangs for going to bed with him because of his relationship to Tim. He wanted to tell her how desperately he needed to see her, to hold her and touch her, but he had to follow her lead.

"Is Uncle Jared coming to watch us play ball this weekend, Mom?" Gary asked.

"I'm afraid not, dear. He's got a business trip to make first thing Monday morning, so it'll be a bit much for him to drive up here for the weekend."

"Aw, shucks," Gordy said.

"I know you're disappointed, but you'll see Uncle Jared

before too long. Now, get ready for lights-out. Tomorrow's a school day, and you both have practice after school."

"Hey, Mom, Coach Gene asked if I knew why you won't go out with him," Gary said.

"I don't know why. He asked me to have lunch with him one time, but I couldn't go because I had made plans with Aunt Corey." Natasha wondered if Gene had sensed something negative when she declined his invitation. It certainly struck her as poor judgment, his trying to get to her through her son. "And maybe I shouldn't say this, but I don't approve of your coach getting you involved."

"Don't you want to go out with him?" Gordy asked in the child-like voice Natasha knew would be history in another few years.

"Not particularly."

"But, Mom, you never go out on dates," Gary protested. "Don't you ever want to get married again?"

His words startled Natasha. Gordy always expressed that the three of them were a package and didn't need anyone else. Apparently her eldest felt differently. "Gary, are you saying you'd like me to remarry?"

"I don't want you to be all alone when you get old. Grandma June has Miss Olivia and Mr. Calvin, but you don't have a mother *or* a boyfriend. What happens when Gordy and I grow up and leave home?"

She took his hand. *But I do have a mother,* she wanted to say. *She just doesn't want to see me.* She pushed the thought out of her mind. That wasn't the issue at hand. Gary clearly felt disturbed by his thoughts of what the future might hold for her. He looked so serious, more serious than any nine-year-old should ever be. "You're really worried about this, aren't you?"

"I don't want you to be all by yourself when Gordy and me get married."

He makes it sound as if they'd be getting married next month, she thought with a mixture of amusement and sadness. Gordy already had a crush on a girl on his soccer team, and Gary liked a girl in his class, but those were just childhood crushes. "Well,

I can always come and live with you and your wife," she said with a smile. "Half the year at your house, the other half at Gordy's. I'll be an equal-opportunity nuisance."

"I know what, Mom," Gordy said. "You could marry Uncle Jared."

"What?"

"You and Uncle Jared. He's got that big house all to himself. And you always seem so happy when he's around."

Natasha stopped being stunned long enough to recognize a golden opportunity to learn how the boys felt. "Are you saying you think my marrying Uncle Jared is a good idea?"

"Sure, Mom," Gary said. "We like Uncle Jared a lot. We have fun with him."

"Well, fellas, I'm glad you're fond of your uncle, but there's a little more to marrying somebody than that."

"Yeah, love and stuff," Gordy said, giggling.

She clapped her hands, effectively putting an end to a conversation that grew more disconcerting by the minute. "All right, that's enough chitchat. It's time for lights-out." She turned off the bedroom light, and the sensory-operated night-light immediately illuminated the room. Natasha bent to kiss her sons. "Sweet dreams to you both. See you in the morning."

Her glance lingered on their sleepy forms in their beds as she quietly closed the door. *My, my. Kids are certainly full of surprises.*

At Saturday's softball game Gene Sanders kept smiling at Natasha, as though he expected her to ask *him* out. He no doubt felt confident that Gary would have relayed his question to her and that any forthcoming invitations would be accepted. She found herself only too glad to get away from the softball game to observe the action at Gordy's soccer match.

Corey had shown up at the park and was watching Gordy perform. "Dad told me he and Barbara stayed home this morning to receive a delivery, so I figured I'd come see my future superstar athlete nephews in action."

"Thanks. Corey, can you do me a favor?"

"Sure. What'd'ya need?"

"Can you go over and watch the rest of Gary's game?"

"Sure. You want to stay put for a change?"

"It's not that. I've never had a problem going back and forth. But Gary's coach has his eye on me, and it's getting uncomfortable."

"Oh, the guy who asked you to lunch before. He seems like a nice guy. Why not go out with him?"

"He's not my type, Corey."

Her brow wrinkled. "Not your type? He's nice looking, is in good shape, likes kids. What's not to like?"

"He just doesn't do anything for me, that's all." She could hardly tell Corey she only had eyes for her brother. "Can you help me?"

"Sure. I'll go right now."

"Thanks. I'll see you when Gordy is finished. I'll send him over, but I'll probably wait here. Maybe the coach will get the message."

Corey ambled off, giving a shout of "Go, Gordy!" and waving before being out of earshot.

After the soccer match ended, Natasha begged off crossing the field with Gordy, saying her legs had given out. "You go on ahead. Aunt Corey is waiting for you. I'll stay here and chill."

"I'm going to get you some water first."

"No, Gordy, those bottles are for the players."

"We've got extra. Hey, Coach, is it okay if my mom gets some water? She doesn't feel good."

Keith smiled at her. "Hello, Natasha. Are you all right?"

"I'm fine. Just a little winded, that's all."

Keith turned to Gordy. "Go get your mother a bottle of water." As Gordy scampered off, he said to Natasha, "Probably all that walking you do across the field to see your other son."

"His aunt is over there with him now."

"Here you go, Mom," Gordy said breathlessly, holding out a small bottle of water.

"Thanks, sweetie. Now, why don't you go over to Aunt Corey. Y'all come meet me in the truck when the game is over, okay?"

"Okay."

Natasha unscrewed the cap and took a swig of the cool liquid. "Oh, that was good."

"Feel better?"

"I feel great." She noticed Keith's female friend staring at them curiously from the refreshment table a few feet away. This woman began showing up at all the games the very next weekend after Gordy introduced Natasha to Keith. She surmised they'd met that same weekend. Natasha viewed the woman's presence as a godsend. As the only unmarried African-American mother of a player, she no longer had to deal with Keith's flirting. How much easier her life would be if Gene, too, found a girlfriend.

Natasha stayed in the Explorer reading a magazine, which she put down when her cell phone began to ring. She recognized her mother-in-law's telephone number in the caller-ID window.

She ended the conversation as Corey and the boys approached the truck. Gary's long face said it all. "Did your team lose?"

"Yeah."

"I'm sorry. Next week you'll probably be on top again. Boys, Grandma has invited you over for lunch and to spend the afternoon. Do you want to go?"

"Sure!" Gordy said.

"I missed them at the game this morning," Gary said.

"I know you did. Their new end tables were delivered this morning, though, so if they had been there they would have missed it."

Corey stood near the driver's side as the boys climbed in back. "Do you have any plans for this afternoon, Natasha?"

"Get ready for the meeting tonight, I suppose. Although all I'm going to do is bake a chocolate cheesecake. I'm getting everything else from the deli or the frozen-food department. You know I'm not much for cooking."

"I promised my mom and grandmother that I'd be by," Corey said. "Why don't you come along? They'd both love to see you."

Natasha joked. "Even without the boys?"

"They like you, Natasha. Of course, they *love* Gary and Gordy."

She laughed. "Your mother really wants grandchildren, you know."

"Her and Dad both. Hey, I'll see you at Barbara's in a few."

Natasha greeted her in-laws and took a few moments to admire their newly delivered accent tables. Corey arrived minutes later.

"Aren't you girls going to stick around long enough to have lunch?" a beaming Ed inquired.

"I don't think so, Dad. You know how Mom and Grandma always insist that anyone who visits them eat," Corey said.

"I'm going to call your mother and ask if she and Olivia can join us for Easter dinner," Barbara said. "Kirk and Tara are coming down. It'll be the first time since Christmas that all of us will be together."

"Actually, Barbara, I think Mom and Grandma are taking a cruise that weekend. Five days to the Keys and San Juan. They leave from Charleston."

"You don't think all that moving about will be too much for Olivia?" Ed said with concern.

"No, I think she'll be fine. Mom says there'll be plenty of seniors on the ship. Calvin is going, too. He'll help Mom care for Grandma. They're going to bring along a wheelchair so she won't have to do a lot of walking. And she's really looking forward to it."

"That's the key to enjoying old age," Barbara said. "Having something to look forward to."

"But that was sweet of you to think of Mom and Grandma, Barbara," Corey said. "Why don't you call, anyway. I could always have the dates of their trip wrong."

"I'll do that."

Corey glanced at her watch. "Natasha, I guess we'd better get going."

"All right. Boys, I'm going out with Aunt Corey for a few hours. You two be good, all right?"

They left the house and got into Corey's Camry. "Oh, my, Kirk and Tara at Easter," Natasha moaned. "Is it time for them again already?"

"I know what you mean. These family get-togethers are getting harder and harder to get through. But they make Barbara so happy, and Dad, too."

"Do you plan to bring Bill to dinner? I'd love to meet him."

Corey didn't answer right away. "Can I tell you something, Natasha?" she finally said.

Natasha sensed a secret was about to be revealed. "Of course."

"You have to promise to keep it to yourself. You can't tell Barbara or my father, which is the same thing."

"I promise, I promise."

Corey took a deep breath. "That wedding I went to in Atlanta. It was actually Bill's daughter who got married."

"His *daughter?* How old is she, fourteen?"

"More like ten years older than that."

"Twenty-four?" Natasha felt as if she was hallucinating. "I don't get it. If Bill's daughter is that old, how old is Bill?"

"Fifty-one."

"Whoa! Corey, you never once said he was an…an older man."

"You make it sound like he's old enough to be my father, Natasha."

"Maybe not, but he's closer to Ed's age than to yours, and you're closer to his daughter's age than you are to his."

"I'm thirty-one. He's only twenty years older than me."

"Only? That's a lot of years, Corey. He was already halfway through college by the time you were born." She paused to let this sink in, then asked, "Do Ed and June know?"

"No," Corey admitted. "I haven't told either one of them. I

don't expect them to be thrilled. But, Natasha, he's just perfect for me. We get along so well. I know it's a cliché, but it's like we were made for each other."

"That feeling is something that comes with time, Corey. You two have only been seeing each other a few months."

"I wish you wouldn't be so judgmental."

Corey sounded so hurt, and Natasha immediately thought of how it went when Terry told her she and Larry were in love. Terry's feelings had been hurt then, just as Corey's were now. But had she really said anything so wrong? It had nothing to do with being hypocritical. She sincerely had doubts about Bill's suitability for Corey. Her feelings for Jared had nothing to do with it.

Still, what would Corey say if she knew they had been to bed together?

"I do trust your judgment, Corey," she said, truly wanting to be supportive. "And if you say this man is your soul mate, I won't dispute it."

"Thanks, Natasha. A little support goes a long way. I know I'll have to introduce Bill to Mom and Dad eventually, but I'd like to put it off as long as I can. I don't think their reactions will be any more enthusiastic than yours."

"Let's not worry about that right now," Natasha said as Corey parked on the street in front of her mother's home. The driveway was empty. "Are you sure your mother is home?"

"It doesn't look like it. Grandma might be there. If not, I've got a key, so we can just go inside and wait."

Olivia answered the door, her gray hair framing her face like cotton candy. "Hello, girls. June mentioned you'd probably be stopping by. She went out to the store, but she'll be back soon. Come in, come in."

Natasha pecked the older woman's smooth cheek. "It's good to see you, Miss Olivia."

"Hi, Grandma," Corey said. Her voice quavered, and she hugged Olivia as if they would never see each other again.

"What's this?" Olivia said. "I haven't even been to the doctor lately, so why are you hugging me like I'm going to die tomorrow?"

Natasha liked the way Olivia joked about her own mortality. If she lived that long, she hoped she, too, could be so down to earth about the inevitable.

"Just a little relationship stress, Grandma," Corey said. "I'm all right, really. Seeing you has always made me feel better, from the time I was a little kid."

Natasha's stomach tightened in envy. How nice it must be for children to have adults to lean on when they felt unsure or worried. She'd never had the luxury of parents or grandparents. As children, she and Robin had cried on each other's shoulders and tried their best to comfort each other, something for which their young ages made them woefully inadequate.

At least she would always be there for Gary and Gordy. As they took seats in the living room she pushed the pain of the past out of her head. Natasha quickly realized that immersing herself in bitterness had caused her to miss part of the conversation between Corey and her grandmother, but when Olivia spoke again Natasha figured Corey must have confided to her about an involvement with a man whom others might not consider appropriate for her.

"A person can't really help who they fall in love with," Olivia said. "Sometimes the choice is atrocious. Look at that mess with, oh, what's her name? Maureen O'Sullivan's daughter. The girl who used to be married to Frank Sinatra."

"Mia Farrow?" Natasha guessed.

"Yes, that's the one. Her boyfriend, that bookish-looking man, had an affair with her daughter. I thought that was awful."

"I think everybody did," Corey said. "It was so lame the way Woody Allen tried to say it was all right because the girl had been adopted. But, Grandma...how did you feel about Mia marrying Sinatra?"

"Oh, there's nothing new about young girls marrying middle-aged men. It's when the situation is reversed that it causes such an uproar. I remember a scandalous case from the late fifties, maybe early sixties. A movie actress named Gloria Grahame— her most famous role was Violet, the town flirt in that Jimmy Stewart Christmas movie, *It's a Wonderful Life*—married a younger man."

"What's so scandalous about that, Grandma?" Corey asked. "It couldn't have been the first time that happened. You told me that Greer Garson married the actor who played her son in *Mrs. Miniver* right after they finished filming, and that was in the forties. And what about Norma Shearer marrying her young ski instructor?" To Natasha she explained, "Grandma has always been a big movie fan."

"Not anymore," Olivia said forlornly. "The movies they put out now are terrible. I'd rather watch the classic movie channel or read biographies of actors from that time. And in answer to your question, Corey, marrying a younger man has been done before. But what made this scandalous was that just a few years before, when her new husband was a teenager, Gloria had been married to his father."

"His *father!*" Natasha and Corey looked at each other, each twisting their features into expressions of disgust.

"Just how young was he, anyway?" Corey asked.

"He was younger than she, but her husband was considerably older, so, no, she wasn't old enough to be his mother. But she had a child with the father and then more children with the son." Olivia shook her head. "Of course, her career was never the same after that."

"My goodness, so her child with the father was the younger children's uncle, as well as their half sibling. That's unreal." Natasha made a face, as if she'd just smelled something unpleasant. The problems her relationship with Jared presented seemed minuscule in comparison. The actress Miss Olivia talked about brazenly had children with a father and a son.

"Of course, that's an extreme case," Miss Olivia said. "Personally, I think it's repulsive, but in most cases you'll be happiest when you listen to your heart."

"And did they stay married the rest of their lives, Grandma?" Corey asked.

"No. I read a biography of her. It lasted longer than her marriage to her father-in-law, but eventually it ended. By then she was in her forties and couldn't get many movie roles. A few years after that she died of cancer. Happy endings in Hollywood happen mostly on film."

Chapter 23

Natasha drew in her breath. The male voice who answered Genae's phone had to be Cliff. When she pictured Genae in her apartment she saw her stretched out on the mauve, striped couch that faced the fireplace in the living room or straightening up her compact kitchen. Cliff didn't fit anywhere into the scenario, but it made perfect sense for him to pick up her phone if she was unavailable.

In the most pleasant tone she could muster, she said, "Hello, Cliff. This is Natasha…Genae's sister." The words still felt odd coming off her tongue, but wonderful.

"Yes?"

"Is Genae in?" she said abruptly, put off by his frigid tone. He deliberately spoke as if he'd never heard of her, just to rile her.

"Yeah, she's in the other room changing her clothes."

Natasha almost wished he'd said Genae had gone out. She felt awkward. She saw no point even attempting to make small talk with Cliff, since he obviously wasn't happy with the idea of her calling.

"So," he said, "are you satisfied?"

His question caught her off guard. She half expected him to slam the phone down and let her wait in silence for Genae. It would be just like him to not bother to tell her she had a call until—no, *unless* she noticed.

She took the bait, prepared to hear something insulting. "What do you mean?"

"Are you satisfied with all the trouble you've caused? I knew this would happen the minute you showed up."

Natasha didn't hesitate to counter with an equally salty reply. "Why, because you were afraid someone would point out to Genae that control doesn't equal love?"

"What the hell is that supposed to mean?"

"It means that when it comes to Genae you're a manipulative tyrant, always telling her what to do or how to think, and throwing tantrums when she resists you. If you'd had your way, she would never have found out that we really are sisters."

"*You're* the one who wants to be in control, pressing her like you did to talk to her mother and bring up matters she wanted to forget."

Her mother? "You're forgetting something, Cliff. Genae's mother is *my* mother, too."

"Yeah, and she was perfectly happy to leave you in the past. You didn't notice her rushing to see you again, did you?"

Natasha winced at the lingering pain of rejection.

Her silence helped Cliff recognize that he'd hit a nerve. "Your own mother didn't even want to see you," he pressed. "All Genae did was open up painful wounds for her, force her to confess that she'd been pregnant and unmarried as a teenager. Mothers are just as entitled to privacy as anyone else. They shouldn't have to share every embarrassing detail of their lives with their children. I'm surprised she even owned up to you."

"But she did, Cliff, she did," Natasha pointed out. Cliff's words, meant to be cruel, suddenly gave her new hope. Her mother could easily have lied to Genae and said she'd never heard of any Natasha. Maybe she really would come around soon.

Cliff sneered. "Probably because Genae's asking about you came as such a shock to her. She never intended for Genae to know about you, or else Genae would have known."

Natasha saw nothing encouraging in his latest barb. Genae's voice in the background spared her from having to respond. "Is this better?" Then she said, "Is that for me?" A moment later she came on the line. "Natasha, is that you?"

"Yes. I was just calling to say hi and ask if you would consider coming down to Greer for Easter. I've been looking forward to seeing you. I'd really like my boys to meet their aunt, even if it means they can't meet their grandmother yet." Her voice sounded high-pitched and unnatural. She hoped Genae wouldn't notice and comment on it. The last thing she wanted was for Cliff to know he'd really gotten to her with that last comment of his.

"Are you all right, Natasha? You sound so funny."

Busted. "No, I'm not all right," she admitted. "But if you want details, you'll have to ask Cliff."

Genae hung up the phone thoughtfully.

"What was that all about?" Cliff asked impatiently.

"Natasha invited me to Greer for Easter."

"I hope you told her you can't go."

"Why would I tell her that, Cliff? And what happened between you two, anyway?"

"Nothing happened between us. I just told her how upset she's made your mother. It's not my fault if she didn't want to hear it. It's the truth." His steady gaze dared her to say otherwise.

She broke eye contact to sigh heavily. "Cliff, why do you dislike my sister?"

"She's your *half* sister. And she's a stranger."

"We're getting to know each other. We talk on the phone all the time. And you never answered my question."

"I don't dislike her. But I've always known she would bring unhappiness. Haven't you ever gotten the feeling that your mother is sad about something?"

"Well, yes, but that's just her way. She's been like that as long as I can remember. But whenever I asked, she always insisted she was fine."

"Genae," he began, taking one of her hands into both of his. She hated it when he did that. It made her feel like such a child. But she knew the drill well. Now would come a patronizing explanation.

"You have to realize that people often hide their pain by pretending it isn't there. It's a coping mechanism. There's a sadness in your mother that no one can reach. When you ran into Natasha at Duane's party and commented on the strong resemblance, I had a feeling we might be opening a Pandora's box. And I was right, wasn't I? Your mother looks sadder than ever these days."

She sat beside him on the sofa. "I guess I'd better have a talk with Mom. Make her understand Natasha wants to put the past behind her and go on from here."

Cliff stared at her. "Genae, haven't you heard what I just said? Knowing that you and Natasha have found each other is what's making your mother so unhappy. She doesn't want the two of you to be in touch. And neither do I."

"Cliff, that's silly. I'm not a child, I'm a grown woman. My mother doesn't pick my friends." *And neither do you,* she added silently. For a moment she felt tempted to share the unflattering opinion her mother had about *him.* That would be sure to ruffle his feathers. "And your concern for my mother is touching, but *I'm* the one you're supposed to be marrying. Doesn't that mean that my happiness should come first?"

Cliff's upper body jerked a bit, as if he found her words startling. "You were happy before you knew Natasha existed. You can be happy without her." He grunted. "See what I mean? This is just what I was afraid of. Now she's causing trouble between you and me."

"There's no reason for trouble between us. You're going to be my husband, Cliff. Natasha is my sister. And just like you're also my friend, so is she. The bond we have will only get stronger when I go South Carolina over Easter."

"Wait a minute. You're going down there?"

He looked almost comical in his shock, she thought, like the favored Oscar winner when they called someone else's name. "Yes. I leave Saturday and I'll be back Tuesday morning. I can get a cheaper flight with a Tuesday return rather than Monday, and Natasha said it's okay to stay till then."

"Well, it's not okay with *me*, Genae. I thought you and I were going to church with my parents." He slapped his thigh. "This is just fine," he said sarcastically. "Along comes your long-lost sister and I get thrown to the curb like an empty can of soda. What am I supposed to do all weekend if you're not here?"

"Go to church with your parents, like you planned. And afterward maybe you could go spend some time with my mother. You know, cheer her up."

Cliff's eyes narrowed. "You trying to be funny?"

"No. But you did express concern over how all of this with Natasha is affecting Mom."

He abruptly stood up. "I'm leaving," he announced.

"But I thought we were going to Carrabba's. She tugged at the hem of her boat-neck cotton sweater. "I even changed for you." Originally she'd put on a pair of jeans with the same blue silk blouse she'd worn to work that day, but Cliff had objected, saying the blouse was too dressy to wear with jeans. Privately she disagreed—a silk blouse went with *anything*—but changed anyway just to get him to stop sulking. Sometimes her fiancé behaved like a five-year-old, pouting when he didn't get his way. He often insisted that she wear a certain style of outfit or accessories and even made suggestions regarding her nail color and design. She generally listened eagerly. After all, Cliff Allen was one of the most sought-after bachelors in the county, and he came from a prominent family. Besides, his being thirteen years her senior meant he knew more about life than she did.

But lately his meticulous nature was beginning to grate on her nerves, especially now that the mere mention of Natasha's name was sure to set him off on another tirade. If she didn't know better she'd swear he felt threatened by her sister.

"I don't see the point. You're obviously more excited about your plans to visit your sister than you are about having dinner with me." He grabbed his golf jacket and left the apartment.

For a few moments Genae simply stared at the closed door, as if she expected him to walk through it again at any moment with a big grin on his face, saying it had all been a joke. When that didn't happen and instead she heard the sound of a car engine starting, she knew he really meant it.

She walked toward her bedroom. No point in soiling a perfectly clean sweater.

Instinctively she knew Cliff wouldn't call tonight. In his mind, she needed to be taught a lesson. She decided to use her free time to check on Natasha.

"Hi, it's me," she said when Natasha answered, loving the casual way they now greeted each other. No further ID needed. "I just called to make sure you're okay."

"Ah. Cliff must have gone home."

"Now, Natasha, you're not being fair. I would've talked longer if you hadn't rushed me off the phone."

"Yes, you're right." She paused, then voiced the question Genae knew she would ask. "Genae, what do you see in Cliff?"

She laughed. "My mother doesn't like him, either. She says he's too much like my daddy."

"Didn't you say Debra introduced the two of you?"

Genae noticed Natasha always referred to their mother by her given name. She supposed it must be difficult to give the title of Mom to someone you hadn't seen in over twenty years. "Yes, she and Mrs. Allen put their heads together one day and decided it would be a good idea if they introduced us."

"Obviously Debra changed her mind."

"Yes. At first she kept telling me what a good catch Cliff was, but then she said…she said he was too controlling."

Natasha grunted. "I can't say I disagree."

"I'd really hoped you and he would get along. But I guess it's not surprising. Cliff doesn't care for most of my friends."

"I'll bet he objects whenever you spend time with them."

"Usually."

"Genae, how can you stand it?"

She sighed. "To be honest, I'm not sure if I can anymore."

Chapter 24

Kirk hung up the phone. "Hey, Tara, you'll never guess what happened! Natasha found her sister."

Tara looked up from the book she held. "She's got a sister?"

"Yes, but she didn't know about her." Kirk hesitated about telling his wife the whole story. Tara could be so mean-spirited sometimes. He'd thought her happiness over the baby would soften her a little, but pregnancy had only made her more disagreeable. He wondered if she had a hormone imbalance or something.

"Her mother had another daughter after she got married and moved to Raleigh, North Carolina," he finally said, neatly summarizing. "Natasha went to her friend Robin's anniversary party in Raleigh, and her sister was there, too, as the date of one of the guests. They noticed how much they looked alike, and they started talking, and one thing led to another."

"Wow. Small world, isn't it?"

"Sure is. Her sister's name is Genae, and she's coming to Spartanburg for Easter. We'll get to meet her."

"Is their mother still alive?"

"Yes, but apparently she won't be coming for Easter."

Natasha drummed her fingers against her thigh. Genae's plane landed ten minutes ago, and passengers filed out through the corridor.

"Do you see her, Mommy?" Gordy asked.

"Not yet. Oh, there she is! Genae! Here we are." She waved vigorously.

Genae waved back. They giggled with happiness as they hugged each other. Genae drew in her breath in mock surprise when she saw the boys looking on curiously. "Look at my two handsome little nephews! Let's see," she said, pointing to Gary. "You must be Gordy. And you must be Gary." She laughed when they shook their heads in vigorous protest. "I'm just kidding. I know who's who. Now give your auntie a hug and a kiss."

The boys did as they were told. As Genae straightened up, Natasha recognized a cell phone ringing to the melody of the 1812 Overture.

"Oops, that's me," Genae said. She pulled a slim silver-colored cell phone out of an outside compartment of her purse.

"Somebody must have known you just landed," Natasha said. She had a pretty good hunch who it was.

All day long Genae's phone rang about every two hours. Cliff even called during the movie they saw after lunch. It annoyed Natasha to no end to hear her sister updating him on everything she'd done since the last time he talked to her. From Genae's answers she surmised that Cliff even wanted to know what she'd eaten for lunch.

"Genae, I've got to ask," she said when the latest brief conversation ended. She stood at the counter, rolling out defrosted bread dough to make steak-and-cheese calzones. She and the boys had enjoyed them in Montclair, but since she couldn't find them on any restaurant menu in the Greer area, she'd learned to

make them herself with Steak-Umms, onion and shredded moz-
zarella baked inside a pocket of bread dough. Genae, at the
cooktop, browned the frozen beef rectangles and sautéed large
chunks of onions. "Does Cliff generally call you this often, or
is he only doing it because you're with me?"

"He usually calls a lot if I'm out without him. I can be
shopping or having dinner with a girlfriend. He does have a
tendency to feel a little insecure." Her sigh hinted at dissatisfac-
tion with Cliff's behavior.

"Too bad he didn't meet my brother-in-law Kirk's wife before
she married him. She's insecure with a capital I, doesn't let him
out of her sight. That would have been a match made in heaven."

"Want to talk about it?"

"Oh, I'll fill you in on all the details after Gary and Gordy
have gone to bed. By the way, I never asked you something important. When's the wedding?" Of course, if her mother hadn't
come around by then, she wouldn't attend rather than cause
conflict for Genae and awkwardness for their mother. The fact
that she hadn't thought to ask about Genae's nuptials until now
suggested that in her subconscious she'd known all along that it
might not be practical to be present.

"We haven't set a date. I'll tell you the truth, Natasha. I'm
having second thoughts. Sometimes Cliff makes me feel like I've
got a plastic bag over my head and I'm smothering."

"Have you told him?"

"No, not yet. You know, he was so upset with me for coming
down here this weekend I half expected *him* to break it off.
Instead he's calling me every five minutes and interrogating me.
I've tried to be patient with him. From the time of our first date
my mother drummed into me what a good catch Cliff is, that he
could get any girl he wants but he wanted *me*. Now she says he's
less of a catch, and I see him as someone who wants to control
me. How I think, what I wear…"

"What you *wear?*"

Genae giggled as she used the edge of a metal spatula to cut the meat into strips. "All the time. His stock line is that he knows more about these things than I do."

"He really wants you to feel like you don't have a brain in your head, doesn't he?"

"That's how he makes me feel sometimes," Genae admitted. "And I'm dreading having to tell him that it's over. He'll insist that I've allowed myself to be manipulated by you."

"It's the old pot-calling-the-kettle-black strategy." Natasha, slotted spoon with steak and onion in hand, suddenly stopped mid transfer and looked at Genae. "You don't think you were influenced by me, do you? Much as I dislike Cliff, I can't say I want the responsibility of a breakup."

"No. Well, maybe just a little."

"Oh, Genae."

"Not directly," she said quickly. "But I noticed how rude Cliff was from that first night at your friends' party. He hated the idea of my even talking to you, and he tried his best to discourage the idea that we could be related."

"I'm sure he wasn't thrilled at the prospect of you having another person in your life. He already wants two hundred percent of you."

"I think that's it. But in the end he'll get zero. I've decided to let some other girl get the great catch."

Jared called that evening. "I got in this morning, but I didn't call until now because I didn't want to interrupt your time with your sister. How's it going?"

That was the reason she'd given herself when wondering why he didn't call. She suspected the incoming call came from him and picked up the kitchen extension so she could speak freely. "Just wonderful, Jared. Gary and Gordy are tickled to have another aunt, and Genae is thrilled to have nephews. We went out for lunch this afternoon and then to the movies. I can't tell you how great it is to have a sibling, someone who has the same bloodline as me, even if it's only partial because we have different fathers. I feel much less alone."

"You've never been alone, Natasha, not from the time you got married."

"Not to take anything away from you and Corey and Barbara and Ed," she clarified, "but this is different. It's so hard to explain."

"Don't worry about it. Just be happy." He paused. "I'm looking forward to seeing you tomorrow. It's been a long time."

That was your *idea, not mine.* "Yes, it has."

"I'll see you at church. Please tell Genae we're all looking forward to meeting her."

"I will. Is Corey there with you?"

"No, she's out with Bill. Or I guess that's where she is. I'm looking forward to meeting him, too. She's trying to be cool about it, but I think she's met her Mr. Right." He paused. "Have you met him?"

"No, I haven't. So what are you going to do with yourself tonight?" Natasha felt uncomfortable discussing Bill with Jared. She suspected that none of the Langstons would be happy with the age difference.

"Oh, I'll just chill out in front of the TV. You?"

"We just got back from the bowling alley. Right now Corey and the boys are playing Uno. We'll probably all go to bed in a little bit." She doubted that would be the case at all, but she said it in case Jared had any ideas about joining them. She wasn't about to lay down the welcome mat for him after he'd shown so little interest in seeing her since the night they made love.

Maybe she *should* get to bed early tonight.

Tomorrow promised to be a challenging day.

Chapter 25

Natasha felt happy and relaxed. Maybe her fears about today hadn't been warranted. Her in-laws accepted Genae with their usual warmth. Even Tara demonstrated tolerable behavior.

Jared provided the only puzzle. When the family gathered in front of the church, Jared grasped her hand in his and kissed her cheek, whispering, "You look delectable," for her ears only in a way that made her knees want to buckle, despite her vow to play it cool. She didn't know what to make of it. If he was so happy to see her, why had he stayed away a month and a half?

"I'm so sorry your mother couldn't travel with you this time, Genae," Barbara said chattily when they returned to the Langston home after services. "We do so look forward to meeting her."

Natasha avoided Jared's eyes. He was the only one besides Robin and, of course, Genae, who knew the truth about Debra. To everyone else, she simply hadn't been able to make it.

"Maybe next time," Genae said.

"Aunt Genae, that's the biggest ring I've ever seen," Gary said, his eyes fastened to her diamond engagement ring. "Doesn't it get in your way?"

"Only when I do housework. I have to take it off to fit rubber gloves over my hand. One time I forgot where I put it."

"Your fiancé wouldn't be too happy about that," Jared observed.

"Try to put it in the same place every time," Tara said, startling Natasha with her participation in the conversation.

Genae just smiled and nodded. Natasha didn't expect her sister to say that her engagement would soon be history.

"Barbara, when do we eat?" Kirk asked. "My nose is getting a few whiffs of that ham, and it smells great."

"As soon as Corey and her friend get here. Everything's ready."

Ed glanced at his watch. "They should be here any minute. It's twenty to four."

"We'll just rush them to the table as soon as they arrive," Natasha said with a laugh. She sounded jovial, but it masked nervousness. The family was about to learn that Bill was much older than Corey, and she didn't know how they would take it.

"Hi, everybody!"

All conversation came to a dead halt as Corey entered the room holding the hand of a handsome man whose gray-sprinkled hair and mustache and general demeanor suggested he was past forty-five. Ed and Barbara exchanged glances, Jared's eyes narrowed, and Tara whispered something to a staring Kirk. Only Genae, Gary and Gordy appeared unruffled.

After stilted introductions, the family went in to dinner. Barbara and Ed's dining-room table had two leaves, both of which had been inserted to make the table long enough to seat twelve. Four padded chairs from their card table provided the necessary additional seating.

During dinner Natasha noticed the numerous glances Bill's way that bordered on staring. Both Barbara and Ed jumped on every opportunity to slip in what they probably believed were natural-sounding questions: When Bill mentioned he worked as a chemical engineer, he was asked how long he'd been in the field. A mention of his family brought up the question of children. Did he have any? How old were they? Then Jared caught everyone off guard by asking Bill if he had grandchildren, a question that prompted Tara to break off into a fit of giggles she didn't even try to control.

Corey glared at her, and Bill put down his utensils. "Mr. Langston, Mrs. Langston—"

"Call us Barbara and Ed," Barbara offered.

Ed's grumble came out loud enough to be heard. "Since we're contemporaries."

"That's just it, Ed. I'd have to be stupid to not get the idea that you don't approve of me because I'm a few years older than Corey."

"Well, since you've brought it up, just how old are you, Bill?" Ed asked.

"I'm fifty-one."

"Fifty-one! That's really *ooooold*."

Natasha turned to Gordy with a frown. She silently placed her index finger to her lips. Gordy covered his mouth with his palm, his eyes growing wide. A meaningful glance at Gary guaranteed that he, too, would keep quiet.

"Last time I checked, Corey was thirty-one. I hardly think twenty years is 'a few,'" Jared pointed out.

"The way you're all behaving is precisely why we waited so long to introduce Bill to you," Corey said, her voice ringing with indignation. "Bill was afraid you'd act this way. I said you wouldn't, but I can see I was mistaken."

"Maybe this has happened to Bill before with previous girl-friends," Ed said.

Corey appeared visibly startled. She looked at Bill, helpless-ness in her eyes.

Bill looked directly at Ed. "Ed, if you're wondering if I make it a habit to date younger women, the answer is no. And I don't mean to be disrespectful, but I'd appreciate it if you were to address me directly instead of referring to me like I'm not here."

"All right. I'll ask you straight out—"

"Ed," Barbara cautioned.

"Ed," Natasha said simultaneously.

"Dad," Jared said.

Corey placed her napkin on the edge of her place mat. "I think it would be best if we left. I don't know about Bill, but I've suddenly lost my appetite. We'll talk another time. I'm sorry."

She pushed her chair back from the table, quickly followed by Bill, who gave a polite nod but didn't speak. She took his hand, and together they left the room. Seconds later, Natasha heard the front door closing.

"Well, that was interesting," Tara remarked.

"I think maybe we should talk about it after dinner," Natasha suggested, cocking her head toward Gary and Gordy, who sat between her and Genae.

"I agree," Barbara said.

Ed pushed his plate away. "They're not the only ones who've lost their appetite."

Comments at the dinner table after Corey and Bill took their leave centered around how tasty the food was. In addition to the spiral-sliced ham, Barbara had also prepared a roasted leg of lamb, macaroni and cheese, collard greens and corn bread. No one wanted to talk about Corey and Bill.

"Come on, boys, let's go watch TV with your auntie," Genae suggested when Gary and Gordy asked to be excused.

Natasha mouthed a silent thank-you to her sister. "I'll be in to join you in a few minutes, after I finish helping Barbara clean the kitchen." She knew cleanup came in a distant second to the crisis with Corey, but she wanted to make sure that Gary and Gordy didn't pop in to see what she was up to, and since both boys found kitchen work boring, they weren't likely to come back this way.

Genae ushered the boys out of the room.

"Cleanup can wait," Barbara said when they were out of earshot. "I think we need to talk about what happened with Corey."

"No wonder she didn't want him to meet us," Ed said angrily. "That was pure crap about being afraid we'd act badly. She knows damn well she's got no business getting involved with a man nearly as old as me." He looked at Jared sharply. "Did you know about this?"

"No, Dad, I didn't. I'm as shocked as you are."

Natasha stared at her feet uncomfortably, not knowing if she should speak up. She decided it would be all right to tell them. After all, Corey's relationship with Bill could no longer be classified as a secret. "I knew," she said softly.

"Natasha!" Barbara exclaimed. "Why didn't you tell us?"

"Because Corey asked me not to."

Barbara nodded in understanding, but Tara, never one to miss an opportunity to criticize, spoke up. "So what'd you do, Natasha, tell her you thought it was a great idea for her to date a man old enough to be her father?"

"He's not quite that old, Tara. And the fact is, I didn't meet Bill before today, but I was just as shocked as you were when she told me he had a grown daughter."

"Well, I think it's awful," Tara said. "I certainly wouldn't want any daughter of mine to be the answer to somebody's midlife crisis." The only one at the table still eating, she popped a piece of corn bread into her mouth and glanced meaningfully at Kirk, who shook his head slightly in some kind of private signal.

"I was caught off guard myself," Kirk said, "but Corey is grown, so it really isn't for us to say."

"I don't care," Ed said stubbornly. "I don't like it."

Barbara mused aloud, "I wonder if June knows." Her gaze settled on Natasha, an unasked question in her eyes.

"I honestly don't know, Barbara," she volunteered.

"Jared, you haven't had much to say," Ed observed. "What do you think about all this?"

Jared shrugged. "I think I shouldn't have asked Bill if he had grandchildren. I'm feeling rather bad about that. I can't even blame Corey for reacting the way she did. I guess I was thinking aloud. But his age came as such a surprise... Corey usually confides in me. But I agree with Kirk. Corey is a grown woman. We have no recourse but to trust her judgment."

"I don't *have* to trust anything," Ed retorted.

Barbara placed her hand on his arm. "Ed, calm down. Kirk and Jared are right. Corey is thirty-one years old. You can hardly forbid her to see this man. Besides, they're only dating. It'll probably go the same route as her other romances."

"I hope so. I can't see her married to that fellow. She's always been an active girl. He, on the other hand, probably won't want to go anywhere, she'll be bored, and then he'll get sick or something, and she'll spend the best years of her life nursing him, and he'll probably leave everything he's got to his kids."

"Dad, there's nothing you can do to stop it if that's what Corey decides she wants," Jared said. At his father's glare he added, "Sometimes people choose partners who seem less than appropriate to others, and everyone wants to talk about how awful it is. But it isn't anyone else's business, and if people stopped sticking their noses where they don't belong, everyone would be a lot happier."

He stood behind Natasha, and she didn't have to see his face to know he referred to their relationship as well as to Corey and Bill. That would, of course, remain their secret.

But her face froze in distress when she felt his hands on her shoulders, his fingers stroking her upper arms. Didn't he realize what signal that would send? Or was he so impassioned by his feelings that he didn't realize the symbolism of his gesture?

If Jared didn't realize it, the others did. Barbara was the first to find her voice. "Jared? Is there something you or Natasha want to tell us?"

"I think he's already told you," Tara said in an amused tone.

"Tara, be quiet," Kirk said.

Jared's fingers abruptly stopped their caressing. He moved to sit on the ottoman in front of Natasha, sitting sideways so his side, rather than his back, faced her. She guessed he wanted to buy some time as he formulated a response. "I didn't realize... Natasha and I are going to ask all of you for privacy right now."

She sat as still as a grandfather clock.

"Jared, are you saying that you and Natasha are...are a *couple?*" Kirk managed to say, his features contorted in disbelief.

Jared glared at him. "Didn't you hear what I just said?"

"Yes, I heard you, and I don't care about your privacy. We're all family here, and I feel you owe us an explanation, given what we just witnessed."

Natasha allowed her eyes to move to Jared. She saw him track the facial expressions of everyone in the room, watched his shoulders droop in defeat. "Our relationship has turned in a different direction," he finally said. "It's new, it's fragile, and frankly, we're not ready to have it dissected and studied like a frog in a biology lab."

"So you two are actually sleeping together," Kirk said in an accusing tone. "Natasha, I'm disappointed in you. How could you do that to Tim?"

"Kirk," Barbara interjected.

"I mean it, Mom. Don't you find this disgusting?"

"Kirk!" Ed's booming voice held a stern warning.

"It's all right, Dad," Jared said. "I can defend myself." He stood up and faced Kirk. "You've got a helluva nerve accusing Natasha of being a traitor to Tim. At least Natasha didn't promise Tim not to get involved with me. But you promised him you would watch out for her, and then you reneged. The last year she lived in New Jersey, you never saw her at all. She could have been hospitalized or deathly ill for all you knew."

Kirk stood firm. "Yeah, like you did such a good job of taking care of her. First you run off to Texas, then you show up three years later and start sleeping with her. I don't think that's what Tim had in mind when he asked you to take care of her. If he had a grave he'd be flipping over in it."

Natasha watched in horror as Jared's hands formed fists.

"That's *enough*," Barbara said harshly.

"Yes, I quite agree," Ed said, this time speaking more quietly. "First of all, we have a guest. This isn't the time to be airing our dirty laundry."

"Natasha and I aren't dirty laundry, Dad." Jared's words sounded hard as steel.

"It was a figure of speech, son."

"Excuse me," Natasha said, finally coming to life. "I have to leave." With as much dignity as she could muster, she got to her feet and left the room, not looking at anyone.

Jared quickly got up and followed her, his hand possessively resting on her shoulder.

"What'd I tell you, Kirk?" Tara said triumphantly. "Natasha put her hooks into Jared when she couldn't get you."

Natasha sniffled and ran away. Jared stopped short. He turned, glaring at Tara with such venom in his eyes that she visibly twitched and linked her arm with Kirk's. But Jared merely shook his head and left the room.

"Tara, that was a terrible thing to say," Barbara said. "What on earth would make you think that Natasha tried to take Kirk away from you?"

"Because she asked him to give up his Saturdays to spend with Gary and Gordy, but whenever they went someplace she always tagged along. If she was so worried about her sons having a male influence, she would have stayed home. I know you guys think I'm such an awful person, but I did the only thing I could to save my marriage." Tara raised her chin defiantly. "And when Kirk and I were here on Christmas, she kept trying to get him alone. I stopped it again, and the next thing I knew she was going off with Jared. I even commented to Kirk about it."

"Yes, she did," Kirk said. "Um…"

"Was there something else?" Barbara prompted.

"Uh…no."

Barbara squared her shoulders. "Well, I'm sorry, Tara, but I think that's all a lot of B.S. I don't believe for one minute that

Natasha set her sights on Kirk, and I certainly don't believe she deliberately set out to get involved with Jared." Barbara looked at Ed for confirmation.

"I think that when people spend considerable time together, sometimes the nature of their relationship can change," Ed said thoughtfully. "I also think that we've all said more than we should. I'm going to excuse myself."

"He's all right, Mom," Kirk said as Ed left the room.

Barbara watched her husband with worried eyes. "I'm not sure. This has been a trying day for him, learning that Corey is dating a man almost old enough to be her father."

"Learning that Jared has secretly been dating Natasha must have come as a shock, too," Kirk added. "I know it shocked *me*. After all, Jared is his son."

His mother shrugged. "Excuse me. I'd better go see after him."

The moment she was gone Kirk turned to Tara. "Why did you say Natasha kept trying to get me alone at Christmas? We've been over that already. *I* was the one who wanted to apologize to her. And she only went off with Jared because you provoked her into saying something cruel and she felt badly about it."

"She *did* try to get you alone, Kirk. You'll never be able to convince me otherwise. I still feel she wanted you to be a replacement for Tim, and not just where the boys were concerned. Like Ed said, the nature of people's relationships can change when they spend time together. Natasha was counting on that with you. I don't care what anybody says, that's what I believe." Tara, elbows resting on the chair's arm rests, calmly patted her thighs.

Kirk shook his head. "What a holiday this turned out to be. I'll tell you something. I'm not worried about Corey. What she does isn't any of my business. But this thing with Jared and Natasha—it's wrong."

Chapter 26

"Natasha, wait. Where are you going?" Jared called.

Nearly at the driver's door of her Explorer with purse in hand, she stopped and slowly turned around. "Home. I've got to get out of here."

"Why don't we talk about it?"

"We just did. I'm not a glutton for punishment, Jared." She sniffled again. "Can I take your car? Genae will need something with a back seat to get the boys home, so I should leave her the truck. Can you tell her how to get back to my place? I promise to bring the Crossfire back to you first thing in the morning."

"Forget about it. I'll bring her." She looked awful, he thought. Her eyes looked dull, her voice quavered and her hands shook. Clearly she held back tears. He wasn't sure if she was physically capable of driving. Who knew what would happen once she got behind the wheel and didn't have to hold back her feelings anymore? But Genae, unfamiliar with Spartanburg County, couldn't be expected to find her own way back to Natasha's.

"I'd like to bunk at your place tonight, if that's all right with you," he said. "Corey knows that showing up with Bill sparked a family feud. She's sure to be especially annoyed at me. I'd like to give her some privacy." As he spoke he knew Natasha needed privacy as well. He cursed himself for having stroked her shoulder the way he had. If not for his unconscious action, the topic of debate would have remained on Corey and Bill. He'd give her the space she needed, but he wanted to be nearby, just in case she broke down and needed him. A person could only take so much. "I could stay at Dad's, of course, but I really don't want to sleep under the same roof as Kirk and Tara."

"It's all right, you can stay at my house. But you'll have to sleep on the pullout in my office, since Genae is using the one in the basement." She dug in her purse and pulled out her car keys.

He took them and handed her his. "We'll probably be leaving soon. I don't think anyone is in the mood for chitchat."

"Uncle Jared, why was everybody shouting?" Gary asked.

"I told them that the grown-ups were having a discussion and that it didn't involve them," Genae explained.

Jared kept his eyes on the road. He nodded. "Fellas, your aunt Genae is right. It's a grown-up thing. All I'll tell you is that you're not to worry. Everything's all right."

"Honest?" Gordy asked.

"Honest."

His confident reply soothed Genae like ice on a burn. She couldn't understand why Natasha had left so suddenly, without saying anything to her or the boys. Sure, Natasha told her that dinner might be awkward because of something her sister-in-law was about to do, but the pieces didn't provide an answer. Obviously the surprise had been that old guy Corey brought to dinner, but she saw no reason for her sister to jump up and leave while the family discussed the matter. What did Corey and her boyfriend have to do with Natasha, anyway? Had she been the one to introduce them or something?

* * *

After Natasha let them in she excused herself, saying she'd been resting in her room. Her pink-tinged eyes, however, told another story. The boys didn't seem to notice, but Jared did. "Fellas, y'all need to hang up your clothes," he said, "and while you're at it get the ball." Gary and Gordy obediently rushed into their room with the nylon garment bag that contained the suits and dress shoes they'd worn to church before changing at their grandparents'. Jared took a step toward Natasha, who shook her head before turning away in the direction of her bedroom. Genae heard her say something to the boys in the hall, and then Gary and Gordy appeared, Gary holding a basketball at his side.

Jared draped his suit coat and his already loosened tie over a chair back. "Okay, let's do it. Remember, the winner gets ice cream." He chuckled. "But so does the one who *doesn't* win." He went out the front door, and the boys followed. Gordy turned to Genae. "Come on, Aunt Genae. Shoot hoops with us."

"You guys go ahead. I'll be out in a minute, after I change clothes." She wanted to talk to Natasha first. She seemed terribly upset about something. Maybe she could help. Wasn't that what sisters were for?

She found her sister in her bedroom, curled up in an armless chair reading a book. She noticed that Natasha at least appeared more relaxed. Now she felt bad for having disturbed her. "Natasha, I just wanted to ask if there's anything I can do."

"No, but there's nothing anyone can do. We'll just have to see what happens next, I guess."

"I heard raised voices. I couldn't hear what anyone was saying, but it seems like this whole thing with your sister-in-law and her boyfriend has snowballed."

At that moment Natasha realized that her sister knew nothing about the matter that overshadowed Corey and Bill. She decided not to fill her in just yet. She felt like she'd been doing hard labor all day, with aching muscles and heavy eyelids. "I'm sure everyone will get over it eventually."

"Well, Gary and Gordy asked about it on the way home."

Panic closed in around her throat. If the boys found out about her and Jared from anyone other than her... "They did?"

"I told them it was grown folks' business, and Jared backed me up. He told them not to worry, that everything's fine."

Natasha exhaled. Of course she had nothing to worry about. Genae clearly had no idea, and the boys seemed fine when they came in. A yawn escaped from her mouth before she could stop it. "Excuse me. I don't know why I'm yawning. It's early still."

"I'm going to let you get some rest. Jared and the boys are shooting baskets out front. I'm going to change clothes and join them. Jared said something about going for ice cream when they're done. Would you like some?"

"No, thanks. I'm just going to read until I get sleepy. I know it's early, but I begin work at five in the morning."

"All right. I'll see you in the morning, huh?"

"Okay. And, Genae?"

"Hmm?"

"Thanks. And please tell Jared I said the same thing."

"Natasha."

Her body jerked, a strange strangled sound coming from her throat at the sound of the male voice just inches from where she lay in the dark.

"Natasha, it's all right. It's me."

She sighed in relief. Her eyes adjusted to the dark, and now she could make out Jared's form sitting in the chair on the other side of her nightstand. "Jared. You scared me half to death."

"You were in a deep sleep. I almost hated to wake you, but I had to talk to you alone."

"What time is it?"

"One o'clock. Everyone's asleep."

She clicked on the bedside lamp, the three-way bulb automatically coming on to its lowest setting, thirty watts. "What's on your mind?"

He chuckled. "Good choice of words. I wanted to ask you about the boys. On the way home they asked Genae and I what all the excitement was about. I'm sure they tried to get something out of you."

"They did, when I kissed them good-night just after they went to bed. Genae had already told me what y'all said, so I just gave them more of the same." She saw the concern in his eyes and found it heartwarming that he took such an intense interest in Gary and Gordy's welfare. She might have doubts about how Jared regarded her, but there could be no doubt that he loved her boys, whom he considered nephews. "I think they were satisfied that nothing's wrong."

Jared leaned forward, his forearms resting just above his knees. "Natasha, I'm so sorry. You know I never would have intentionally told the family about us. I was talking, and I didn't realize I was caressing you. I, uh, guess you're mad at me."

She chose her words carefully, being honest. "I can't say I'm angry, but I'm far from pleased. I wanted so badly to keep what we have to ourselves. Whatever it is."

He straightened, and lowered his chin. "What's *that* supposed to mean?"

She cursed herself for letting that last remark slip out. Now she would sound possessive and domineering, no better than Tara. But she'd opened the door; she had no choice but to walk through it. "It means," she said, "that I don't know how to classify us. Are we having an affair? Did we just sleep together one time? It happened weeks ago, and you haven't been back to town since. When you did come through you wanted to arrange a…a tryst in a hotel room, like I'm your South Carolina squeeze you see when you're passing through. Yet, when you finally do get here for a visit, you seem happy to see me. What am I supposed to think?" She let out her breath. "I should apologize. I know you said no strings—"

"I said that for your benefit, Natasha. I wanted to give you an out if you wanted one."

"You can't put this all on me, Jared. Yes, I worried about how the family would feel. But I wish you would admit that you're not sure how you feel about Gary and Gordy. Not about them personally—I know you care about them—but the fact that you have reservations about getting involved with me because as their mother I'm responsible for them twenty-four hours a day, seven days a week. To quote you, I have 'baggage.'"

He winced as if he'd just gotten a rabies shot. "I don't deny I've used that term, but I don't recall ever saying it in front of you," he said quietly.

"No, you haven't. Someone quoted you under quite innocent circumstances."

"It's been a long time since I said that to anyone. I don't think it's fair for you to use it against me now. It was years before I thought of you romantically."

"Maybe so, but that doesn't change the fact that you meant what you said. You'll never give serious consideration to any woman who has children."

Natasha rolled onto her back. For the last hour she'd alternated between lying on her side, her stomach and her back, with the same end result. She couldn't sleep.

She kept seeing that pained look on Jared's face when she'd confronted him with his stated feelings about women with children. He'd recovered quickly, bade her a cool good-night and returned to the pull-out bed in her office.

He hadn't denied it. His failure to object only served to confirm her fears. Nothing of any substance could ever happen between them. That was why he'd stayed away all these weeks. That was why he'd invited her for a rendezvous at a hotel, and why he couldn't keep his hands off her tonight. She represented an eager sex partner, a good time. No strings, like he'd said.

Now that everything was out in the open and she knew for sure, why didn't she just turn out the light and go back to sleep? She should be sleeping like a newborn infant, now that she at last had the answer to a question that had troubled her for months.

She rolled onto her side and punched her pillow. She'd get to sleep within the next fifteen minutes for sure.

Twenty minutes later she rolled to her other side. Suddenly she sat up. She couldn't stand this anymore. Yes, she'd spoken the truth, but she hated the idea of Jared feeling hurt. She cared about him too much. It didn't matter how he viewed her.

She grabbed her robe from the edge of the bed and slid her arms into it. She would just make sure Jared was sleeping. If he slept, she'd be able to sleep as well.

She opened her bedroom door, only to see him standing on the other side.

"Jared!"

"Natasha!"

Having spoken simultaneously, they both began to laugh. Natasha put her hand over her mouth to muffle the sound in the quiet hall.

"I was just coming to see you," he said.

"I wanted to see you, too. Jared, I feel awful about what I said earlier. Please don't think I blame you for how you feel. It's just my own disappointment. I needed to hear you say it so I could put a stop to any foolish ideas in my head, once and for all. We can just put what happened at your place behind us and continue to be friends. I promise to never bring it up—" She gasped as his strong arms wrapped around her back and pulled her close to him. She stared at him, bewilderment in her eyes. "Jared?"

"I love you, Natasha," he whispered before touching his lips to hers. He kissed her hungrily, and in a reflexive action she raised her body on her toes, her arms going around his neck. She leaned into him, allowing herself to forget about everything except his soft lips and demanding tongue.

When their mouths broke apart they remained in an embrace,

her head nestled comfortably against his shoulder. "You had no idea, did you?" he said.

"No. But if you love me, why did you stay away so long? Don't you know what it did to me? That it made me feel like I'd been abandoned again?"

"Oh, Natasha. Sweetheart, I'm sorry." His arms tightened around her. "That wasn't it at all. Remember, we spoke often, even if we were in different states. I stayed away because I couldn't stand the thought of seeing you and not being able to make love to you."

"Is that all there was to it?"

"You have to learn to try not to complicate matters. The reason for other people's actions are usually a lot simpler than you think."

"You know," she began, "we probably shouldn't be standing out here in the hall where anyone can see us."

"Since it's two-thirty in the morning and everyone else is fast asleep, I doubt that'll be a problem."

She pulled away from him and took his hand, leading him along as she stepped backward into her bedroom.

He closed the door behind them, but not without protest. "Natasha, I'm not sure this is such a good idea."

"*I* am. You want to make love to me, don't you? Now you've got the chance."

Eyes closed and lips parted, Natasha's back arched as she raised her hips to meet his thrusts. Each time his sex filled her body a soft moan escaped from her throat. If this wasn't heaven she didn't know what was.

"Look at me, Natasha."

She opened her eyes.

"Tell me you want me."

She smiled. "I want you, Jared. And I love you. That's why I was hurting so much when you didn't come back to Greer."

He lowered his body so he could kiss her. "If I have my way you'll never hurt again." Then he moved back and increased the tempo of his movements. Natasha's eager hands reached out to touch the hard muscles of his chest. She raised her knees higher, and he filled her deeper. Drops of sweat fell from his chest onto hers as he moved faster and faster. Jared called her name as his body began to tremble. She clung to him and cried out. They rocked together in an explosive moment, and then all was still.

He lay on his back and put his arm around her as she snuggled up to him on her side. "Stay the night here with me, Jared," she said. "I'll make sure you get up before anyone else does. I know that pullout is way too small for you."

"I am a little tall to be sleeping in a twin bed," he acknowledged. "But I've got to tell you, now that I'm able to think with the right head—" he chuckled "—I feel a little strange sleeping in this bed, at least with you next to me."

She knew what he meant. He felt guilty about having made love to her in the same bed she had once shared with Tim. "It's only a piece of furniture. People don't go out and buy all new things just because they've changed partners. It's not practical. What if I still lived in the same house in Montclair? Would you want me to sell it?"

"Of course not. All right, so I'm being a little silly."

"Inanimate objects don't pose a problem for us, Jared. It's the *people,* those who live and breathe, who we have to worry about."

"Don't worry, Natasha. I'll talk to Dad and Barbara about it before I leave. As for Kirk and Tara, they can think whatever the hell they want to."

"I'm so disappointed in Kirk. He sounded so hypocritical."

"Forget him. I think we should tell Gary and Gordy the truth."

"That would be a little awkward, with Genae here."

"Well, tell her, too. She's your sister. She might as well know. Hey, did your mother maybe send you a message through Genae? Happy Easter or something like that?"

"No," she said sadly. "Not a word."

In spite of her sadness over her mother's continued silence, her worry over facing Barbara and Ed's displeasure, and her fears about Gary and Gordy's acceptance of the situation, Natasha felt content as she fell asleep nestled in Jared's arms. Jared loved her. He'd only tried to protect her when he'd said their relationship had no strings. She couldn't remember the last time she'd felt so optimistic. It was an old cliché to think that love could give a person the power to leap over tall buildings, but it did make her believe in her heart that somehow everything would all work out.

Chapter 27

Natasha opened her eyes and glanced at her alarm clock. She shook Jared's upper arm. "Jared, it's six-thirty."

He tightened his arms around her. "But I don't wanna go to school," he whined.

She gave his shoulder a playful slap. "Come on, get up. The kids will be awake within an hour."

"That's an hour from now."

"The idea is for them not to know we slept together. You've got to go *now*."

"All right, all right." He threw the covers back and did a whole-body stretch, exposing his naked form, complete with morning erection.

Natasha had to force herself not to stare. Instead, she got out of bed and gathered his undershorts, shirt and suit pants, which he'd simply dropped on the floor last night in his haste to get out of them. "I can press these for you."

"Nah, they're all right. My suit has to go to the cleaners

anyway." He slipped into his clothing, leaving his shirt unbuttoned. "I'll only sleep for about an hour or so. I'd like to have that chat with the boys right after breakfast. If we're going to have a problem, best to know about it sooner rather than later."

Natasha climbed back into bed after he slipped out of the room, snuggling up to the pillow on which his head had rested. She knew she should worry about the boys' reactions to their affair, but she couldn't. How could anything that felt so right possibly be wrong?

When she woke up she took a shower and dressed in a T-shirt and jeans. Gary and Gordy were already up, in the kitchen, pouring cereal. "Tell you what," she said. "Since today's the last day of Easter vacation and I'm off, why don't I make us pancakes."

Gary promptly poured the cereal back into the plastic container while Gordy whooped, "Pancakes, yeah!"

Natasha took down a large bowl from the cabinet and prepared pancake mix from scratch, as was her custom. Genae, fully dressed, showed up as she was heating the electric griddle. "Morning. Why don't I make some bacon and sausage to go along with the pancakes," she suggested.

"Sure. Put some of that ham Jared brought home from Barbara's in there, too."

The scent of frying pork drifting through the house roused Jared. He wandered into the kitchen as Genae removed the cooked meat from the large iron skillet. "Fee fi fo fum. I smell bacon."

"It's almost ready," Natasha called out cheerfully.

"I'm going to fix some eggs," Genae said. "Nothing like having your ham and eggs in Carolina, as that song goes. Would anyone like some?"

"I would," Jared said. "Over easy, if that's okay. I'll take my pancakes on the side."

"I take my eggs the same way, so that's fine. But, Jared, I've got to ask you, where does it all go? You look too thin to be able to eat so much."

Natasha could only smile as she listened to the exchange. She knew about the well-developed body that hid under Jared's tailored shirt.

They sat down to breakfast at the kitchen table. As a surprise for Gary and Gordy, Natasha had defrosted some blueberries and mixed them into part of the batter so that they could have blueberry pancakes, which they loved.

She had just given them their plates and was about to fix one for herself when the phone began to ring.

"Do you want me to get that for you?" Genae offered.

"No, I've got it." She made space for her empty plate on the counter and reached for the extension. "Hello," she said breathlessly.

"Good morning, Natasha. It's Barbara."

"Hi," she said tentatively.

"You left so quickly last night. I didn't get a chance to talk to you. Now, I want you to hear me out, even if you can't say anything because you aren't alone."

"That's precisely the case, at least right now." She gestured to the others to excuse her and walked with the cordless phone out to the living room, where she sat on the edge of a chair.

"Natasha, I know you think Ed and I disapprove of you and Jared getting involved. But that's not true."

"What?"

"We think it's a wonderful idea. We used to talk about it all the time after Jared moved closer, saying how nice it would be if the two of you got together. After all these months we'd all but given up on it. Learning that you haven't is like getting a gift."

"But...I don't understand. You seemed so shocked. And Ed went into the other room, like he didn't even want to look at us." Natasha spoke in a tone just above a whisper, not wanting anyone to overhear her.

"Well, it did come as a shock. We figured if nothing had happened between you two by now it never would. What had Ed upset was Corey and Bill. He's still upset. Plus, he was furious at Kirk for saying what he did. That was the main reason he left the room. He was afraid he would upset me if he told Kirk off like he wanted to."

Natasha's mouth dropped open. What was it that Jared said about the reasons for people's actions usually being simple? He'd been so right.

"I admit we were being a little selfish in our hopes," Barbara continued. "We had this inner fear that you would eventually remarry and we wouldn't see you and the boys as much. And Jared, although we're biased, is a fine man. We think you two would make a great match. And don't think twice about those cruel things Kirk said. You haven't disgraced Tim's memory. If anyone's guilty of that, I'm afraid it's him."

"I'm so relieved, Barbara. I thought you and Ed would disown me." She bowed her head for a moment to say a silent prayer while Barbara reassured her. When she raised her head she saw Jared's tall frame in the doorway, his mouth set in an unforgiving flat line. She gestured for him to pick up the living-room extension. "Jared's going to pick up, Barbara."

"Good. Ed is here, too. He wanted to talk to both of you."

The line clicked as both Jared and his father picked up.

"Natasha, I hope Barbara assured you that we're not upset," Ed said in his authoritative voice.

"Yes, she did. I can't tell you how happy I am about that."

"I'm sorry if you had a bad night because of it. But there's one thing we're concerned about."

"What's that, Dad?" Jared asked.

"Gary and Gordy. We're afraid they might object to this new role you have in Natasha's life."

"We're planning to tell them about us after breakfast," Jared said. "We'll find out then if we have a problem."

"I know you have a good relationship with them as an uncle," Ed said, "but kids can sometimes be possessive of their mothers.

They might not like the idea of you taking over the role of boyfriend to Natasha."

"Especially Gary, since he still remembers his father," Barbara added.

Natasha spoke up. "I don't think that'll be a problem. You see, Gary's been trying to fix me up with his softball coach. A couple of weeks ago I finally came out and told him I wasn't interested. He and Gordy said they thought it would be nice if I had a boyfriend. Then they said that Jared would make a nice boyfriend for me."

"They did?"

"Hey, you didn't tell me they said that," Jared remarked with surprise.

"It wasn't a good time to mention it," she said quietly. Her pointed gaze reminded him that this occurred during his prolonged absence.

"Well, please be sure to tell us how it goes," Barbara said. "I'm going to hang up now. I think Ed wants to talk to Jared."

Natasha took that as her cue to hang up as well. She said goodbye and clicked off the phone, then returned to the kitchen.

"Is everything okay, Mommy?" Gary asked anxiously.

"Oh, sure. I just spoke with Grandma for a few minutes, and now Jared is talking to Grandpa Ed." She filled her plate, covered it with a paper towel and placed it in the microwave. On noticing Genae's curious stare, she realized that her sister had to wonder what had caused the ear-to-ear grin she now wore. She pursed her lips, forcing them into a more natural expression.

The boys both ate seconds while Jared finished his breakfast. Natasha could barely finish her first helping. Her stomach was practically dancing from the good news she'd just received.

When she could eat no more, she joined Genae in cleaning the kitchen, loading the dishwasher and wiping down the countertops and cooktop. "It seems like Sunday, doesn't it?" Genae remarked.

"It sure does."

"Mommy, are we going anywhere today?" Gordy asked as he got up from the table.

"Maybe we'll do something later on. But don't get up just yet."

"Huh?"

"Sports, there's something I have to tell you," Jared said. "And your aunt Genae as well. So everybody sit down for a minute."

Genae promptly put down the dish towel she held and sat, a will-somebody-please-tell-me-what's-going-on look on her face. Natasha took a little longer, scraping food particles off the boys' and Jared's plates and putting them in the dishwasher, then rinsing her hands and drying them on a paper towel. Her casual movements concealed the turmoil churning inside her.

"All right, here's the deal," Jared began after she finally joined them at the table. "Since I moved to Atlanta last December I've been coming up to Greer and Spartanburg pretty regularly. I've really gotten to know you fellas, and we've had a lot of fun together."

"You're not going to move far away again, are you?" Gary asked, alarm in his voice.

"No, sport. If anything, I hope you'll see me even more often. But I've got to ask you something. Would either of you object if I…if your mother and I went out on a date?"

Gary's forehead wrinkled. "A date? Like boyfriend and girlfriend?"

"Uh…that's the idea, yes."

Genae beamed, first at Natasha and then at Jared. But Natasha's gaze was fixed on her sons, anxious to hear their responses.

"Does that mean you're getting married?" Gordy asked hopefully.

Tears sprang to Natasha's eyes. Her youngest son, with no retained memories of Tim, desperately wanted a father. She tried to speak, but didn't know what to say.

Jared came to her rescue. "Well, that would be getting ahead of ourselves, so that question really can't be answered. No one knows what the future holds for any of us. But one thing I can promise both of you. No matter what happens between your mother and me, I'll always be part of your lives. Remember, we're family. Okay?"

The boys spoke in unison. "Okay."

"So you're all right with me taking your mother out?"

They nodded.

Jared turned to Natasha. "Well, that's a load off our minds."

"But will you play ball with us today, Uncle Jared?" Gordy asked.

"I'm afraid I can't, sport. I've got to get over to Dad's and change clothes, and then I have to see Corey before I leave for home. But you'll see me next weekend, okay? Maybe you guys can drive down to Atlanta after your games Saturday."

"I think you boys should go get dressed now," Natasha said. "But first tell Uncle Jared goodbye, since he's getting ready to leave."

She watched in happy satisfaction as Gary and Gordy took turns hugging Jared. He lifted them in the air as usual, and she didn't think she imagined that he seemed to squeeze them tighter than usual.

She walked Jared outside to his car. "You're not really in a rush to change your clothes. Besides, your clothes are at Corey's, not at Ed's. What's really going on?"

"Kirk and Tara are getting ready to leave, and I want to say a few things to them before they do."

Her feet quit moving. "Now, Jared, it doesn't really matter what they think."

"No, it doesn't. But Kirk shared his thoughts with us, and they were rather unpleasant, to say nothing of insulting. I'm not going to let him get away with that." He rested his palms on her shoulders. "Don't worry. I'm not going to start World War Three. But there are some things that need to be said, and I'm going to say them. And I really do want to check on Corey. Yesterday was pretty difficult for her. I know she's disappointed in the way I behaved at dinner. I owe her an apology. All together, I'm looking at a couple of hours. I doubt I'll be on the road before this afternoon. I'll call you then." He moved in and kissed her briefly, his hand circling her waist. "I don't know about you, but I feel pretty good about the future."

As Natasha expected, Genae stood waiting when she returned inside after waving goodbye to Jared as he drove off.

"Natasha, I just wanted to say I think it's wonderful, you and Jared. I had no idea."

She chuckled. "I think we caught everybody by surprise. I'm sorry I didn't tell you about our relationship, but it's still very new, and we decided to keep it to ourselves because it's such a sensitive situation. But Barbara and Ed didn't object. Only Kirk and Tara thought it was wrong. Things got rather ugly at Barbara's yesterday afternoon."

Genae's eyes widened. "Is that what you guys were talking about yesterday? I thought all the uproar was about Corey and that guy Bill."

"Well, it started off that way. But Jared got a little carried away with his body language when making a point about people getting into other people's business. He kind of gave it away. After that, all anyone wanted to talk about was us." She looked around anxiously. "Are the boys still in their room?"

"Yes, they haven't come out. I'm sure they're dressed by now. Maybe they're talking out how they feel. They seemed pretty thrilled about the prospect. Frankly, so am I."

"Hold the rice packets, Genae. Jared's mother and grandmother still don't know, and they might feel it's not right because Tim and Jared were stepbrothers."

"I gathered from something someone said yesterday that they're on a cruise?"

"Yes. They'll be back tomorrow."

"Don't worry, Natasha. I'm sure they won't think you and Jared have done wrong. It would be kind of messy if they were full brothers, especially if you were to have more kids. I mean, would they be cousins or half siblings?"

Natasha sighed. "I feel quite fortunate that I don't have to deal with that. I've got enough problems than to have to worry about complicated bloodlines. But I know I'll feel a lot better when it's all out in the open. My own mother gave up on me. I couldn't handle if Jared's mother gives him the cold shoulder because of me."

Chapter 28

Kirk knew the moment he and Tara got into the car that she would begin to grill him.

He wasn't disappointed.

"What happened in there?" she said.

"Jared and I had a talk, and then we talked to Mom and Ed."

"I *know* that, Kirk. I was politely asked to excuse all of you, remember? First you and Kirk, and then your mother and Ed."

"Tara, I'm sorry if you felt slighted, but believe me, it has nothing to do with you."

"Fine. First you tell me how I'm a member of the family, and then you insinuate that I was left out because it's a family matter and has nothing to do with me. You need to make up your mind." She sat rigidly in the passenger seat, staring straight ahead.

"That's not it. If anything, Jared was being considerate. He pointed some things out to me that are best left between him and I. If you'd been there it only would have made things worse."

"Why do you say that, Kirk?"

He sighed. She wasn't going to let up on him until she knew exactly what had transpired. He didn't know how much more of her strangulation tactics he could take. "Because he reminded me that I promised Tim as he lay suffocating in smoke that I would always watch out for Natasha and the boys, and then I left them hanging after you complained about me spending a little bit of time with them."

"How many times do I have to tell you, Kirk? I *had* to stop you. Natasha was trying to take you from me!"

"She was *not* after me, Tara."

"So it's just a coincidence that now she's with your step-brother?"

"Precisely. That just happens to be how things went. Can't you see that there's a much more important issue here? As much as I tried not to think about it, Jared forced me to. I didn't honor my brother's dying wish. I broke my promise to him because of you, Tara, because it made you unhappy. But all you can do is sit here and go on and on about some foolishness about Natasha's motives. How insecure can you be?"

She turned her neck to look at him. "How dare you call me insecure! *Natasha* is the one who's insecure. Only an insecure woman goes after every man she sees."

He took his right hand off the steering wheel to hold it palm out in her direction. "I want you to do me a favor, Tara. Don't say another word until we get back to Jersey."

Natasha tried to read as she nervously waited for Jared's call. Genae, bless her, had offered to take the boys to Chuck E. Cheese's for pizza and games. She'd said she wanted to bond with her newfound nephews, but Natasha knew she wanted to give her some time alone. But it was two in the afternoon and they'd been gone for an hour. Surely Jared was on his way back to Atlanta by now.

When the phone finally did ring she grabbed the receiver on the first ring.

"Calm down, it's only me."

"Jared, what happened? How's Corey?"

"She's annoyed at me. I apologized to her and said I wished she'd given us some warning about the age difference. I told her it wasn't fair for her to be upset because we were all so shocked, that she should have told us what to expect. How would she feel if I'd been dating someone for months and when I brought her to meet everyone she was bound to a wheelchair? Of course, she said a physical infirmity isn't the same as an age difference, but I said it is, at least from this perspective. The shock value is just as great when you aren't expecting it."

"Is she still upset?"

"Yes. She's hurt about the things Dad and I said to Bill at dinner. She really loves that man, Natasha."

"Yes, I believe she does."

"Anyway, it made her happy to learn that you and I are seeing each other. She said she didn't know what took me so long to see that the perfect woman was right in front of me."

Natasha didn't realize until the *whoosh* sound that came from between her lips that she'd been holding her breath. "So that means the only ones who have to be told are your mother and Miss Olivia."

"I'll call them when they get back from their trip. They'll be fine with it."

"I think your grandmother will, at least." Natasha recalled Miss Olivia's encouraging words about relationships that weren't viewed as appropriate, even if they weren't quite as distasteful as that Hollywood scandal she recounted from so many years ago, or the more recent one involving Woody Allen and Mia Farrow. "Actually, I think she might be more understanding of Corey's situation than the rest of us were."

"It's generous of you to include yourself, but it was really just Dad and me who were openly critical."

"I was a little critical myself when Corey first told me how old Bill was. But I'm sure her feelings toward everyone will mend." She couldn't wait any longer to move on to the topic foremost on her mind. "Uh, how'd you make out with Kirk?"

"We got into a fistfight."

Her spine straightened. "Jared, no!"

"Relax, I'm just messing with you. I said what I had to say, and that was that." He didn't feel it prudent to inform Natasha that not only had he berated Kirk for saying that he felt repulsed by their relationship, but he had also pointed out that Tara's paranoia was becoming more and more irrational. Again he pointed out the irony of Kirk's accusation that he and Natasha had sullied Tim's memory by beginning an affair, asking Kirk how he slept at night knowing that he'd gone back on his word to Tim. Kirk appeared to take it with stoicism, but his lack of response made Jared suspect he'd hit a nerve.

Natasha tried to look straight ahead as she walked down the aisle in time with the music, but she couldn't help looking from side to side and smiling at the guests on both sides of the hotel banquet room. Vivid red poinsettias on pedestals of varying heights reflected the season. Happy occasions like this gave a person a new zest for life. She felt better than she had in months…and the last months had been pretty doggone good.

She spotted Gary sitting with Jared in chairs near the aisle and winked at them, then gave a cover-girl smile as Jared snapped a photo. Gordy would follow her, the rings he carried secured to a pillow with a loose stitch.

She was glad that Terry had opted for the opulent wedding she'd always dreamed of having instead of settling for a dismal, nondescript ceremony at city hall out of respect for Wendell's memory. Neither she nor Larry had ever been married before. Why not go all out? They had no need to feel guilty.

Natasha felt confident, after all she'd gone through to keep her relationship with Jared a secret, only to learn that just about everyone approved of the idea, that she would never feel culpable again.

In addition to asking Natasha to be her matron of honor, Terry also asked Gordy to be the ring bearer. Gordy insisted he could balance the rings on the pillow and they didn't have to be secured, but Terry pointed out that the satin pillow was quite slippery, diplomatically soothing any fears the now eight-year-old Gordy had about being treated like a baby. One day she would make a great mother, Natasha thought.

At the end of the processional, when Terry and Larry turned to face each other, Natasha bent to arrange Terry's train behind her. Then she took Terry's bouquet to free her friend's hands and stepped back with the bridesmaids to observe the ceremony.

She spotted Jared, who stood out in the sea of faces because of his height, and smiled ever so slightly, like the Mona Lisa.

As Jared predicted, his mother and grandmother were delighted about their romance. Once their relationship was out in the open, she and Jared saw each other regularly, with each weekend finding either him driving to South Carolina or her driving to Georgia. In October they took a vacation together, a cruise to Mexico's Yucatán Peninsula. Gary and Gordy came along too, since the services offered on the ship included organized children's activities all day and into the evening.

The cruise had been a welcome respite after her somber trip to New York for the commemoration of the September eleventh attacks. Jared had offered to go with her, but Natasha told him it wasn't necessary. She cited her plans to spend a few days with the boys' paternal grandfather and her desire to avoid any awkward moments. While she knew Kirk had told his father about her relationship with Jared, she nevertheless didn't feel it right to flaunt the fact that she had moved on to her father-in-law, who'd just recently emerged from nearly disabling grief.

Stephen Lawrence and Ginny, his second wife, welcomed Natasha and the boys warmly, and Gary and Gordy happily reconnected with their grandfather. Best of all, Stephen said to her as they were leaving, "You look happy, Natasha. I hope to one day meet the man who put that sparkle back in your eyes." The remark told her he didn't share Kirk's objections to her relationship with Jared.

Natasha had another reason for wanting to travel to New York alone. She knew she would become emotional and shed tears at the memorial, and she didn't know how Jared would react to seeing her cry at the loss of Tim. Then, at the actual event, she saw Terry crying openly as Larry, a single tear running down the side of his face, tried to comfort her. At that moment she realized that Wendell, who had been Larry's oldest and dearest friend, meant as much to him as he had to Terry, and suddenly she felt ashamed of herself for wanting to conceal her emotions from Jared. She had loved Tim. Even now, her memories of him were filled with love. If he were here they would still be husband and wife. Gordy would have a father he remembered. And Gary wouldn't have turned to her with a tear-stained face and said, "I wish Uncle Jared was here."

Tim belonged in the past. Jared knew that. He wouldn't be insulted by her sorrow, or feel that she cared less for him. This was a time to remember Tim, not to think about their resulting entanglement. She vowed that next year all four of them would make the trip together.

Like on this trip to attend Terry's wedding to Larry Bishop. With reception halls, country clubs and hotels often booked for weddings up to two years in advance, Terry and Larry's only choice for a hastily arranged but large wedding was in the hectic days just before Christmas, when bookings tended to drop off a bit. Even with that, the only day available was Thursday evening.

While in the area they drove past their old house in Montclair, which had been decorated beautifully for the holiday, with a Nativity scene on the front lawn and sparkling white lights in the trees and at the edge of the roof, even framing the windows. Whoever lived in the house now clearly loved it. It filled Natasha's heart with happiness to think of it being a happy home, full of laughter and cozy moments.

Kirk and Tara lived nearby in West Orange, but they did not

stop to see them. Neither Natasha nor Jared had spoken to Kirk since the Easter debacle last spring. Tara gave birth to a baby girl in early November, and while Natasha had her doubts about someone as paranoid as Tara raising a child, she did send a frilly outfit for the infant via Barbara and Ed when they drove up to see the family's newest addition. Tara promptly mailed a rather stiff, formal thank-you note that sounded about as sincere as a politician's campaign promise to clean up blighted areas.

Natasha had long since learned not to let Tara's antics trouble her. If Kirk felt repelled by her and Jared, so be it. The bottom line was that she hadn't been this happy since before Tim died. But after eight months the constant travel back and forth to Georgia was beginning to wear thin. It was no secret she and Jared loved each other, but as she stood listening to "I, Teresa, take thee, Lawrence," she found herself wondering if his old fears about "baggage" would make it impossible for him to ever commit to being a true father to Gary and Gordy.

They returned to their hotel after the reception, exhausted. "Let's not leave to go home too early tomorrow, huh, Jared?" Natasha suggested.

"I've got a better idea. Why don't we stay another day and get an early start the day after tomorrow."

"Stay another day?" Her bewildered tone conveyed how little she thought of that idea.

"Why not? Neither one of us has to work until after the holiday. And I'd rather not drive through the Appalachians after dark."

She hadn't thought of that. It did get dark awfully early these days. "Yes, I suppose it's best to take those inclines in daylight. And it's a cinch we won't be up to hitting the road at 7:00 a.m." She sighed. "All right, we'll stay another day. Maybe I can get some last-minute Christmas shopping done."

"I'll talk to the front-desk clerk and extend our stay. It shouldn't be a problem. I doubt they have many people checking in this time of year."

* * *

Natasha slept until seven forty-five, which for her was nearly three hours after her norm. She stretched. She had a room all to herself; Jared had suggested the boys stay with him. She'd shower, comb her hair—she'd had the braids taken out for good just a few weeks before—and get down to the lobby for the Continental breakfast before they stopped serving at nine. Maybe later this morning they could all go to the Kohl's in nearby Clifton, stop for lunch and do some shopping. If Jared and the boys didn't want to deal with the inevitable pre-holiday crowds they could go to a movie or something.

To her surprise, Gary, Gordy and Jared were not at the buffet when she got there. Might they still be sleeping?

Impulsively she picked up the courtesy phone and dialed their room. When the voice mail came on she hung up, the first lines of worry forming across her forehead. Where could they be?

She went to the front desk. "I'm Natasha Lawrence from room 414. My sons are staying in 416 with…well, they usually come down for breakfast, and they don't answer the phone in their room…."

"Oh, yes, Mrs. Lawrence, we have a message for you." The clerk handed her a folded paper.

Natasha took it and read the bold strokes of Jared's handwriting:

Gone to pick up a surprise for you. We'll be back soon.
Love you. Jared.

She sighed in relief. "Thank you," she said to the clerk.

She returned to the buffet area and made herself a waffle. Usually there was a line for the twin waffle makers, but this morning no other hotel guests sat in the breakfast area. The few guests in the hotel had probably eaten already, since she'd been later than usual to get downstairs and it was twenty minutes to nine. Activity around the hotel would probably increase on Monday, Christmas Eve, when people coming to spend the holidays with family members unable to put them up would check in.

As she waited for the timer of the waffle iron to count down, she wondered about the surprise Jared mentioned in his note. What kind of surprise could he and the boys possibly have in store for her on a Friday morning in New Jersey?

She ate with an eye on the television, which was hoisted on the wall and tuned to CNN, but she had no interest in the news of the day. Her gaze kept wandering over to the entry hall.

Her three favorite guys returned just as she took the last gulp of her orange juice. "Hi, Mom!" the boys said, putting their arms around her.

With Gary on one side and Gordy on the other and two sets of arms around her, Natasha felt like Medusa, with her ringlets of snakes draped around her neck. Speaking in a deliberate raspy Donald Duck voice, she said, "I can't breathe. I can't breathe."

When they removed their arms she gazed at all of them expectantly, her eyes wide as she looked for something different. "I got your note."

"And you're wondering where's your surprise," Jared finished.

She shrugged. "You can't blame me for being curious."

"We wanted to make sure you're ready. The boys can go get it. I'll stay with you and make sure you don't peek."

"Now, Uncle Jared?" Gary asked eagerly.

"Yeah, you two go ahead."

Gary immediately took off running. "C'mon, Gordy!"

"And don't run!" Jared called out after them. He chuckled and came around to stand behind Natasha. "It won't be long now," he said as he massaged her shoulders with his large hands.

"I can't imagine what it is."

"Oops. Here it comes. Can't let you see until we're ready."

Everything went black as Jared moved his hands to cover her eyes.

"I can't take too much of this," she warned.

"Okay. One, two, three...*surprise!*"

He removed his hands, revealing a beaming Gary and Gordy flanking a woman in a camel-hair coat and matching hat. It took Natasha a few seconds to realize the woman's identity. She stared openmouthed at Debra Simms.

Her mother.

Chapter 29

"Hello, Natasha," Debra said haltingly, smiling through tears and love in her eyes. "Look at you. You've matured into a lovely woman."

"Thank you." Natasha felt as if she was having an out-of-body experience. Could this really be her, holding a polite conversation with the mother she hadn't seen in over a quarter of a century, who now stood not three feet away?

"I'm sure you're wondering why I'm here. Genae has convinced me that I owe you an explanation. I hope you won't hate me."

Stunned, she shook her head in disagreement. "I could never hate you…Mom." Suddenly feeling like she was eight years old again, she got up and ran into the arms of the woman she'd alternately loved and hated, and the feel of her mother's palm against her back made tears come to her eyes.

"I think it would be a good thing for the two of you to go up to your room to talk, Natasha," Jared suggested. "Don't worry about the boys. I'll keep them entertained."

Natasha stepped back, her arm still around her mother, whose height she had eclipsed by several inches. "But how... how did you ever manage to pull this off without my knowing? I truly had no idea."

"It was Genae's and Jared's doing," Debra explained. "Genae has been at me for months to reconcile with you. Natasha, you don't know how much I wanted to, but I was so afraid you'd hate me for the way I vanished from your life." She squeezed Natasha's arm. "I planned a trip to Newark so I could tell my parents in person that my deep dark secret was out, and that I was going to...beg you, if I had to, to let me into your life." She sighed, her eyes momentarily closing.

Natasha imagined the confrontation hadn't gone smoothly.

After a few seconds Debra resumed her explanation. "Genae said you would be coming to Montclair for a friend's wedding and said she would find out the exact date so I could be in Newark at the same time. So here I am. Jared was nice enough to come and pick me up."

Natasha looked at Jared in astonishment. "You and Genae arranged all this?"

"Guilty as charged," Jared said with a big smile. "Genae called me and told me her idea. She said she'd finally gotten your mother to agree that she needed to see you."

"But I don't get it. What if we'd left town this morning like we planned to originally?"

"We wouldn't have. The fact that we were all exhausted made it easy to come up with an excuse. Otherwise I would have had to come up with another reason for keeping you here. I guess I would have come down with some kind of twenty-four-hour bug in order to stay another day."

Natasha eyed her sons. "And when did you two rascals find out about this?"

"A little while ago when Uncle Jared brought us to meet Nana," Gary said. He, too, wore an ear-to-ear smile.

"She asked if we would call her Nana, since we already have

a grandma," Gordy added. "Two grandmas, if you count Grandma June."

Natasha's hand went to her heart, and she found herself unable to speak.

"Are you all right, Mommy?" Gordy asked.

"She's just happy, you nitwit," Gary said as Natasha managed to nod.

"Come on, dear, let's go talk," Debra said, linking her arm through Natasha's. To Jared she said, "We'll probably need an hour or two."

"Take all the time you need, Debra. Call when you're ready. Natasha has my cell number. By then we'll be ready for some lunch."

"Thanks so much, Jared."

"Yes, Jared," Natasha said, finally finding her voice. "Boys, Mommy is going to spend a few hours catching up with your nana. We haven't seen each other in a very long time."

In the privacy of her room, Natasha sat in an easy chair and waited as her mother removed her jacket and laid it across the foot of the room's lone queen bed. Debra then seated herself on the love seat facing her. "Well," she said brightly.

"I guess I don't have to tell you I've got a million questions for you," Natasha said.

"I know. Natasha, you don't know how much I wish I could turn back the clock. I was young and foolish, and I let everyone tell me what I ought to be doing.

"My parents were aghast when I got pregnant," Debra continued after a brief pause. "The first thing they said was that no one must know."

"Were they wealthy?" Natasha asked curiously. She knew virtually nothing about her mother's family, but she did know that folks with money tried to avoid scandal at all costs, often with success.

"No, we were lower middle class. Not much money, but a lot of pride. To this day, they never let me forget how I shamed them, how none of my sisters ever got pregnant outside of marriage in spite of the bad example I set for them." She shook her head. "They sent me to Lakewood to live with a great-aunt and -uncle before I started to show, but the rumor mill got hold of it, or maybe somebody just made a lucky guess. For all I know, Freddie told everyone," she said, alluding to the young man who'd fathered Natasha, "since he and his parents where the only other ones who knew. Anyway, the whispers and pointing followed me around from the time I got back."

Natasha remembered her mother telling her how much she wanted to get out of Newark. "It sounds like it wasn't a happy time for you."

"It's been a real long time since I knew what happy was. It's impossible when you're constantly being manipulated. First my parents, then my husband. My parents were dead set against my ever getting you out of that home. They encouraged me to give up my parental rights, to stop going to see you. My mother said my having a baby would mean I'd never get a good husband. But I wouldn't just forget about you, Natasha. Then after I met Lyle I told him how I hoped to take you to live with me one day."

"And he refused."

"No, not outright. He said it was a big step and we had to think about it from all angles. He said that by this time your personality was all formed and that you probably resented my not taking you out of the home earlier. He said you would probably be a problem child, difficult to control. He said he wasn't sure he wanted the responsibility, especially since you weren't his child."

Natasha nodded knowingly. She'd figured as much.

"Then, when I met his mother, she told me outright that she didn't want her son marrying into a ready-made family, and that she didn't think it was fair for him to shoulder the financial burden of raising someone else's child. You already know that Freddie, your father, was never involved in your upbringing."

"Yes, I know." She'd never had any curiosity about her father. Even her mother's minimal involvement had been sufficient to cause years of emotional turmoil after her sudden disappearance.

"Anyway, I was so sure I could get Lyle to change his mind. He promised to take me out of Newark, and I was desperate to get out. All the fellows looked on me as easy because of the rumors that I'd had a secret baby. They all talked about how high and mighty I thought I was, and how they knew I didn't act like that behind closed doors." Her gaze dropped lower. "I know my parents wanted the best for me, but I honestly think it would have been easier if I'd just stayed at home and not tried to hide my pregnancy. I was hardly the first girl to have a baby out of wedlock, and at least I was sixteen, not twelve. By the time you were born I'd turned seventeen. And even with that I still managed to go to college and get a nursing degree. Having a baby as an unmarried teenager isn't something anyone wants to aspire to, but it doesn't have to mean your whole life is down the tubes."

"So what happened, Mom?"

Debra sighed. "Lyle became more and more controlling after we got married. I got pregnant a few months afterward, and that was when he decided it was time to move to Raleigh. That was when I came to see you…that last time, although back then I didn't know that would be the case. I still hoped I could convince him to let me get you and bring you with us, but he kept putting me off, saying he was thinking about it. After Genae was born his 'maybe' about you suddenly became a definite 'no.' He gave the reasons I told you before.

"In Raleigh he became even more domineering. Genae reminded me so much of you, Natasha. Having a new baby is supposed to be a joyous time, but I was miserable. Lyle did keep his word about taking care of me. I had everything except the one thing that would make my life complete, and without you the rest of it didn't mean much."

"Why did you stay with him?"

"I just didn't have the backbone to leave. I kept telling myself that one day I would. When Genae got older I switched to full-time. Lyle was furious." She shrugged. "We finally had the showdown that we'd been building up toward for years. That's when we separated. So my life changed more than I thought. I went from being a housewife to a single working mother."

"Why didn't you try to find me after you and Lyle broke up, Mom?"

"Because by then so much time had gone by and you would have been in your early twenties. I was so sure you hated me for disappearing like I did, especially after I told you what I had planned."

"I did," Natasha confessed.

"I don't blame you, Natasha. But I do hope we can try to make up for lost time."

"I'd like that, Mom."

"Genae told me how you lost your husband in the World Trade Center. I'm so sorry I wasn't there for you."

Natasha looked down. "It was the worst time of my life." Then, raising her gaze, she said, "Did Genae also tell you about Jared?"

"Yes. She said his father is married to your husband's mother."

"Yes. Does it shock you that he and I are involved?"

"It might be considered unconventional by some, but I see nothing wrong with it. Genae spoke highly of him, and now that I've met him I agree. He seems to be a good influence on my grandsons, and he obviously cares for you very much."

"Home again," Jared said as he turned the Explorer into the driveway alongside his Crossfire.

"At last. That was a heck of a long drive," Natasha said.

"That's because you're used to flying."

In the back seat the boys, who'd both been napping, stretched and yawned.

"We're home, kids," Natasha said. "Won't it feel good to sleep in your own beds?"

"It sure will," Gary agreed. "But it was good to meet Nana."

"Yes, Gary, it was," she agreed. She and her mother spent the previous morning talking, covering just about anything that came to their minds. Debra confided that when she realized Cliff Allen had a dominating personality she feared God was punishing her for disappearing from Natasha's life by making Genae's life as unfulfilling as hers had been. "I was so happy when she broke it off with him," she'd said.

At the day's end Natasha went along on the ride back to Newark. She looked at the modest two-story home of her grandparents and felt nothing. These people had discouraged her mother from having any contact with her. They had no interest in her whatsoever, and she was their own flesh and blood. How heartless could people be?

"Nana said she was visiting her family in Newark," Gary said now. "When do we get to meet them?"

"I'm sorry to disappoint you, Gary, but we won't be meeting them. You see, they never showed any interest in me. None of them ever visited me when I was growing up. They saw me as someone who shouldn't even have been born." As his forehead wrinkled in confusion, she added, "I know this is hard for you to understand, but when someone sends you signals that they don't really care if you live or die, you shouldn't waste time being curious about them. So I'm afraid you'll have to forget about ever meeting your great-grandparents, aunts and uncles."

"Wow. I've got great-grandparents?"

"Yes."

"They must be really old, like Miss Olivia."

"I suppose. You have to remember that Nana is only—" she added seventeen to her own age of thirty-four "—fifty-one."

"That's old, too."

She rubbed the top of his head. "Not from where I stand." She turned to see what was going on behind her. Jared had finally gotten Gordy to wake up and helped him step out of the back seat without falling. "He's okay," he said to her.

A still-sleepy Gordy took Jared's hand as he rubbed his eyes with the other. "Uncle Jared, I wish you were with us all the time," he added wistfully.

Natasha and Jared exchanged another glance. Jared turned his head to smile at Natasha. "Cheer up, chum. I'll be in town until New Year's."

Christmas this year was completely different from the year before. Kirk and Tara decided to stay at home in New Jersey with their baby and spend the holiday with her family. Corey, likewise, spent the day with Bill. Natasha sensed the real reason they all stayed away was lingering bad feelings from Easter.

"Where is everybody, Grandma?" Gordy asked as they sat down to dinner.

"It's just going to be the six of us this Christmas, dear."

"I thought I was gonna get to see Uncle Kirk's new baby," Gary said forlornly.

"I'm disappointed too, Gary," Barbara said.

"Why isn't Aunt Corey here?" Gordy pressed on. "She lives right here in Spartanburg."

"Aunt Corey is with her boyfriend, Gordy," Natasha said quickly. "When you're a grown-up and you have a serious girlfriend or even a wife, you'll find that sometimes it's difficult to split yourselves between both your families, so you have to take turns."

"But Aunt Corey wasn't here on Thanksgiving, either, Mommy," Gordy pressed.

This time Ed saved the moment. "I do have good news for you boys," he said. "This evening we've been invited out for dessert with Miss Olivia and Grandma June and her friend Calvin. You know Calvin, don't you?"

"Yes, he's nice," Gary said.

"They're all having dinner together with Calvin's children and grandchildren. I think you fellas will have a good time. There'll be a number of kids there your age. Won't that be nice?"

"Yes, Grandpa Ed," Gordy said. "But I wish my aunt Genae and my nana were here, too, so we could all have Christmas together."

"Gordy, we talked about that," Natasha said patiently. "Your aunt and nana already had plans for Christmas. They couldn't change them at the last minute. But they'll be coming to visit us, just like we'll be going to visit them."

"Remember, Gordy, Christmas will come again next year," Barbara said. "Everyone will have time to make plans to be together."

"That's a long time from now, Grandma."

"Not so long."

Natasha watched as Gary put his hand over the side of his mouth and whispered something to Jared. "Gary, you know better than to whisper at the table," she chided.

"I'm sorry, Mom. I was just asking Uncle Jared if we can ask you now."

"Ask me what?" She waited as Jared spooned out mashed potatoes from the large glass bowl onto his plate. "What?" she repeated.

"Well, it's like this," Jared said in a maddeningly slow manner. "Gordy said something the other night that got me thinking."

"What did he say?" Barbara asked, obviously curious.

"We were just getting in from Jersey. Gordy said he was happy to be home, but that he wished I was with them all the time instead of just on the weekends."

Natasha's shoulders tensed against her chair back. She, too, hadn't been able to put Gordy's remark out of her head. He clearly wanted a father figure.

"That's understandable," Ed said easily. "With all due respect to Tim, you're like a father to the boys."

"The three of us had a talk after Natasha went to bed," Jared continued. "They told me what they really wanted for Christmas was for their mother and I to get married."

She gasped.

Barbara leaned forward eagerly. "And what did you say, Jared?"

"I suggested we take a vote, and we did. It was unanimous. But I suggested we wait until Christmas Day to ask." He turned to Natasha. "So how about it?"

She hadn't moved since he'd said the word *married.* Just a few days ago, as she watched Terry and Larry pledge to love each other forever, she doubted that Jared could do the same for her, which meant doing the same for her children. Her mother's husband hadn't been able to do that for her, and she knew he wasn't alone.

The fact that Jared had just publicly proposed meant he was willing to be a father to two young boys, eight and ten years old. She no longer had any reason to doubt his commitment to Gary and Gordy.

She broke into a smile. Five years ago she thought her life was over. Now, wonderful things were happening for her. The mother she thought she'd never see again was now a part of her life, and she had a sister she adored. Best of all, everyone who mattered had accepted her being with Jared. And they would be together the rest of their lives.

His voice broke into her thoughts. "Natasha? I see you smiling. Is that a yes?"

She looked around the table at the expectant faces of her in-laws and her sons. "Yes!"

Everyone got up, and she and Jared exchanged one quick kiss before squatting to pick up the boys to join them in a group hug.

"This is wonderful!" Barbara exclaimed. "And the best part is that I'm not really losing a daughter-in-law. You're just moving over to Ed's side of the family."

"And we're thrilled to have you," Ed said, planting a kiss on her cheek. Then he clapped his hands. "Okay, everybody. We've all gotten the Christmas gift we wanted. Now, let's eat!"

Chapter 30

They married a week later, just after midnight on New Year's Day, in a ceremony held in Ed and Barbara's living room. Natasha's minister officiated. The entire family witnessed the ceremony: June, Olivia, Ed, Barbara, Corey, Genae, Debra. It thrilled Natasha to have her mother present. She'd missed her marriage to Tim, but at least she witnessed this one, which Natasha knew in her heart would be her last.

Also present were Tim's father, Stephen, his wife Ginny, Robin and Duane Davis, and, to everyone's surprise, Kirk. Even Terry and Larry Bishop, just a few days back from a Paradise Island honeymoon, managed to make it to Spartanburg.

Corey came alone. Natasha knew that presented a dilemma for her. "I'm sorry you didn't bring Bill," she said when they were alone. "He really should be here with you, especially since your being here meant you couldn't be together at midnight." She remembered how Bill had sat out spending last New Year's with Corey, because their relationship was still new and even then was kept secret.

"We both felt it would be best if he didn't come. Today's your day, and Jared's. We didn't want to cause any discomfort for anyone."

"Believe me, I know how you feel. I vividly remember feeling the same way last Christmas."

Corey lowered her voice. "Wasn't that something about Kirk and Tara?"

Natasha nodded. Kirk surprised them all by showing up for the wedding alone. When Barbara questioned him, he confessed that he and Tara had separated.

"Do you know anything about what happened?"

"Yes," Natasha said. "Apparently she spotted him going into a restaurant with an attractive female colleague, and she followed them inside and caused an embarrassing scene, accusing him of cheating on her. It turns out the woman was his new boss."

"Oh, no!"

"I feel sorry for him, Corey. Their baby is only a few weeks old, but he said he can't take Tara's suspicions anymore."

"Maybe they'll work it out."

"I don't know. That would require Tara admitting she's got a problem, and I just don't see that happening."

Kirk sought out Natasha and Jared after the ceremony. "I said some things last spring that weren't right. Jared really pointed out what a jerk I'd been. My father had a few things to say about it, too. I wanted you both to know that I'm sorry for what I said, for what Tara said. I wish you many happy returns."

Natasha hugged him. "We're family, Kirk. Maybe we won't always agree or even get along, but we have a bond that really can't be broken. Maybe one day Tara will understand that."

Jared embraced his stepbrother. "Let us know if there's anything we can do to help out. We'll be there for you."

Kirk patted his back. "Thanks, Jared, but it's my problem. I'll handle it."

* * *

"We're going to be busy the next few weeks," Natasha remarked as she brushed her hair. She and Jared had returned to her house to spend what was left of the night before departing for a romantic but brief, hastily arranged honeymoon in Asheville. Gary and Gordy had stayed with Ed and Barbara.

"That's why we both took so much time off. We'll handle it." A bare-chested Jared came up behind her and massaged her shoulders. "We just have to take one step at a time. First, we'll put this place up for sale. Then we'll get settled in Duluth, get the boys registered in school and get your computer set up so you can work. We'll get workmen in to put up dry wall between the stairs and the den so the boys can have the privacy of a closed-in room. You'll be so busy getting the house decorated that you won't realize how fast the time has passed. And as soon as school lets out for the summer we'll take a real honeymoon, to an island where there's nothing to do but lie around and make love day and night." He nuzzled her neck. "Stephen already asked if the boys could spend a few weeks with him and Ginny on Long Island. You know Dad and Barbara will expect them to spend time with them as well, and Debra, too. Between all the grandparents there won't be a problem for us to get away for some one-on-one. Why don't you stop worrying and come to bed."

"Why are you in such a hurry? It's nearly four in the morning. I figured you'd be too tired to do anything except go to sleep."

"Are you kidding? I'm not about to let this first opportunity to make love to my wife pass me by."

She stood up and faced him, taking his hands, as she'd done just a few hours ago. "That's right. I'm your wife. For as long as you live." She raised on tiptoe to kiss him.

Epilogue

Eighteen months from now

"Remember, Gordy, you have to be careful with his head," Natasha warned.

"I've got him, Mom."

"It's my turn to hold him," Gary said.

"Not yet it isn't. Wait a minute."

She smiled at her sons, all three of them. The boys were competitive as ever, but they adored their baby brother.

Jared appeared, camera in hand. "If that's not a Kodak moment I don't know what is," he said as he held the camera in front of his eye and preserved the image.

"Isn't the flash going to hurt the baby's eyes, Uncle Jared?" Gary asked.

"Not at all. It's artificial light. It's the natural light, like the sun, that you have to watch out for. Here, let me take him." He took the blanketed bundle from Gordy's arms. "You fellas finish getting ready. Our guests will be here shortly."

"Okay, Uncle Jared."

Although Jared had easily slipped into the role of father figure for the boys, and they loved him dearly, they continued to address him the same way they had all their lives. Natasha and Jared saw no need to push them to change, although they'd had an embarrassing moment when registering the boys in the local school. Gordy expressed to the school administrator that Jared "used to be my uncle, but now he's married to Mom, so he's my stepfather." The woman had been unable to conceal her shock, and Natasha said only, "It's not what you think. He's not *that* type of uncle. He's actually—"

But Jared had cut her off. "I'm sure Mrs. Bennett isn't interested in hearing our history." When they were alone he told her gently but firmly to never allow anyone to make her feel ashamed of them, or feel obligated to give anyone an explanation. She resolved she wouldn't. Her days of feeling guilt because of her love for Jared were in the past.

Natasha enjoyed living in suburban Atlanta. They frequently visited Ed and Barbara, and June and Olivia, in Spartanburg.

The happy mood at the church extended to all present. In addition to the friends Jared and Natasha had made in Duluth, most of the family traveled for the occasion of the baby's christening as well. Genae and Debra, Ed and Barbara, June and Olivia, thrilled to be a great-grandmother at last. Corey attended with Bill, whom after a rocky start the family had come to accept. Corey wore a diamond engagement ring Bill gave her on Valentine's Day. They planned to be married in the fall.

Stephen and Ginny Lawrence sent regrets and a savings bond, as did Terry and Larry Bishop, who expected a baby of their own in a few weeks and chose not to make the trip. Robin Davis was also pregnant, but not as far along. She and Duane came with their daughter. The Davises already knew from fetal tests that their baby would be a boy. "Our sons are going to be the best of friends," Robin predicted. "Just like us."

To no one's surprise, Kirk and Tara had been unable to patch up their marriage. Now divorced, Kirk participated avidly in the upbringing of his daughter, who was now a year and a half old. Natasha watched with interest as Kirk stood talking with Genae. Wouldn't it be nice…

"Forget it," Jared whispered. "They're only talking. Probably about the weather."

"I confess, I was entertaining nice thoughts about the two of them hooking up. Oh, Jared, you know me too well."

"That's what husbands are for." He bent to kiss her.

When the ceremony began, Natasha held her two-month-old son in her arms. Against a background of organ music the minister said, "Name this child."

She nodded to Jared, who spoke out clearly. "Timothy Lawrence Langston."

They looked down at Timmy, who gurgled and smiled, as if he knew everything…whom he had been named for, his family history and just how much he was loved.

Leila Owens didn't know
how to love herself let alone
an abandoned baby
but Garret Grayson knew
how to love them both.

She's My Baby

Adrianne Byrd

(Kimani Romance #10)